BLOODY MARY

ALSO BY SHARON SOLWITZ

Blood and Milk (1997)

BLOODY
MARY

A NOVEL

Sharon Solwitz

Sarabande Books
LOUISVILLE, KENTUCKY

Managing Editor
Sarabande Books, Inc.
2234 Dundee Road, Suite 200
Louisville, KY 40205

Library of Congress Cataloging-in-Publication Data

Solwitz, Sharon, 1945–
Bloody Mary : a novel / by Sharon Solwitz.— 1st ed.
p.   cm.
ISBN 1-889330-93-0 (pbk. : alk. paper)
1. Girls—Fiction. 2. City and town life—Fiction. 3. Chicago (Ill.)—Fiction.
4. Mothers and daughters—Fiction. 5. Jewish families—Fiction. I. Title.
PS3569.O6514 B58 2003
813'.54—dc21   2002015503

Cover image: *Mutter und Tochter*, 1913 by Egon Schiele. Bleistift, Gouache/Papier 47.9 x 31.9 cm. Provided courtesy of Leopold Museum — Privatstiftung, Vienna.

Cover and text design by Charles Casey Martin

Manufactured in the United States of America
This book is printed on acid-free paper

Sarabande Books is a nonprofit literary organization.

FIRST EDITION

For Jesse Silesky, 1987–2001. My darling.

ACKNOWLEDGMENTS

I am grateful to many people for their help on this manuscript. Barry Silesky, for one, whose faith in me is indispensable. Seth Silesky, who continues to challenge me (and who provided a valuable critique of current adolescent-diction). And the brilliant women in my writing workshop: Sandi Wisenberg, a gifted line-editor, and Tsivia Cohen, Garnett Kilberg Cohen, Peggy Shinner and Terry Mathes for all their insights and suggestions. Other terrific readers and advisors include Sara Skolnik, Rosellen Brown, Joyce Winer, Mitchell Newman, and Sandor Goodhart. Thanks also to Maria Massie who found the best place for this book, and to Sarah Gorham who welcomed it in, and to the editors at Sarabande, Kristina McGrath and Kirby Gann, who lovingly clarified and simplified, and bore with my fanatic revising. Thank you all, and may your own work flourish.

I am also grateful to the Illinois Arts Council for grants and fellowships that have given me time to do this work.

ONE

CHAPTER ONE

Tumble

Claire locates the place at the top of the stairs where the carpet is loose. With a crowbar in one hand, a hammer in the other, she rips, stepping back and down. Earlier this morning Hadley lied to her. A pointless lie, the lie of someone in the habit of lying. But Claire doesn't have to think about it. She's close to happy in this simple, absorbing physical work almost like a dream.

With another small backstep she yanks at the stiff, dirty, gold-colored shag and tattered foam pad, turning away from the cloud of old dust. Carpet springs free of the tacking strips, shoves her backward down the stairs, unwieldy slab almost toppling her, she has to stay ahead of it, backstepping, nimble dancer with large, clumsy partner, *one, two, cha cha cha*-ing down and down. At the landing, she drops her tools, pushes open the screen door. Carpet is caught on the doorframe; she pushes it out, a heavy tangle on the stoop, spilling down to the walk. Should she drag it back to the alley for the garbage pickers? This is her part in the cycle of city dailiness, a middling part, not too high or too low. Stick your head up above the crowd and you'll get it cut off, her mother had said. She coughs, feels a bit dizzy. Leo can handle it. Another small piece of ugliness, gone from her house and her life.

She sits on the bottom step, on the newly exposed wood, which is not pristine. Marred by spatters of paint and nails, carpet tacks, some sticking up like tiny hurdles, others embedded. It's a big job. She imagines the wide, curving maple staircase as it will be someday, polished dark red, the handsomer for its past abuses. Stressed wood, a value in the world of Victorian rehabs. She runs soothing fingertips over the surface. Pictures Nora three years from now in a prom dress at the top of the stairs. Ten years from now (conscientiously finished with graduate or medical school) Nora in a wedding gown with a jeweled train, Persian runner softening her footfalls en route to the eager, appreciating world below. Actually Hadley will probably get married first, while Nora, bright and supremely responsible, will marry only after everyone has given up on her, at thirty-five a celebrated doctor or a full professor with lines around her mouth. At thirty-five Nora can still have children but she'll choose to adopt, Claire imagines, a handicapped Third-World orphan, to limit the totality of pain in the world. Something else not to think about. She retrieves pliers and a screwdriver from Leo's workbench and starts in on the tacks. Many are loose and yield to a twist of the wrist. A breeze blows in with the smell of the city and the warm October morning.

But when a certain kind of thinking starts, it has a life of its own. Taking root in the brain's greenhouse, stamping out less aggressive thoughts, till, rootbound, it occupies all available space. She pulls five tacks in a row; the problem zips along with her. When a lie comes to the lips as easily as the truth, there are other things that have been lied about, not to mention the as-yet-unknown causal complex beneath the lying. If Hadley's lying is a pattern, she'll have to do something about it, and she's not good at this sort of doing, especially with daughters who laugh at her taste in clothes and movies (Hadley) or treat her with patronizing compassion (Nora). Once she asked her own mother what were the best years of her life, if there had been best years, and her mother said, "When the kids were little," the kids being Claire and her older brother. Claire had felt bad for her mother, whose best years were long gone, but now unfortunately she understands. When Nora was little, Claire taught her to read, delighted by Nora's delight in her unfurling new power. Hadley's pleasure was Marshall Field's, the El ride downtown, and the store itself, beaming clerks behind glittering counters. Then lunch in the high-ceilinged Walnut Room. Those were good times.

With the claw of her hammer Claire pries at a tack buried in the wood. Tries a screwdriver, digging at embedded metal that she can scarcely feel with her fingertip. Driving Hadley to Rachel's this morning, she asked her what she had eaten for breakfast—a reasonable question, a mother's prerogative—and was told milk and cereal, and back home she found the milk not even opened, a Diet Coke in the trash. Thirteen is a rough age, she thinks, for parents as well as children (though Nora at thirteen was not like Hadley). Worst was the look she saw on Hadley's face, not even blank. Sincere like an angel. Who is Hadley anyway, this girl who used to love her best, who at dinner *had* to sit next to her, who wouldn't go to sleep without a glass of water delivered by her alone? Rocking the screwdriver from side to side under the tack, Claire gets some leverage; the tack shoots back over her shoulder, pings on the storm door. For a moment, the air in her lungs goes thick as syrup. The steps rise endlessly before her, the upper landing invisible behind the curtain of mist.

She takes two Tylenols and sets to work on the next tack.

When the phone rings she's on the third stair and going strong. But it's Eileen, whom she has known since college, with whom she plays tennis on Sundays. There's new vibrato in Eileen's voice, a string pulled tight. Claire brings the cordless over to the stairs so that she can work while Eileen worries to her about things in her life that are essentially enviable, in this case her gifted son unhappy at Juilliard. His classes are boring; his roommate's a pig.

"He's homesick," Claire says, soothing her friend with Nora's sometimes troubling solitariness and Hadley's reading problems—"She won't open a book!"—considerately not mentioning that Hadley's phone rings off the hook and that Nora, a sophomore, made varsity track. Phone to her shoulder, rocking her pliers over the handle of her screwdriver, she pulls out the staples in the riser, pine probably, delicately retentive, like the skin under an eyebrow, while Eileen segues to her wealthy brother-in-law, whom she disliked till six months ago when he was diagnosed with multiple sclerosis. Now Eileen feels terrible, for him and for her sister who doesn't realize the miseries in store.

"There's something new in medicine every week," Claire says.

Eileen brings up her husband, who has an anger problem. Claire suggests management strategies, rejoicing in Leo's mild temper and her own beneficence as a friend, poking her screwdriver at a protruding finishing nail. The moment it dawns that she should just hammer it down, she remembers Hadley's gratuitous lie, which for some reason she hasn't mentioned to Eileen—was it unimportant? Or too important?—and the screwdriver skids off the tiny nailhead into the fleshy underside of her thumb. She sucks, then looks. Blood wells along the line of the cut. Thumb in her mouth, phone shouldered to her ear, she staggers to the kitchen and snaps off a paper towel.

She's on automatic now, fully occupied. She wraps her thumb, tapes it, murmuring in the occasional spaces between Eileen's concerns. Pulls a chair toward the high cupboard over the refrigerator, where she keeps the iodine, Drano, Raid, and Strip-Eeze.

Eileen's voice is trembling nakedly. Claire's head aches a little behind one eye. She takes another Tylenol (how many is that now?), then climbs up on the chair, blood seeping through the toweling. Her good hand is clamped to the bottle of iodine in the back of the cupboard when Eileen hits emotional rock bottom. She has fallen in love with someone not her husband, a man ten years younger than she, skinny as a boy. He teaches tennis and racquetball at her club and tells her funny, tender things in bed. She has a step class in ten minutes; she talks fast, describing him in bed, how inspired he is—it's the only word— how he touches her as if it's all new to him. As if she, Eileen, is new and beautiful. He has beautiful, even, white teeth. Afterward he looks at her as if she has given him an exquisite gift. She can't introduce him to her friends or her children, this voyage into vicarious youthfulness is disgusting maybe, but she can't think about that now. "I'm gone, Claire. Remember how we used to say 'on the bus or off the bus'? I'm on the bus. I've got to see where it'll take me."

"I never said 'on the bus or off the bus'!"

"It's from *The Electric Kool-Aid Acid Test*."

"What about Dan?" Claire says, wondering if she sounds mean-spirited. Her heart beats hard in her thumb. She doesn't remember reading the book.

"God, that's what Nancy would say!" Eileen's voice rises. Then she giggles. "But all of a sudden I'm alive, Claire. Do you know what I mean?" A pause. "Claire, are you there?"

"I'm here," she says more sharply than she meant to. "Why bring up Nancy?"

Antiseptic in hand, Claire feels something bubble and fume at her attempt at empathy. She works with Nancy; she knows her a lot better than Eileen does. Nancy, who listens almost devoutly to Dr. Laura's radio advice, is a joke they have shared. Nancy and Dr. Laura believe in ethics, not empathy, in rational choice, while Claire and Eileen like to identify with or, at worst, laugh at, the occasional misadventures of their many girlfriends. Claire loves Eileen, a source of continual, slightly wild energy, like a campfire she can warm herself by and keep in bounds with her good sense. But Eileen has passed some boundary now.

"Hey, your class, isn't it starting?" Claire starts to say, and her chair begins to sway. Her head pounds like a heart. "God," she says, more to herself than to her friend.

She looks at the tiny bottle in her hand, thinking she has opened it. She hasn't opened it. The greasy dust on its cap divides before her eyes into discrete silvery particles. The white granulated top of the refrigerator pulses violet, fuchsia, chartreuse like oil on water. The skin of her arms is made of the same gorgeous substance, arranged in small circular bundles. The holes in the mouthpiece of the phone have widened slightly. She smells apricots. It seems the most wonderful thing in the world is about to happen.

"Claire? Hey, say something or I'm hanging up on you!"

The light has rearranged itself to form a face with a high,

noble forehead but mottled, like bread mold. If she can remember a name, or at least where this has happened before, she can stand firm. But even as she understands the rules of the game, her thoughts are blurring. She can no longer remember the name of the friend with whom she has been speaking. The name of her husband whom she loves and is faithful to. The glass thing falls out of her hand and clunks on the floor. *Floor*, she murmurs, reaching a foot back and down for the stability of something whose name vanishes as she flails for it.

When she was too young for school, too young, almost, to remember things, Claire had seizures in which she'd stiffen like a branch, and when she came to, hours later, she wouldn't be able to speak, transfixed by a picture in her head that wouldn't let go.

Phenobarbital was prescribed but made her sleepy and irritable (she'd been a quick, sweet child), but she took it twice a day till they came up with Dilantin, which she took till her gums began to grow down over her teeth. The doctor stopped the medication, said kids sometimes grow out of this business of seizing (he did not say epilepsy), said just keep an eye on her. And in fact her brain scans were normal. A year passed and the "non-epileptic seizures" ceased as abruptly as they began. But her mother's younger sister had died at twenty-two when a vein burst in her brain, her mother couldn't look at her without a crease between the eyes, and Claire took over the business of watching herself. She wasn't afraid of what had happened to her aunt, and of the seizures she recalled mostly a fuchsia-toned euphoria. But something lingered in her mind's outreaches, the feeling that the area of the world marked "safe" was small, and the terrors beyond so unspeakable that only an idiot would trespass, or a crazy person.

Even when she was old enough to see that certain people lived as if there were no boundaries and suffered no visible damage—many of her girlfriends in high school, for example, and her brother Eric—she didn't relax her guard. Her friends copied each other's homework, stayed out past their curfews. Wild Eric, suspended from school for smoking pot, tried to hitchhike to Miami Beach. He got as far as Cincinnati, came home to tears and hugs. Claire, though, had no urge to test limits. Maybe because the image of herself as fragile was formed so early it was all she knew. Maybe she saw herself as made of a different substance from her friends. She had a bridal doll once with a starched, multi-tiered net gown that could be taken off. When the dress got dirty she put it in the hamper, to be washed along with her own dirty clothes, and it came out a rag, something to clean windows with, linked only by the color white to its former self. She had nightmares about that dress. To stay alive and sane in a world where objects sagged from their appointed shapes, where colors started to run or hum, she had to work strenuously.

By second grade, she could sit through class without asking to go to the toilet, releasing only at lunchtime a hard hot stream that went on for minutes. She could avert hiccups by swallowing at the first squeeze of the larynx, following up with a series of firm, quick pants. She also assumed full and minute control over the movements of her limbs. She took art lessons at the Highland Park Community House, and with tiny, careful crosshatching, inked two realistically proportioned, reclining girls connected by swirls of phone wire, a drawing chosen for an exhibit of children's art at the School of the Art Institute. She took ballet from a downtown teacher, learned to stretch tendons into the required postures of unnatural beauty, danced the lead in the junior high production of *The Red Shoes*. Onstage or off, she walked as if she had a basket of eggs on top of her head. She obeyed her parents and Eric, and overstudied for tests. And although no medical evidence showed seizures as amenable to the power of will, they did not return. Her sophomore year at college, when she became engaged to Leo Winger, an intelligent, considerate medical student with a vein of amusing cynicism, she quit the dance classes she was still taking twice a week and transferred from Fine Arts to the School of Nursing. Eileen, her roommate, gave her a hard time about it, but dancing truly wasn't what she needed. Dance provided only partial, limited control of the nightmare forces. Dance was a mere symbol of control, while soon-to-be Dr. Leo Winger was a train she could ride forever.

Then, the month before her wedding, Eric, who'd made it back from Vietnam with his limbs intact and most of his mind, took her to dinner at an Indian restaurant where they ran into one of his friends. It was summer, 1975. Nixon was disgraced and gone; the confusing War had lurched to its end. Her father was diagnosed with emphysema; the folks were moving to Florida. Fast Forward, as the friend called himself, had scraggly strawberry-colored hair and the face of an aging angel.

Shy as usual with strangers, Claire watched Eric's friend lift clumps of yellow rice to his mouth with the first three fingers of his right hand. Later at his apartment he and her brother lit a water pipe, and as the hash smoke burbled up the long tentacle arms she started laughing about something she couldn't explain. Eric congratulated her on having achieved a "contact high." Fast Forward touched his foot to her foot. She felt the bud of an exotic flower in her chest begin to open. When Eric left, she hardly noticed. She and his friend took off their shoes and began massaging each other's feet. He had huge hands and feet, knuckles like small walnuts, long fingers with bitten-down nails so ugly they were hard to look at, but they seemed to know even more than she knew about the configuration of nerves under her skin. She trembled with pleasure as he pulled her toes nearly to the point of pain, as he bent her arch farther forward and back than it had ever gone before.

He didn't talk a lot, nor did she, but parts of her childhood that she'd forgotten returned to her forcefully that night. She had loved Greek and Roman myths, and when the books went back to the library, she'd draw scenes from the uncanny, bloody stories. With her 64-pack of Crayolas she drew Andromeda beautiful, naked, and chained to a rock, a monster rising from the sea to devour her. She drew valiant Prometheus also naked and chained, his tender side exposed to the vulture's talons. When the crayons wore down, she resharpened them in the back of the box. Her aim was close detail—the vulture's yellow claws tipped in the red of the hero's blood, the man's open eyes fearless despite the pain he knew would come again. What was this interest of hers in heroism and pain? In torture and chains?

Until this night with Eric's friend, she had made love with exactly two men, her high school boyfriend after a year and a half spent gathering clues to weave into the assurance that if they broke up it would be her idea, and Leo, her fiancé. But this lanky elf, this faun of a man Fast Forward, was trembling so hard she was afraid something was wrong, and then she was shaking too, kissing his hands, his face, his neck, the hairs of his chest, the sour hair of his groin. She told him that once, mistaking *Last Exit to Brooklyn* for *A Tree Grows in Brooklyn*, she read the former cover to cover, looking for the beauty and hope her teacher had mentioned in this recommended book about poor people in New York. She was twelve, engrossed and horrified. He laughed. It was funny, he said. Sad and funny. That was how she saw it too. They drank tequila that he'd brought back from Mexico. "I love you," she said, and he looked at her as if he didn't fathom, but it didn't matter. It was hysterically funny. Grating and beautiful, Dylan's voice on the stereo hurt the bones of her skull. She pulled him inside her. Then woke on unpadded carpet in a pool of sweat, in her head the picture she'd worked so hard to escape—the sun gelatinous, gray-yellow, swollen three times its normal size, and she flying straight toward the putrid heat, hair ablaze, her charred skull cracking open onto the intricate meat of her intelligence. Years later when she described the experience to Eric, he said she had dreamed of Napalm.

For two weeks afterward she sat in the back of her classes taking frantic, detailed notes that the next day made no sense at all. The feeling of Fast Forward's hands and of an oncoming train kept mixing together in her mind. When Leo touched her she had to swallow in order not to gag. One morning Leo asked her if she wanted to call off the wedding, and then told her, simply, that even if she didn't, it would probably be best for both of them if he did. "Please, no!" she said. She loved his brown, open eyes, his firm, narrow, still teenage-looking body, and how smart he was, speaking thoughts with a beginning, middle, and end. He said what he thought. She trusted him. She held both his hands, told him about the Indian dinner, the interesting (weird, she said) hippie guy and drinking too much (but not the sex, or the fainting spell that maybe was and maybe wasn't a seizure), promising never again to relax into danger. She would devote herself to him and the family they would create, help him build a shelter where they'd both be safe from her mind.

She wakes on the kitchen floor to the ringing doorbell. Her side hurts. The tile is cold under her back. Someone pounds on her door. "Claire, are you in there?" She sits up slowly, keeping her head upright as if something in it might spill. Eileen runs in.

"Crazy woman, how can you leave your door unlocked?" Eileen kneels down beside her. "Jesus, is that blood? Is that *your* blood?"

Claire follows her gaze to the linoleum tile, a black and white pattern that the saleslady convinced her was coming back in. The European look. Cheaper than wood and ceramic, and it holds up better. Easy on dropped glassware. Claire picks up the bottom half of the broken bottle. "It's mostly iodine."

"God, it looks like a murder scene."

Claire is annoyed, and she's never annoyed with her girl-friends, least of all Eileen. But she feels interrupted. In the middle of what, she doesn't know, but she wants it to go on. She tells Eileen about her hand and about the tumble—what a spaz she is!—but not about the disturbing vision. She puts the chunk of glass into the trash. Her hip hurts; she cancels their tennis tomorrow. Offers to pay for the court if Eileen can't find a partner.

"Oh, please. Just take care of yourself!" Eileen washes and bandages her hand, blots up the spill, picks up the rest of the glass. She admires the work on the stairs, obsessive as it seems. She gestures out the door at the trail of carpet splaying down the stoop, tacks protruding. "I had to fight my way through that to get to you. Like Sleeping Beauty. Oh, God! Then what does that make me?" She laughs, gives Claire a goodbye hug. "Don't you ever slow down?"

Claire shakes her head. There's more to say but she doesn't know what it is.

By the time Leo gets home, midafternoon, she has washed the

dried blood off the floor and scrubbed the iodine to a faint pink in the white squares. She even hauled the old carpet around back. On her finger is a neat, flesh-colored Band-Aid. Go to him. Touch him. He is happy with his day which comprised two surgeries followed by nine holes of golf at the city course. He smells of spreading lawns and expensive soap, which he has earned, Dr. Leo of the sure hands. Modest, he calls himself a mechanic. But where, these days, can you find a good mechanic? Who can tweeze out a fogged cataract, reattach tiny retinal veins, laser a hemorrhagic artery without touching the optic nerve? His decisions not normally life-and-death, but light and darkness, the former of which, for his patients, normally prevails, along with improved visual acuity. I'm okay, you're okay, and if not I'll fix it: Leo, the conscientious optimist. She puts her arms around him. "Let's eat in tonight."

He licks her face, an expression of affection she has always liked. "And skip the party?"

What was she thinking? They're invited to dinner in Evanston with three other couples. Followed by slides from the host's trip to Nepal. "I forgot. I've had a headache all day." Which is true, though such a small part of true. She confesses her double mishap, the cut and the fall, focusing on the mess, the superlative clean-up. As far as she knows she didn't lose consciousness. No concussion unless her head's on her butt (ha ha). Still she must wait, seated, while he retrieves his ophthalmoscope, shines it at the back of each eye. "Any tumors, honey?" she says, loving him and how important she is to him. "Any signs of macular degeneration?"

He pockets the light. Kisses the top of her head. "You could take some Tylenol. Or Motrin."

"And call you in the morning?"

He laughs. "Just don't call me late to dinner." It's a line his grandfather used repeatedly, that used to irritate Leo. Now it's a legacy, a toast to history, to the life she and Leo carry on together. While he examines the bones of her skull, she smiles into his shirtfront. The smile of someone who recognizes her good fortune.

Shortly afterward, Nora returns from track practice. She takes a pear from the fridge and goes upstairs to read. Later, she and friends will go out to hear jazz. Her friends, the sophomore intellectuals, too gifted and ethnically diverse to be nerds.

Hadley calls. She's sleeping at Rachel's.

Claire takes a couple of Motrins, though she feels overmedicated.

The dinner party is no different from other dinner parties, but, smiling and nodding, Claire wonders how she ever got through them. She drinks more than usual and falls asleep during the slide show, although a long time ago her brother traveled in Nepal. Followed sherpas up and down mountains, so the story went. Now he tends bees on a communal farm in Tennessee. The nation's last extant commune? She doesn't bring it up.

She sleeps in the car, then in bed lies awake. After a while she calls Leo's name, a murmur, so as to let him sleep if he is so inclined.

He rolls over toward her, his eyes closed.

18

"Leo?" Still soft, almost a breath. This isn't the best time. "I'm worried about Hadley." If she can get it out, maybe she can sleep. "You know what she said to me this morning?"

He stretches, lays a heavy leg across her legs. He has thickened in the twenty years of their marriage, but not with fat. He's a runner, hard solid limbs, looking taller than he really is. He opens one eye, ready to be amused.

When she tells him, she can tell it doesn't sound that bad to him. All kids lie about something or other. It's a passage, a developmental phase, an assertion of independence or identity. Actually, he'd be worried if she didn't lie. That's what he says. (I'm okay, you're okay. He, she, it's okay.)

Normally, in the warmth of his plausible optimism she is glad to be soothed. But now, for some reason, she feels almost angry. Not all children tell lies, as a child *she* didn't lie, she had no need or use for lying, and her one lie as a young adult was a lie of omission—not that she excused herself, but it was for a reason, and at least she knew it was wrong.

This is what passes through her mind as they make love—a diatribe against Leo's vision of the world, what she'd say to him if there were no consequences. Like the dinner party, their lovemaking leaves almost no memory. When, afterward, he looks at her with a question on his face, she emits a sigh of pleasure. And then a sigh she must suppress, it having arisen from her apprehension of her own fakery.

———

She had to take a sleeping pill and wakes up late. Hadley is back from Rachel's. Claire bribes her and Nora into helping with the stairs. The pay is six dollars an hour. She passes out tools, turns on classical music. Outside on the stoop Leo is reading the paper, talking occasionally to a dog-walking neighbor. He wears a wool shirt, his down vest. It's bright outside but cooler than yesterday. The wind blows through the screen, cooling her face. The girls work at the top of the staircase, she at the bottom, a family tableau of harmony.

After half an hour Nora has moved to her second stair, while Hadley sits upon the original, leaning against the wall, examining strands of her light brown hair. Hadley dislikes (hates, she says) its natural curl. Has been campaigning for permission to straighten it.

Hadley sees Claire looking at her. "This is so boring and pointless."

Claire smiles like a TV mother. "I never promised you a rose garden."

"That's brilliant, Mom." She plucks something from the end of a long strand, flicks it off the tip of her finger. "I have a question. Why are we doing this? If we're going to put down more carpeting?"

"We're not," Nora says. "We're putting down a runner."

"Nobody asked you."

Nora continues with the same unflappable mildness, "I don't mind doing this."

"You don't mind anything. You wouldn't mind a nuclear bomb."

"How long," Nora says softly, "do you plan to just sit there?"

"She's telling," Hadley says to Claire. "It's the *same* as telling!"

"Now *you're* telling."

Claire would like to go on dreaming but the conversational pitch requires something. She looks at Hadley sprawled in seeming exhaustion. "How late did you girls stay up last night?"

Hadley yawns. "Not that late."

Claire smiles brightly. "No pay till you do at least *one*."

Hadley stands up. "I have my allowance. And what Grandma sent. I don't need your blood money."

Claire feels a psychic slap on the face, but before a response comes to mind Hadley has breezed down the stairs and out the door, hair a banner behind her. "See you guys."

For some moments, Claire and Nora breathe the fumes of silence. Then Nora says, "You shouldn't let her get away with that."

"Who's the mother in this family?" She meant to joke, but it came out testy. "Are you the mother?" She sounds not just hostile but completely false, ineffectual. Who *is* the mother? She wants to explain to Nora the problem with curbing a teenager's rudeness but she's not sure if it's a universal problem or only her problem. But increasingly it seems to her that mothering consists in *not* saying or doing. Protecting your children from yourself. She eyes Nora, alert for signs of disrespect. "She's maturing so fast. Physically, I mean. She already has a figure." Nora regards her sweetly, overlooking the parental archaism. "I don't want her to feel ashamed," Claire says, feeling foolish and petty in the face of her older daughter's tranquility. "She's so tall, I mean. She's starting to hunch her shoulders."

At the end of the hour Claire gives Nora a twenty-dollar bill, the extra to salve the guilt she feels toward just about everything. Nora, though, keeps pulling up carpet tacks. "I sort of like this. It's fun in a creepy, anal sort of way."

"Anal? What, are you going to be a psychiatrist?" Nora's steady gaze burns right through her attempts at irony. "I feel bad, honey, seeing you work so hard."

"Don't you want my help, *chère maman*?" In her third year of French, Nora uses it in certain moods to enhance the general conversation.

"I'd rather see you having fun."

"*Quoique tu veux.*" She sets the pliers down and goes up to her room.

With Nora gone, Claire resumes work on her project but now the tools feel clumsy in her hands. When Leo passes her on his way inside, she sits up with a stiff smile on her face. She has failed Nora. She has failed Hadley. The thoughts make no sense but sit like boulders in the middle of her mind, too big to walk around. By dinner time, too tired to chop vegetables, she orders in a pizza. When it comes, no one complains. Hadley is ebullient. Claire feels even worse.

"It's not that healthy," she reminds Hadley, who has taken a large piece from the pizza's gooey center.

"Then why did you buy it for us?" Without waiting for an answer she goes to the fridge, returns with a Diet Coke.

Claire, normally careful not to overwhelm the girls with eating rules, especially at the dinner table, is too weary tonight to hold her tongue. "That's even worse."

Hadley shrugs. "You said we could have pop on Sunday nights."

"Not when you had it for breakfast."

"Who said I had it for breakfast?"

Claire stands up. All three of them are looking at her but it's almost a relief, this chance to speak. She has been pent up too long. "Don't lie to me, Hadley."

Hadley starts to cry. "I didn't have pop for breakfast, I swear I didn't!"

"You had it yesterday. Didn't you?"

Hadley takes a breath, looking back toward the cloudy regions of yesterday. Nora looks at her mother as if she doesn't recognize her. Leo, busy opening a bottle of wine, acknowledges her unaccustomed tone with a slightly raised eyebrow, but the rest of his face maintains his characteristic enjoyment of things. He pours her a glass of wine. One part of Claire sees that Hadley has no idea what she drank for breakfast yesterday, or for lunch or dinner, but Claire's rage has its own life.

"It's wrong to lie, don't you know that by now? It destroys trust and love and everything!"

Hadley's sobs come in sharp, painful hiccups. Claire puts her arms around her. Tears are running from her own eyes, but whether they're from this seeming reconciliation or from her own confused shame, she doesn't know.

On Monday, without acknowledging to herself any fear of a recurrence of her "fainting" episode, instead of driving to work she takes the El. At the hospital she's briskly competent as usual, impersonally friendly. It's the premier children's hospital in the state and maybe the country, an honor to be working there, a special honor to work hematology-oncology, which occupies an entire floor. People ask if it's depressing in hem-onc, but most of the time it isn't at all. The children are surprisingly upbeat, even funny at times. Sometimes on the way home, she'll want to cry at what she knows or guesses. But mostly she manages to care for the children the way she imagines God cares for the universe—tenderly but without undue sentiment. Besides, although the children have sickle cell or some form of cancer, they live moment to moment and entice the people around them to do the same. If they're free of pain, most of them are ready to be amused. She's good at "pain management," able to insert an IV quickly into a nearly collapsed vein, meticulous with dosages.

Toward the end of her shift she takes her own emotional temperature, an old habit that resurfaces in times of stress, and marks herself normal; if anything's wrong, it's buried deep enough to let her work. During break she tries to talk to Nancy, who's assured in a way that doesn't question itself. They're alone in the nurses' lounge, a large closet with a table, chairs, refrigerator, and coffee machine. Claire says as casually as she can, "Do you ever think that you're a terrible person?" Tears well in her eyes. "I have the worst thoughts."

"What thoughts?"

She shakes her head. Tries to gather a thought, an image. It's a mess in there.

"When did this start?"

"Sunday. But it's been brewing all weekend." It doesn't sound right. "It's like this is how I've been all my life. How I really am."

That statement rings true. She feels a little better.

"We all get depressed," Nancy says, pouring herself coffee. She adds powdered creamer. "Do you want a cup?" Claire declines. "Just don't wallow in it," Nancy says. "Don't feed it. You have a family to take care of."

"I know that. But—" She wants to tell Nancy that she's afraid she's scaring her family. She thinks she *is* scaring them. She is definitely scaring herself.

"And these kids here. What they have to go through. And look at them!"

"I know."

She looks at Nancy's regular features, which, for some reason aren't beautiful or even pretty, and resolves to take control of herself. She has indeed been wallowing.

She makes the final rounds. Temperature, pulse, respiration.

Meds. She lingers with Josh Potrero, who got a fancy computer from Make A Wish and who played Internet chess while his doctor and parents discussed amputating his leg. Later, legless beneath the sheet (one leg, taken just above the knee), Josh made puns about needing a leg up and not having a leg to stand on and his computer upgrade that cost an arm and a leg. Well, a leg. Once his little brother tried to commiserate by saying, "Don't you just hate lying here?" and Josh replied, "It's not so bad." Simply, as if he meant it. Now Josh, who has had a recurrence, is in for a week of cytoxin/topotecan. She can't help but see the sticks of his arms out the sleeves of his hospital gown, from out of which also runs the double tube of his central line to the bag that supplies a hundred percent nutrition. She hooks up the cyto-topo, attaches it to his second tube, fixes the infusion rate and says what she always says. "Let's marshal the forces of good. Go, chemo!"

"Go, chemo," he tries, then turns to the bag hanging over his bed. "I hate to look at it. It makes me gag."

It's an ugly color, off-yellow like spoiled egg yolk. "Don't look. I'll take care of it. Just close your eyes."

She runs to Clean Utility and returns with a pillowcase. She drapes it over the bag. Smiles at him. "You can look now!" She smiles at his mother, sitting beside him in a wooden rocking chair, a plaque at the back of which reads, *In Memory of William Tyler Fleming.* Taped to the foot of his bed, a sheet of paper adorned with a smiley face says, *My name is Josh. I am 12 years old.*

I have no known allergies. His morphine drip is almost empty. She installs a new one. "Is there anything else I can do for you?" For once she doesn't know what else to say.

Josh says, in a voice surprisingly robust, "You are my favorite nurse."

She nods brightly. Thank you, she wants to say. I love you. But she feels a little dizzy.

She walks to the bathroom but it's occupied. Tries Clean Utility; someone's mother asks for a second pillow. Her face refuses to smile. Her skull seems to be filling with liquid again. Although she doesn't know where she's going, she walks rapidly; people get out of her way. She passes Nancy, who looks at her. "Are you all right?" She shrugs. Nancy follows her down one hall, up another. "Claire, what are you looking for?"

Now she knows what she's looking for. Purse. Jacket. What's going to happen must not happen here. "I think I'm sick. I'm going to be sick."

Does Nancy hear her? She lets Nancy help her into her jacket, accepts the gift of her purse. It's just past three, she has two more beds, logs to fill out, this has never happened before. "Don't worry," says Nancy, "I'll let Jackie know. We're okay, I'll cover for you. How are you getting home?"

"I'm sorry," she says to the fourth floor in general. While Nancy is calling a cab for her, she heads for the stairs.

In the chilly air of outside her head clears a bit. She hails a cab, flirts histrionically with the pink-faced, hefty young driver.

In front of her house, embarrassed, she gives him a twenty and tells him to keep the change.

"Thanks, babe."

Babe? She soothes her pique by giving the man an ugly name she remembers from Sunday School, Og, a local warrior-king who tried to keep the Jews out of Palestine, Og, whom, in Sunday School at age seven she imagined stupid and clumsy, falling off his ox onto the swords of the band of determined Jewish refugees. Of this latter day Og she amasses details for Eileen: his missing front tooth, the Christian saint medallion around his neck. How dare he call her "babe," as if he had her number? As if he knew her to be as brainless and helpless as she felt right now? In their college days she and Eileen had a name for men who were offensive to women and completely oblivious to it. They were Single-Celled Organisms. A Single-Celled Organism might say, for example, withdrawing his dick from a woman's mouth, "Thanks, babe." In Og's West Side accent Claire repeats the utterance, drawing out the *a*, omitting the final *b*-sound. She's not a babe, she's old and frowsy, but no one has a right to mock her. She sits down at the kitchen table. Smells something like the odor of old chicken.

She walks from room to room but the smell persists. Surfaces breathe in and out, walls, fingernails. She calls Eileen.

Eileen sounds happy to hear from her, but too full of her own bursting life to pay much attention. Eileen's lover is thinking of moving to L.A. to run some prep-school athletic program. Her pained laugh rises up like a kite. "Maybe he won't go," Claire murmurs. Hangs up. Remembers what she wanted to ask Eileen. Was she a bad mother? Not that Eileen would necessarily tell her the truth. She can't remember if she said goodbye. Should she call Leo? Or her mother in Florida, the remaining grandparent, source of unflagging, wearisome, comforting worry about her?

She picks up the receiver and starts to gag. She sets it back on the hook, swallowing sour saliva. Peels a banana, takes a little bite; bumps rise on her tongue. The backs of her hands look scaly as if she has developed a sun allergy. A cluster of warts seem to be rising under the skin of her wrists. She saw a movie once about a man whose human parts flaked off one by one—ear, nose, hair—to show the face of a giant housefly. She touches the skin on the back of her hand without looking down at it. The air shines with a sickly pink light.

She labors to manage her augmenting fear as she did as a child in the grip of a nightmare. With the beast bearing down on her she'd half awake, heart thudding, and alter the dream scenario, giving herself more strength or speed. Then back in her dream, she'd outrun whatever was chasing her, through the door that slammed behind her just in time. Now she walks from room to room in her house, seeking images of safety. The stairs close to finished. The girls coming home from school. From her bedroom window she looks down on the tree in the small yard, a maple, there when they purchased the house. Its leaves are edged in orange. She thinks also of the medicine chest in the master bathroom, the bottle of newly-prescribed sleeping pills.

If she could fall asleep right now, before she's outrun and captured. She thinks she can do it.

Bottle in hand she walks downstairs for the purified drinking water she keeps in the fridge. How many to take? She swallowed three and once even four Tylenol with no dire effect. On the third stair from the bottom she stops to read the fine print: *In case of accidental overdose consult a poison control center.* She presses and turns the childproof cap. Then there's Nora coming up the walk, sweet, good Nora with a load of books in her arms—through the new glass panel alongside the front door Claire watches her approach. Nora stops for a moment, half-hidden by the tree trunk, but she's clear in Claire's mind, the books, her new sweater, so red it looks like burning. In the orange leaves of the maple tree, red is starting at the orange edge, bleeding into the orange, invisible but she can smell it, sweet-bitter like orange rind. Then the pills are flying and she is falling again, holding tight to the empty bottle as if it will save her life.

CHAPTER TWO

Nonentity

From her desk, row three, seat four, Hadley could see the general shape on the board of Darnell Jones' sample introductory paragraph, and knowing Darnell there were spelling errors and probably it didn't make complete sense, but even with her eyes in slits, which would one day crease the top of her nose, she couldn't read it, and she thought of the food she might have eaten today— an English muffin from the box Nora had opened for breakfast, lasagna in the cafeteria, a bag of Rachel's chips. In the private inside of her desk, her hand found a bite-size Peanut Butter Cup. Unwrapping, she knew what she'd say if Boltz called on her—*I really like it!* Which would make the teacher stumble on her words. And the boys in the back row who cracked their knuckles and broke their pencils in half would laugh.

But Felice Pinter was waving her hand back and forth. Felice sat one row down and one over—round pink cheeks, lips smiling around the right answer. Felice was nice to people, and there was nothing wrong with the way she looked, but for some reason nobody liked her. Chocolate and peanut butter melting on her tongue, Hadley pondered the oddity. Then a sheet of paper appeared on her desk, a grid with names down the left margin and across the top, of the twenty-nine students in the seventh-grade language arts class.

In the horizontal row of boxes by her own name was *100%* and *FUN!* and *LOVE HER!* (the *o* in the shape of a heart). Not even Rachel or May Sun were so beloved. Every once in a while she wondered at her popularity (she was too tall) but mostly she accepted it like the fact she had to kiss relatives she didn't like, and that, although her parents had plenty of money, at restaurants she wasn't allowed to order lobster tail (market price) or filet mignon. Of the boys, only Fletcher Lawson had scores as high as hers. Fletcher was new this year in Edison Magnet. He came from Texas and talked like a cowboy—Yes Ma'am, No Sir— but he seemed to think that was how you were supposed to talk and you took his word for it.

By Felice's name someone had written *NONENTITY.*

Hadley traced the comment up the page to *SHERELLE*, who

had introduced "nonentity" into the class vocabulary, who said whatever she thought, even mean things, in a flat nasal voice completely free of self-doubt. By *EMILY BACKOS*, who wore glasses and too-small Kmart blouses, Sherelle had written *PATHETIC*; hairs rose on the back of Hadley's neck. For a moment she wanted to label Sherelle *PATHETIC* though Sherelle had called her *PRETTY COOL*. Upon Felice she'd bestow *KINDA FUN!* Last year Ms. Macauley, who was nicer than Mrs. Boltz, had asked the class whether, in life, they planned to side with good or evil—did they act with moral courage? it was their choice!—and she'd read to them about Joan of Arc, who at fourteen led her country against the English tyrants and was burned at the stake, and Hadley was moved by her sense of this courage, that she had been afraid she didn't have. She had loved Ms. Macauley.

Now she gazed hard at the back of Felice's neck, pink with a fringe of hairs too short for her Scrungi. Felice glanced back with a smile that was truly pathetic, but Hadley, by choice, could make Felice feel good or feel bad; courage like heat coursed from her heart into her arms, her hands. *Felice is Fun!* she said to herself, and in the box where her name coming down met Felice's across, in indelible blue ballpoint she began, *FU*... Then, maybe because she was lightheaded from sugar on an empty stomach, the heat went away. She started to shiver, twined her legs around each other, bent close to the desk. Her *FU* bypassed *FUCKED UP* and became *FUNNY LOOKING*.

She felt bad for the rest of the day. She even knew why she felt bad but couldn't fix it. She talked fast and happy and didn't look at Felice. When school let out she declined Rachel's invitation to her house and let the bus ride off without her.

The October day was bright but cold, but she'd left her jacket in her locker; didn't want to go back for it. She had some books; hoped they were the ones she had homework in. She had her lunch money; she could take the bus home, or the El. She imagined herself already home, on the couch watching TV, eating Oreos, waiting for her mother to come home from work. Her mother had gray flecks in the blue of her eyes and strong, thin ankles and wrists, and shiny black hair like Snow White. Lips as red as blood, skin as white as snow. She'd been a dancer in college and she walked like a dancer even in her cloddy nursing shoes. But sometimes now she looked at Hadley as if she didn't recognize her, cold and beautiful like Snow White's stepmother.

Hadley took the Brown Line downtown, squinting to see the freshly-painted back porches with their hanging flowerpots on some of the three-flats they passed, turning away from others with boarded-up windows, grassless, junk-filled yards. They'd almost finished their circle of the Loop when she remembered to get off. She walked toward Michigan Avenue and the Art Institute, then north past windows with fancy jewelry and shoes, and streams of handsome, fast-walking men and women.

It was almost dinnertime when she got off the bus at Waveland, three blocks from her house. It was getting colder, the wind starting up. She could really use her jacket. Rounding the corner onto her street, she thought of Felice and moral courage and whether she'd give her jacket—if she had it with her—to a poor person who was colder than she, and whether, in a world war, she'd rise to the nobility of Joan of Arc. Then the flashing red lights down the street turned into an ambulance, and although she used to want to be a model, she imagined herself a doctor in a poor, war-torn country, operating while the bullets flew. She felt bad for the sick children her mother took care of, and for the old people who lived on their block, especially for Mrs. Sayres across the street who walked with a walker and every time she planted grass in front of her house her dogs pawed it up. Poor Mrs. Sayres. The ambulance was parked in front of Mrs. Sayres' house. She couldn't stand to grow up and be Mrs. Sayres.

The ambulance pulled away with a scream of sirens and she saw her father standing on the sidewalk in front of their house. He was holding Nora's hand. Nora was crying. "Hadley!" he called out. "Sweetheart!"

Hadley's teeth started to chatter. It was too early for him to be home. His face looked sad and stupid. She wanted to run. To get on the Red Line and ride it down into the tunnel, pressing her nose to the dark glass and the air whistling along the invisible walls and the wheels screaming on the tracks blotting out everything. She had, though, to let him put his arms around her. She let him explain: Her mother had fallen down and hurt her head. She was going to the Emergency Room. Scary, but she was conscious. He didn't think she had a concussion. She'd be home tomorrow, or maybe even tonight. She'd be all right.

Hadley looked at his face, serious and unhandsome and squeezed with worry. But he was looking at Nora; in his talking was a secret for Nora, not her; she gazed over their heads out of the way of the secret. The ambulance was gone now. There were lots of green leaves on the row of trees along the street but some had fallen already, yellow red brown on the gray of the pavement. The low sun hit the chain-link fence in front of their house and the leaves of trees, and the shadows of leaves were dark on the pavement.

"I'm going to the hospital now," her father said. "You girls stay here, fix dinner for yourselves, get your homework done—"

"It's *done!*" Nora said. "Please, Dad, I want—" He gave her an over-the-shoulder look as he headed for the car. Nora followed him, "Dad, I understand what's going on, don't think you have to keep it from me, there's no point!" but he didn't turn around. Nora glared after him.

"What was that all about?" Hadley said.

"Nothing."

"You think you're great, don't you? You think you're better than everyone."

Nora gave her a look of lingering pity.

Hadley wanted to shrivel Nora to rind and dust. She could say some of the swears she knew as well as anyone at school. She followed Nora into the house, watched her set pasta water to boil

36

on the stove. Nora set up her violin stand in the living room and began to practice. Hadley was trembling. She didn't want to see her mother sick in the hospital. She didn't want to stay here alone with Nora. She took her mother's *Redbook* up to her room, lay down on her bed and read an article about movie actors with imperfect faces. There were pictures of Meryl Streep, Frances McDormand, and Jodie Foster from angles that showed their noses. Jodie Foster looked all right. The phone rang: it was Rachel wanting to know where she'd gone after school. Rachel had gone to Sherelle's. Sherelle had mouthed off in the extreme, and her mother grabbed the Palmolive from under the sink and squirted it onto her tongue.

Hadley started laughing.

"What about you?" Rachel said. "Were you sick or something?"

Hadley's laughter went on. Every time it started to fade she pictured Sherelle with dish detergent in her mouth, and it fanned into life again. She was the type of person who didn't dwell on sad things, unlike Rachel who thought when she coughed she had AIDS; in *Redbook* there was an article, "Your Daughter Says She Has AIDS!"

"I've decided," she said between gasps. "I'm going to be an actor."

CHAPTER THREE

Medicated

At home the next day, even skim milk and salt-free chicken broth burn the cut place on her tongue. By Wednesday, though, she can eat again. I lost it, she tells herself, a nod to the experience that turns it zany and light, an episode from a sit-com. The CAT-scan showed no tumors or other oddities. Her EEG was sine-curve smooth. Next time she'll remember her smelling salts, she tells the friends who call to see how she is. That, or "I was abducted by aliens." It gets a laugh.

But Leo, who rarely worries if he can find a reason not to, doesn't like the two falling incidents, three weeks apart and so similar. And unusual for her, normally the opposite of clumsy. He makes her an appointment for an MRI on Saturday afternoon when he can accompany her. She can't object to a plan obviously in her interest. But she has no reason to think she didn't simply trip coming down the stairs, or faint after a stressful day, biting her tongue from the force of the fall. Having ultra-low blood pressure, she almost always gets dizzy when she stands after sitting too long. If she eats better, sleeps more, drinks less or not at all, she'll maintain her not-so-frail hold on consciousness.

To reduce stress she takes the rest of the week off from work, planning to return the following Monday. In the meantime she de-nails the rest of the stairs, then starts the stripping, watching the maple emerge a clear, pale mustard. She plays tennis with Eileen and beats her two games out of three, slightly better than usual. By Friday the thing feels so remote it might have happened in someone else's life.

That morning, unusually relaxed and energetic, she calls Hadley's school and asks to speak to her language arts teacher. A good mother should know whether the teacher sucks, as Hadley says, or hates her, as Hadley also says, or whether Hadley simply isn't turning in her work. When will she get the call back? At lunchtime, possibly, though she may have to wait till after school. Mrs. Boltz is very busy.

Mrs. Boltz is busy through lunch. In the meantime Claire sands the stairs with increasingly fine sandpaper, stopping every once in a while to hear Dr. Quentin Young on "848" on the need

40

for universal single-payer healthcare. Dr. Quentin Young speaks slowly and sounds elderly, but is very smart and sure of himself. She too believes in universal healthcare although, thank God, they don't need it. She imagines herself elderly and tranquil, beyond neurosis and pettiness like Quentin Young. Then the door opens with a rush of fall air. It's Nora, who has come home right after school every day this week to be with her.

Nora kneels down beside her. She looks into her daughter's face. Says "I love you." Though Nora's vigilance is making her crazy. But she adores Nora, so intelligent and honest and good; a seeker.

"Mom," Nora whispers though no one else is home, "are you happy?"

She smiles. "I'm probably as happy as most people." The crease in Nora's brow deepens. She looks like a thirty-year-old woman. Claire passes a hand over her daughter's forehead. "Why wouldn't I be happy? I have you and Hadley and Dad. I have a good job. A nice house. I'm very lucky."

Nora presses her hands to her cheeks, as if molding the words that will emerge. "But sometimes, don't they, people get depressed for no reason. I have a friend who's on Zoloft. And this girl at school who looks like a model—she's taking Prozac."

"How do you know she's on Prozac?"

"Everybody knows. It's no big deal." Nora rubs the back of her head, dark curly hair that she rarely bothers to comb. Thick and coarse like Leo's. "I'd take it if I had to. I mean, it's better

41

than..." She pushes her hair away from her forehead, eyes her sharply.

"Better than what?"

"Well, obviously, better than, well—than ending it." Nora speaks with uncharacteristic lightness, as if embarrassed by what she is saying.

"God, you're morbid!" She touches Nora's arm, feels her flinch. "I hope you don't talk to your sister like this."

"Why would I talk to fuzz-brain about anything? Why are you changing the subject, *Maman*?" She picks up her books, walks out of the room.

Claire moves to the couch, lies down. Shuts her eyes, vaguely aware of a radio-news announcement. A bombing of a U.S. embassy. A country is named but she can't make it out. Her good mood is gone now.

She thinks of Leo, whose role, till now, was to counter her tendency to worry too much. He was okay and so was she. She would mock his persistent optimism, his refusal to entertain ugly or painful possibilities, but she counted on it. But now, according to Leo, she might not be okay. It makes her feel not okay. And Nora, with the same depressing attitude. Sometimes climbing the stairs Claire feels Nora behind her, arms out to catch her. How can she live like that, with only Hadley free of the image of Sicko Mom?

Claire has to reach back in memory for the normality they think she has lost. She wasn't a dominating conversationalist, was she? She must therefore stop herself from going on too long. She was, or thinks she was, affectionate. She must remember now to hug and kiss the girls when they come home from school. And Leo, of course. She has been called controlling, or at least "in control." That's probably true. She knows the location of keys and backpacks, and everyone's plans, who needs picking up when. But she also remembers being out of control. Hadley told her a lie and she yelled. Screamed, until Hadley cried. At which she felt relief and some pleasure, wanting not Hadley's moral reformation but evidence of her own impact. This is not who she wants to be.

Aswirl, she's almost glad when the phone rings. It's Mrs. Boltz.

The teacher sounds eager to talk about Hadley. "I've known her since she came here, what, three or four years ago? She was the sweetest child, so eager to please. But this year she has a little chip on her shoulder. Do you know what I'm talking about?"

Claire has always had respect for teachers. She tries to listen with an open mind, though it's as if her own conduct is under scrutiny. "No one's ever complained about her before." She believes this is true. Hadley's grades weren't like Nora's, but everything was at least satisfactory.

"I'm so glad to have you on the phone," says Mrs. Boltz. "Hadley's a beautiful girl. Extremely likeable. A natural leader. But she has trouble focusing on anything that doesn't completely absorb her. Most girls her age can concentrate for a class period. Have you ever had her tested for Attention Deficit Disorder?

Some children do marvelously once they're on Ritalin. Would you like to have her tested?"

She would like to hang up. She tries to remember what she'd called about. "I've been a little worried about her grades this year. Last year she was getting *B*'s. Ms. Macauley seemed to like the way she wrote."

"Seventh grade is demanding. She's changing classes now. And going through puberty, no doubt."

Claire labors not to be defensive. "I don't think *that's* the issue. She's tall, so people think she's older and expect more of her. Actually we're all late bloomers in this family." This is true. Neither Nora nor she got their periods till age fourteen. Nora had worried about it.

The teacher clears her throat. "Please don't take offense but I wouldn't feel right concealing this. I'm not sure if Hadley is always—" She pauses. Claire hears her loud breath. She holds the receiver out from her ear. "—If she has been entirely forthright with me. I'm sorry but I must ask. I don't mean to be tactless. Did you—did Hadley recently lose a grandparent?"

"Uh yes," says Claire, although her mother was alive and well in her condo-complex in Boca and her father had died ten years ago. Leo's folks were long gone. "Her grandpa. They were very close."

Mrs. Boltz takes a breath. "I am so sorry."

"Thank you. And thank you for calling back!"

Stimulated by the interaction (though aware it's not her normal pattern), she goes up to Nora's room with a glass of iced tea. Nora is reading but moves to give her room on the bed. Answers without anger or irony her questions about friends, movies, her teachers, her busy schedule, seeming to be, actually, glad for the company. She tells Claire about her fundamentalist Christian coach who makes them pray before and after practice. Nora wrote an editorial to the school paper stating her opposition as a Jewish agnostic, then withdrew it when she realized she no longer minded the prayer. In fact, it made her feel peaceful. "Do you know what I mean, Mom?" Claire nods, glad, simply, that Nora is talking to her.

Claire is trying to find another harmless, interesting topic of conversation, when Nora says in her voice of a Supreme Court Justice, "You think I'm too young, don't you? To know things?" Claire laughs—she's feeling so much better—but Nora doesn't laugh. "I already *know*," Nora says, fixing her with her pale gray eyes. "So there's no need to tell me."

"Know what?" Claire laughs merrily. "What do you know?"

Nora shakes her head. "I won't bring it up anymore, I promise. But you have to promise me it won't happen again. No matter what."

"Nora, what are you thinking? You talk like I—" She won't conclude the ridiculous statement. Nora eyes her some more, which Claire reads as pure fakery. But it's unnerving to hear your own admonishments in your children's mouths. *Promise that it won't happen again.* "You have an interesting mind, honey. But, really, truly, you don't have to worry about me."

45

"Promise," says Nora.

Claire giggles. "Promise what? To hold onto the banister?"

"Promise."

Claire does so. And is pleased to feel Nora feeling easier. Nora allows a hug. Then Hadley comes upstairs with a story about a girl on the bus who acted stupid. Nora rolls her eyes. Claire smiles, suppressing her lecture on tolerance. On the way downstairs she hears Nora say to Hadley, "Do you think Mom's acting, you know, different?"

She freezes, hand on the banister, for Hadley's response, but can't make it out. She thinks Hadley said, "Truly. She's nicer!"

She stays calm throughout the MRI, picturing a little red-roofed town in the south of France where Eileen and Dan went last year (they sent a postcard). She's fine the seventy minutes they spend waiting for the neurologist, one of the best in the field, according to Leo. In his office, having received no apology or explanation, still she lets him run on to her and Leo about the many things wrong with her. Until she can't stand it anymore, she has to break in, "I'm sorry, Dr. Patel, I just want to know, if the MRI is 'inconclusive,' as you say, why do I have to take— Even when I was little, they never said for sure that I—" She swallows hard. Any more words and she might cry. She sits straight up, hands on the arms of her chair.

"Listen to me, Mrs. Winger. Whether we call it epilepsy or nerves or a good old English fit, the treatment is the same. You probably had a grand mal seizure. You may have another one. Do you want to go on working? You're a nurse, yes? Do you want to drive a car? If so, you must take medication. There are drugs on the market that reduce the incidence of seizures by as much as ninety percent. That's good news, Mrs. Winger."

She looks at Leo, waiting for him to say something. She has a right to ask a question, doesn't she, without being made to feel brainless (when she already feels sufficiently brainless)? But Leo's nodding at him. The cronies discuss drugs, benefits and side effects. Patel is small, fiftyish, with dark skin and bright dark eyes, like a squirrel. His large corner office overlooks the Loop. She gazes out the window without seeing anything.

Afterward in the car Leo agrees that Patel was needlessly highhanded. But when she calls him unprofessional, Leo says nothing. When she calls him an asshole, Leo just smiles at her. He stops at a drugstore and fills the prescription. Back home he pours her a glass of water, hands her a pill. Watches her swallow it. Says from high above and far away, "If you have any problems we can get him to prescribe something else. Or we'll find you a new doctor."

He sounds reasonable. He is reasonable. What can she do but agree? On the wall of the nurses' lounge Nancy put up a plaque that reads: *Grant me the Courage to fight the Battles that I can win, the Strength to decline those I cannot win, and the Wisdom to know the Difference.* Is she strong, then? She doesn't feel wise. But she'll take the medication, as directed, even, by Herr Patel, if Leo will agree not mention her problem to the girls. It's a need-to-know situation. The girls do not need to know. He has to promise.

He embraces, kisses her. Seems to find her in some way touching. "You're ashamed, honey, and you don't need to be." He laughs, he's in a very good mood about something. "The best people get epilepsy," he says. "Dostoevsky had epilepsy."

"*You* don't have epilepsy."

He nods—restrained, compassionate. She pulls back from him. "Look, they're teenage girls, they have their own problems, they don't need mine." She looks at him, still shaking his condescending head at her. "It makes me highly uncomfortable. If you insist on telling them—in fact, Leo, if you say another word to me now, I am going to hate you. This is not a joke."

"Look, look, look, look, look—"

"Fuck you."

"But what if you seize right in front of them?"

Now, although the argument runs on for a while, he is taking her seriously. "That's why," she says, "I'm taking medication."

"It takes time to work."

"If I have another, whatever, episode? If it happens again I'll tell them. But not until."

"All right," he says. "All right."

He buys her a pure white cat with one blue and one green eye. Nora names it Cassandra. It sleeps between them, purring loudly, silky under her hand.

———

Leo is as happy as she has ever seen him. He has started doing radical keratotomies, and comes home infused with the pleasure and gratitude of patients who no longer need glasses to see stars in the sky. "At least the patients that live in the suburbs," he jokes. She laughs, sharing with him the city dweller's snobbery toward the suburbs, where both grew up. Enjoying his excitement at what he can do for people. "The scales literally fall from their eyes!" He kisses her as if terribly aware of how precious she is.

She has gone back to work, as planned. She takes her meds, as prescribed. She hasn't fallen again, or fainted or seized. But it's November now, under a cold, white sky. She spends less time thinking, or thinking about thinking, but small things have started to annoy her, noises like the hum of the hospital heating system. Maybe it's the medication, but an undertone in the speech of certain people gives her a lump in the throat. As if there was, once, a veil or screen between her and the world, and now it's gone. Sensations prick her like manicure scissors. Sometimes in the middle of the night, full of daytime energy, she walks downstairs, mists her plants, dances around the empty living room to the music in her head. Then the spirit shuts off. She sinks onto the living room rug, or at the door of her and Leo's room. At the hospital she has four ten-hour shifts, Monday through Thursday, and she continues to work them. But sometimes she trips on her way out the revolving doors while other times her movements are briskly purposeful. Either way it's dangerous to come close. She runs behind her cart down supermarket aisles tossing in cartons and jars.

She wants to stop the Tegretol but she's afraid. She starts seeing Kara, who has an MSW, wears short skirts over long muscular legs, and believes in talk therapy. At the second session, Claire unearths her old childhood envy of Eric, who scored ninety points higher than she on most achievement tests and got *A*'s without trying. "Good work," says Kara. According to Kara, Claire is as brilliant as Eric but needs to prove it to herself. She must try new things. Be daring. She finds a four-week adult ed. ceramics class at Francis Parker, a nearby private school. She tries to feel hopeful.

In early December, the air crackling with the promise of winter, she arrives home from her first session, washes the clay off her hands. The girls are in bed, the front and back doors locked, thermopanes shut, furnace blowing warm air into all the rooms of the house. Leo opens a bottle of wine. At the kitchen table, while Cassandra purrs on her lap, occasionally looking up with her blank, beautiful mismatched eyes, they drink and toast things. The art of ceramics. Ms. Kara, MSW. Life's complexities, "which we can handle," says Leo.

They toast their marriage, which has taken some recent hits, but which is fundamentally sound.

"We're lucky, Claire."

"It scares me."

"A lot of things scare you."

"Fuck you."

He looks at her. She puts a hand over her mouth. She can tell she doesn't sound like herself. She wonders if she should apologize. She's been swearing a lot lately.

"You've been watching those R-rated movies again."

She pretends to hang her head. "Honestly, I don't know where that came from!" She tries to laugh, feeling a little nervous.

He takes her hand, and chews the fleshy side of it. "The devil made you do it?" She laughs.

He tells her about the red string his bubbie tied around the leg of his crib to protect him from the evil eye, a spirit that punishes families arrogant and foolish enough to revel in their good fortune, as if it were their due. They discuss whether, after the ceramics course, she should take another or join a book-discussion group at the University of Chicago. They finish the Chardonnay, then start in on the only other bottle they have, sweet grape wine from last Passover. They make love on the living room floor. And fall asleep on the rug. And wake, thank God, in the early morning when a daughter's alarm goes off upstairs.

From her course at Francis Parker, Claire emerged with a set of oatmeal-glazed bowls that wobbled and scratched the tabletop. Then, in January, she enrolled in a sculpture class at the School of the Art Institute. It ran all day on Saturday, nine till four. She left with her hands dry from plaster, or bruised by the hard, cold metal and splintery wood.

But Claire loves the materials. She loves the class. She admires the work of the other students, especially of a girl who carves nightmare masks from tree bark, and another whose knee-high bald plaster women have grotesquely large hands and feet. She chats sometimes with the girl who works at the table beside her, amusing her with gaps in her awareness of pop culture. Sometimes she stays after class trying to mold out of clay a small, accurately proportioned female body. Every once in a while in the cafeteria she drinks tea with her teacher Professor Ko, an elderly man with ebony button eyes, whose first name is so contemporary white-professional-American (Vic? Steve?) she can never remember it. But she's at ease with Professor Ko, who does not impinge on her erratic store of energy. Without responding directly to anything she said, he speaks gravely, looking her right in the eye; she feels sometimes as if she's conversing profoundly with someone from Mars.

During one of these surreal conversations, she's sitting outside and slightly above herself, watching her mouth and hands act out a scene from a Japanese play, when she feels a shift in the atmosphere of the room, as if all the dust motes, vapor droplets, and air molecules have started flowing in a single direction. The clatter halts a moment, then resumes louder than before. Her head turns toward a table, one row down and one over, where ten or twelve students have gathered. Professor Ko beams at her his thoughtful, random amiability but she keeps an eye out. Wanting a glimpse of the student beauty queen who must be the focus of the intensity. A chair scrapes away from the table. A laughing shriek rockets up. Someone screams, "That is so sick!" She no longer gives Ko even the husk of a response. The rapid speech at the nearby table is urgent, significant. And behind it a voice so low and steady it might have been her own pulse. When one o'clock signals the start of the afternoon session, she picks up her tray and strolls past the crowded table. With the students is an older man who could be anywhere between forty and sixty. He has pale reddish hair, a beak of a nose, leathery skin over strong bones, good-looking in an ugly way like a cartoon CEO. He talks with a loose smile on his lips, as if he has an oblique relationship with what he's saying. As if daring you to challenge him.

He looks up. His glance crosses hers.

The moment stays with her, in part because she can't exactly describe it. For days afterward it plays in her mind: There shot from his face to hers and back again—could it be? for sure?—a small, distinct flame of white light. It sent a stab of pleasure and pain to the base of her throat. She ran her tray over to a pile at the back of the room, out of range of his eyes, the palest blue they could have been without being colorless.

At the door she caught up with Professor Ko. "They look so *engrossed*," she said casually, cocking her head toward the crowded lunch table.

His smile showed small, startling white teeth. "Yes, here it is so very messy and soiled."

That night Claire and Leo lie in bed critiquing how well they're getting along and how they might improve, a ritual that began just after Hadley was born. Normal procedure is to say a few necessary though possibly hurtful things, like swimmers sticking their toes into icy water. Then they back away toward the cabana of their mutual love and respect.

Leo begins. "I don't know why you persist in ignoring the street-cleaning signs. I'm tired of paying the city fifty dollars a crack."

"I know. I hate it, too. I'll try and be more careful."

"Try?"

"No, I'll work on it. I promise." She takes a breath, a courteous gap between her apology and her own small complaint. "If you came home earlier on Tuesday and Thursday you could pick Nora up from track practice. As it is, I'm back from Children's making dinner and I have to drive over to Whitney Young."

She has mentioned this before. Tuesdays and Thursdays after his last surgical round he goes to the gym and works out. Thirty minutes on the treadmill, three circuits of strength training. With his shower it takes him an hour and a half. It has never seemed fair to her, since she can only exercise on weekends. She doesn't expect him to change, though. Wednesday he has surgery board, Monday he does the shopping. She waits for his apology and for her own pulse of irritation. He has no trouble apologizing but nothing changes in his behavior. Maybe because he *has* no trouble. He seems to like to apologize. She tries to remember if he has ever conformed to a desire of hers. Ever changed in the smallest way.

"Nora's almost sixteen," he says. "Isn't she old enough to come home on her own?"

"You want her to take the bus past Cabrini-Green?"

"I don't mean at night. She's done at five o'clock, right? Besides, they're tearing down Cabrini-Green."

"Yes."

"What's the matter? Why are you looking at me like that?"

She looks away. She has nothing to say. Tears have sprung to her eyes, but they make no sense; this is not a major issue.

"Claire, all right. I'll skip the exercise. I'll die early, of a heart attack, like my father. Claire, what? I'm trying to be funny, honey."

She looks at his face—eyes, nose, mouth. His ears look too small, his eyes too close together.

"Earth to Claire. Hey, put your arms around me."

She edges toward him, allows him to pull her into his warmth. The familiar smell of his hair and breath. She breathes it in.

"You are beautiful, Claire. I'm lucky to have such a young and beautiful wife. I mean that."

"Thank you."

"Thank you?"

He sounds so comically outraged she's forced to laugh. They make love. As always he's sensitive and painstaking but for some reason now, the feeling doesn't come through completely. She thinks of a woman in one of Oliver Sacks's books, whose skin didn't feel anything. She had a nerve disease. She felt completely cut off from human life.

Afterward Leo kisses her all over her face. "There couldn't be anyone better than you for me."

"I know," she murmurs.

"*What* do you know?" He's teasing, looking for her usual affection.

"Eat your heart out," she says, a devilish response that makes him laugh and at the same time makes her feel better.

In her dream, in a peach-colored body suit, she lies on the grass of a high mountain-meadow. A man kneels down beside her. She's afraid to open her eyes but she feels good, on the verge of happy, except for an annoying buzz in her ear, of a fly or mosquito.

"Mom, I can't sleep, Mom."

Claire feels a soft hand on her shoulder.

"Hey, deadhead."

"What," Claire murmurs, trying to preserve the thread back to her dream.

Hadley leans in, whispers loud in her ear, "It's this game at school. We look in the mirror and say *Bloody Mary, Bloody Mary*."

She keeps her eyes closed but the dream is gone.

"I don't like it at all," Hadley says.

"Then maybe you should stop playing it?"

"Brilliant, Mama."

Claire sighs. "Bloody Mary. What kind of game is that? Have your girlfriends started drinking?"

"Don't joke."

"I'm sorry," Claire says. "But who's Bloody Mary?"

"What difference does it make!"

"Shhhh." Claire reaches in the dark for Hadley's hand but can't find it. "Honey, what do you expect to see in the mirror? If you look for monsters you're going to find monsters."

"What grade am I in, Mom? *Kindergarten?*"

Leo turns over and puts the pillow over his head.

"Hsssh! Don't wake your father."

Cassandra has been lying between her pillow and Leo's. Suddenly the cat arches her back like a witch's cat. She emits a brief yowl, then recurls in the nest of her hair, purring ferociously. Claire says,"I love you, Hadley. There are no monsters in our house. Now go back to bed."

"Can I sleep in here?"

"Your own bed is much more comfortable." Nearly awake now, Claire puts an arm around her daughter and kisses her cheek. Hadley draws back.

"That's great! I'm a poster girl. Have you hugged your kid today?"

Claire sighs. "Honey, you're going to have to give me a break. I am really tired."

Hadley is silent a moment; is she caught in the first throes of empathy? Claire holds her breath. Then Hadley whispers in her ear so loud it almost hurts, "I don't say *Bloody Mary,* I don't even look in the mirror." There are tears in her voice. "When I do, I look like I'm old already."

"All right. All right." She's already sitting up. She sets her feet on the floor. "Go to the bathroom, Had. I'm right behind you. Be quiet now."

In the deep darkness of the master bathroom Claire closes the door, turns on the night light. In the medicine chest is a new bottle of Nyquil. She removes the safety cap, pours an ounce of the heavy liquid into the plastic dispenser cup. The air seethes with the smell of manufactured cherry. "It's for colds, but it works like a sleeping pill."

Hadley looks at the cup in Claire's hand, the gelatinous red shining black in the low light. "This is your brain, Mama." She makes a hissing noise. "This is your brain on drugs. Ssssssss!"

"It's up to you." She sets the cup on the counter. "Well?" Hadley doesn't move. Claire opens the door, peers out toward the gray swamp of the marital bed and the surprising whiteness of Cassandra. The cat, with one blue eye and one green eye, turned out to be deaf. Hadley is a surface from which sounds ricochet just below the threshold of hearing. Claire dumps the medicine. "Go," she whispers, "or you'll be tired for school."

"Ooh. That's up-front thinking, Mom."

Claire leans forward to kiss her goodnight, but Hadley recedes, shrinks, winks out, and is gone. Claire swallows two Excedrin PMs, lies down beside Cassandra, and tries to remember the name of Hadley's game. Asleep, she dreams she's driving her car so fast it's almost like falling.

CHAPTER FOUR

Normal

Hadley wanted to be normal, that was all, clear and pure like apple juice, the kind of girl who passed through a room leaving the scent of fresh air. But forces in science class beyond her control had situated her directly in front of Mr. Raskin, between two boys who would have punched each other out, then and there, if not for the desk between them, *her* desk, over which they evil-eyed each other, it was like a war zone, and besides it made her out the only bad one. Really she didn't mind getting in trouble along with her friends, but alone was sad. And infuriating, since Rachel had talked just as much as she, and at this moment

May Sun and Winston Baines were probably passing notes to each other.

She cast a quick glance behind her but her friends were miles away. All she had to look at were the words on the blackboard (easier to read from here but so what?) and the flower diagram on the easel with all the parts labeled, *pistil, stamen*. Maybe she'd get smarter up here. Competition for Nora.

As well as she could under the circumstances she tried to absorb what Raskin was saying. The subject was plant reproduction (ooh, dirty) but it was hard to listen without someone to roll your eyes to every once in a while, and really hard not to yawn, and the yawn wanted to come right now, it was coming. Last night she'd slept less than four hours (she lay awake watching the clock's glowing red digits), and God, she'd better listen now because Raskin liked to call on you in the middle of a yawn, and if you looked blank he'd say, "Are we keeping you up, dear?" Pistil fertilized stamen, right? Or was it the other way around?

She was near dozing when she felt a prick on the back of her head. She flicked a cool glance at Fletcher Lawson behind her, who had poked her with what felt like a pencil. She glared at him. Yee ha! But there was no assurance that Raskin wouldn't yell at her for turning around in her chair, or send her, chair and all, to the outer Siberia of the hall, or, even, because he got irrational sometimes, down to the principal, who'd call her parents, who wouldn't do anything, but their concern, however mild, would sit on her brain.

With the mirror of the compact from her mother's purse (her mother never noticed small missing things) she checked out Fletcher Lawson, who had a grin on his face. Angry tears sprang to her eyes. The dingbat beside him was grinning, too, at the bigger dingbat Aaron Rappaport who supposedly had a crush on her. Aaron Rappaport's cheeks were red, and he was leaning back from his desk, like there was a worm on it, or a turd. She angled the mirror toward Rachel in the hazy, comfy middle of the room where she used to sit. With a pair of crossed fingers Rachel signaled encouragement. Hadley trained the mirror on May Sun, who was half turned toward to Winston, whom she supposedly talked to every night from seven-thirty to eight-thirty. Hadley directed the mirror toward her own mouth and nose, gazed with some pleasure at the small, fine-haired nostrils, the two smooth, narrow scallops of her upper lip. She liked the shine of her hair falling over her ear. Then she heard the words *Bloody Mary*, as distinct as if someone had whispered them. With a shudder, she snapped the mirror shut.

For the past months the other girls had loved this game but so far Hadley had only pretended to play. She'd turn her back to the mirror or close her eyes and instead of the words that were to summon the bloody image, she'd say *Blood Money. Bill Murray. Bad Manners. Black Magic.* But now, to make a bad day wholly unspeakable, she began to wonder if her trick had been noticed. If a so-called friend—Sherelle?—had told Fletcher what to whisper to her? Before she could dispel the queasy thought, the back of her head twitched again, and she turned in time to see exactly what Fletcher Lawson had given Darnell to place on Aaron Rappaport's desk—one of her long straight brown hairs.

Her cheeks went sick hot. This was her future all of a sudden rolling out before her like some terrible country. She couldn't stand Aaron Rappaport, his round red face, his jeans with the three horizontal creases below the stomach. She didn't have an hour's worth of anything to say on the phone to a boy, let alone Aaron Rappaport. She wanted Fletcher in the principal's office. She wanted his mother called. She wanted him suspended. She raised her hand and waved it back and forth like the goody-goodies dying to give their answers.

"Yes, Hadley?" Raskin smiled, as if Hadley were someone he'd been wanting to meet for a long time.

Hadley giggled her shame into the compact in her hand. What could she say, what could anybody? That Fletcher Lawson had pulled a hair out of her head and given it to Aaron Rappaport? Tears filled her eyes.

"Hadley," Raskin said, "you had a contribution?"

Hadley tried to blank everything from her face but earnest thoughtfulness. "I forgot."

"About how pollen is disseminated?" he urged gently.

"The pistil fertilizes the stamen," she ventured.

Raskin's mouth turned down. "Dissemination, not fertilization. How pollen spreads from flower to flower. Hadley, you're in dreamland again."

"I mean the stamen fertilizes the pistil." She smiled like a good-natured idiot, rapping herself on the side of her head. Raskin walked over to her, stared down over her shoulder.

"What's that in your hand?"

She shrank from the heat that radiated from his body, and his smell of cologne and cigarettes. She studied her own hand, the uncurling of her fingers, like petals opening on a stamen or was it a pistil?

"Ask me for it later," Raskin said.

She placed the compact in the teacher's large dry palm. She gazed straight ahead at the labeled flower diagram as her one link to the society of her girlfriends through the long, bleak morning vanished into Raskin's desk. Fixed on the diagram, she allowed but didn't welcome the drab words of science into herself. Then, as Raskin put the easel away, a folded scrap of notepaper plopped softly onto her desk. She nudged it onto her lap, opened it with a secret hand. *Dear Hadley I am very sorry Fletcher Lawson.*

She put her hand over her mouth, trying not to cry. Her hand smelled of the compact, like a fancy ladies' room or the word boudoir. Like her mother's skin.

That night Hadley woke up again and tiptoed in to her mother.

This time she watched her sleep, her black hair spread out on the pillow. Her mother looked beautiful asleep, and Hadley prayed God that when she grew up she'd look exactly like her mother. She walked to the master bathroom, closed the door, turned on the light and swallowed a capful of green Nyquil, considerately rinsing the cap before screwing it back on. Then she opened the drawer that held her mother's jewelry box and pulled out her diamond bracelet.

Back in her room Hadley held her braceleted wrist up to the arc of lights around her dresser mirror, standing just out of range of where her face would show. Bold and crazy like Joan of Arc, she swam her arm back and forth under the lights, within the glinting stones. Then an undulation took her too far forward. In the mirror was *what*—a flash of nose? Eyelid? Heart beating wildly she turned, hurled herself into bed. Across the expanse of varnished floor was the white oblong of the switch plate. She burrowed under the covers. Mom, Mama, someone, please come turn off the light please!

She knew better than to scream. Teeth faintly chattering, she put a pillow over her head, wedged another under her stomach, adjusting her arm so that the flat underside of the precious stones lay against her wrist. The bracelet, a gift from her father to her mother, was flashily, assertively beautiful, the kind of gift she hoped one day a man would buy for her. Her mother wore it to fancy parties. But her mother's eyes on her, and everything, were dreamy these days, absent-minded, and Hadley already suspected there was nothing fixed in the arrangement of wishes, lies, and other people's notions that made up herself. There was some *give* here. An opportunity to impose some will. She had listened to Nora on the phone, and incorporated in her own voice the same appealing laughing underlay. The word "gnarly" in her lunchtime chatter came from her second cousin in California, a chubby girl who had a million friends and got elected to everything. She had memorized the eye chart in her father's office—the tiny fifth row O F L C T, and the tinier sixth T Z V E C L—and each year he commended her eyesight, so much better than his at her age, and marked her blurred vision 20/20. (She was not a girl who wore glasses or even contact lenses.)

Her mother's diamonds would be a sort of garnish on the personality she was developing in the halls and classrooms of middle school, the embodiment of a new hard glamor. Tomorrow, braceleted, she'd ignore Fletcher Lawson, whose apology made up for nothing. She was absent and beautiful like her mother, who was more beautiful than her girlfriends' mothers, who made women out of clay that looked like tiny goddesses.

CHAPTER FIVE

A Foreign Country

Next Saturday in the cafeteria no groupie cliques assembled; she might have forgotten the red-haired man except for a little residue at the bottom of her dreams. Ko had recommended an exhibit of Illinois sculpture at the Museum. After class that day, she threaded her way along the art school corridors to the public building.

The exhibit irritates and confuses her. She likes realism and, even more, expressionism. Distortions in the world that suggest hidden human lives. That shed light, or seem to, on her own hidden life. Of the pieces on display, the only thing vaguely understandable is a sandstone block with a vertical cleft entitled "Genitalia." Worst is a ceiling-high tower of black crenelated restaurant ashtrays that lists to one side. On the nearest wall a poster declares:

1. Every year the Tower of Pisa leans an additional .083 degrees.
2. The universe is flying apart at a calculated 80.6 miles per second.
3. Every year 20,000 Americans die from diseases linked to the smoking of cigarettes.
4. During World War II when meat was scarce, the rate of Scottish women with breast cancer dropped a startling 20%.
5. These statements have nothing to do with each other or to any of the artifacts that you may have been looking at.
6. Or to factual truth.

The lobes of her brain begin to swell. Behind her a man says to a woman, "What am I missing?" Claire smiles at him. His companion replies, "But isn't that the point?"

Her fingers feel thick, her hands clubs at the end of her arms. She bends over a plank of what looks like close-grained wood. It's a plank-shaped canvas with meticulously applied sworls of brown and gold paint. She wants to to sink down onto the museum floor, lay her head down. Close her eyes. Nap for a moment; she is so tired. She glances around—is she behaving oddly?—and sees the man and woman locked in the kind of daytime embrace associated with teenagers. He has a bald spot the size of a headlight. They are nearly her age. Out the nearest door, she finds herself in a smaller room, narrow and shadowy.

The dark room seems empty at first though murmurs dot the air like clouds of insects. Faint yellow light comes from a table lamp by the far wall, part of a stage set of a living room *circa* 1960—TV console, blond wood table, salmon-pink upholstered chair under plastic, on a square of sculpted green carpet. On top of the TV is a large framed portrait of President and Jackie Kennedy and their two children. A rifle leans against the console, casual as a broom. In front, in a semicircle of chairs two teenage boys begin to laugh. A woman hugs the little girl on her lap, who looks like a princess in her white bunny-fur coat. "Mom," the girl says, "this is *stu*pid."

Claire is about to leave, but then a woman in a powder blue suit and squash-heels limps onto the square of carpet. Claire thinks it's a woman, though her face is hidden under a milky plastic Mixmaster cover. On her arm hangs a bulging flowered carry-all. She sets the bag down, then seats herself on the edge of the pink chair and removes the appliance cover. Her face is very young, eighteen or nineteen at most, and looks younger still with her bright red lipstick. "Hello, dear ones," she says, and her red mouth opens and shuts like a doll's. "Jack is dead but something of him remains with all of us."

Claire sits down in the empty seat, unable to take her eyes off this ghoul-Jackie Kennedy, whose thin sweet voice heightens the impression of overwhelming grief. Tears hang in her eyes, sweat beads her upper lip, her fingers tremble—she's either consumed by her role or on the brink of a nervous breakdown. "I ought to be sad," says Jackie, "but, to tell you the truth, I don't exist."

A hoot comes from somewhere in the small audience. The woman picks up her daughter and departs.

Jackie dips into her carry-all and starts handing out to members of the audience repellent artifacts linked to the death of JFK. There's a bullet painted with blood-red nail polish, a white sock frozen to the approximate shape of a lung, melting limp and soggy, a plate of scrambled eggs topped with pink hand lotion, announced as "his brains." Claire sits mouth-breathing against the pink sweetness. This is strange, yes. But she and all of them are part of the strangeness.

They remain silent, motionless, as the young woman steps back onto the carpet and begins taking off her clothes. Her skirt falls to the floor, then the matching jacket, a string of pearls. She yanks her slip up over her head. Soon all she has on are a bra and a girdle, between which squeeze out parallel rims of young-girl fat. From the audience comes an intake of breath, all the eyes and minds in sudden unison. Cutting diagonally across her midriff is the black trestle of a scar, obviously daubed on with marker or eyebrow pencil but still troubling.

That seems to be the climax of the little play, if that's what it is. The actor, if that is what she is, bows amid scattered applause.

One of the boys gives a wolf whistle. Jackie's fingers tremble, hands holding each other at her waist. A heavy-set man at the other end of the row hands her a plaid flannel robe.

The boys stroll out, but the handful of people who remain begin to critique the performance. "I had a problem, uh, with the level of invention," says a small, bearded man. "I'd like to have discovered something else under your clothing. More provocative than a scar. Less, er, cliche."

A woman nods. She has snow-white hair and a young face. "The act of stripping is itself a cliche."

"I do admire the gesture though," says the bearded man.

Somebody else was bothered by the fuzzy "idea-content." What did the artist mean to create through this grotesque Jackie Kennedy? Does she represent bourgeois America, or a certain kind of American woman? Or the myth of female purity?

"All of the above," says ghoul-Jackie with some fire. Claire sits curling and uncurling her toes to test their ability to bear her away, but she can't take her eyes from the young woman's face— its mix of frailty and pure crazy guts.

"The real problem," says the white-haired woman, "is how to be outrageous these days. What myths do we believe in enough to care if they're obliterated? The just State? The myth of female purity? The sanctity of the naked body? Outrage is dead!"

"I know that," the girl says. "Do you think I just wanted to offend you? I *couldn't* offend you. You all sat like it was a cocktail party. That was my *point!*" Her voice is loud but thin, as if it will break if any more stress is applied. Claire aches for the young artist, whose wide mouth registers increasingly large quantities of pain. "Well, thank you all very much," she says, thick with controlled tears.

The girl stands up, and Claire rises as well, her arms wanting to reach out. In this young woman she feels her own pure, fragile, crazy soul.

But the young woman is heading toward the heavy-set man at the end of the row. He puts an arm around her, lays his cheek, briefly, to her cheek. She is nearly his height, but he's bulkier, his stance wide like a wrestler's. In his paternal embrace the young woman releases a quiet sob. There's a lump in Claire's throat. Her father was a sad, nervous man, so easily hurt she had to protect him. This man is the opposite of nervous. He has curly reddish hair. His lazy voice carries. "Take in what you can and save the rest to mull later. It was a ballsy performance. Now, onward."

Claire nods though no one is looking at her.

Then the man turns, showing her his face, his eyes the pale blue-gray of cigarette smoke. It's the man who'd held court last week in the cafeteria. His pupils gleam like black beads. Sick and exhilarated like a voyeur, she walks out of the room.

The following week, after the morning session of her sculpture class, Claire visits the Office of the Registrar. "I'm looking for the course that, uh, teaches you to do bizarre things in front of, uh, an audience?" She sounds like a valley girl. The bored-looking work-study student looks more painfully bored.

"You mean 4-D. Performance."

Claire nods, though she had no idea. She smiles warmly. The girl yawns.

Performance, she explains, is art in four dimensions, the usual three plus time. "2-D's painting and drawing, 3-D's like—sculpture, and 4-D's—"

"Like a crazy play?" Claire tries not to giggle.

The girl shrugs, looks through the course catalogue, so oppressed by the inanity of her duties and the people she has to deal with, it must be a pose. But if she sees her as a ditzy middle-aged woman, Claire doesn't mind. She feels oddly buoyant, like herself a long time ago when her future seemed a wide, shining road to anywhere.

There are two instructors of 4-D, Jennifer Rosencrantz and Bodey Marcus. "Bodey? Is that a man?" Claire asks.

"It depends on your definition. No, I'm kidding. Marcus is obviously a . . . He won't let you forget." Her voice trails off. "It's in 26B. Most of the time it runs late."

"You're sweet," Claire says giddily. "You'll go far in life."

The girl doesn't look up, but Claire puts a hand to her mouth, surprised by her mockery. What else will come out of her? Who would name their son Bodey? Body? Bawdy?

26B is low-ceilinged, windowless, fluorescent bright like a

Hopper painting, and full of motion that makes no immediate sense. The students mill, forming and reforming small groups, talking, gesturing. Conspicuous in his isolation is a tall, lanky boy whose head seems too heavy for the stem of his neck. He stands at the edge of one of the groups, grinning as if at a joke he doesn't get, while the teacher, the red-haired, pale-eyed man, observes the proceedings from a chair across the room. The boy approaches a second group of students. He speaks but gets no response. The instructor, Bodey Marcus, calls out, loud over the murmuring, "You have five minutes to establish your presence or you are out of here!" Claire stiffens but the man pushes on, "What's the smirk all about, Peter? Come on, we don't have to like you to acknowledge your lousy existence!"

Peter's head hangs lower. He speaks to a sari-clad redhead who addresses the girl beside her, "I saw a crazy bird last night. A white bird with a yellow comb on its head. It was sitting on the railing of our little balcony. In the morning it was still there." A third party declares, or so Claire believes, "Henry James is a fag."

"Tallyho," says Bodey Marcus.

Claire rubs a spot between her eyebrows; any appeal this Bodey Marcus might have had for her is completely gone. In fact, she'll write a letter to the Dean of Students about the nasty game he's making his students play. How could they employ such a man?

The conversations, if that's what they are, proceed a few more minutes, then Bodey Marcus raises his hand. Silence falls.

Peter looks up, wiping his damp forehead. Everyone is watching him. "You're good actors," he says, his voice quavering but without a trace of smirk. "God, you almost had me believing it."

"Believing what?" Bodey Marcus steps closer, smiling his knowledge of exactly what Peter will say. The conductor. The ringmaster.

"I was in a foreign country. I was a stranger. I was completely out of it." He takes a breath. "It was freaky." He's upset but regrouping now. A girl puts an arm through his arm. Someone pats his shoulder.

"Good work," says Bodey Marcus. He looks at his watch. "Lunchtime. But first, volunteers. At one o'clock who wants to run the next gauntlet?"

Hands go up. The class straggles toward the door, Claire among them. Bodey Marcus touches her sleeve, lightly, with a finger. "I've seen you before."

He is standing regulation distance from her but seems to press down on her, maybe because of his size. He's at least a head taller than she, and probably fifty pounds overweight. She wants to step back but forces herself to hold her ground. "That was quite a show."

"You appreciated it. Not everybody does."

Claire's face feels hot. But his gaze is so purposeful and interested, she wonders what she'll say next. She expects to enjoy saying it.

"I'm not sure I appreciated anything. I was going to report you to the Dean."

"Uh oh."

She smiles. She feels in charge now, though she fears he's allowing her to feel in charge. "You were abusive," she says firmly.

He touches the back of her wrist. "You said to yourself, 'There's something wrong with a guy who treats his students like that.'"

"Not just your students! Anyone!"

His grip is light rather than firm, but even after he lets go she can't move for a moment. She shifts her weight, relocates the door.

"But then you said to yourself, 'It's generally not useful to formulate an opinion until all the information is in.'" He emits a gunshot laugh. "See, I know you."

His voice resonates with self-love. It irritates but also excites her. As if somehow he does know her. She feels more than usually distinct.

The following Saturday, in sculpture, she learns from the friendly young woman who works beside her that Bodey Marcus is living with a former grad student, an art prodigy who by age twenty-two had her first Museum show. Claire is done thinking about the subject. She begins work on a large clay head, inside of which she installs a chewed pencil, a receipt from a hair appointment, a scrap cut—right there in class—from the hem of her T-shirt, insignificant things whose confluence makes her hands feel weak. On his inspection round, Mr. Ko breathes in her ear, "You have turned a

76

corner." She resolves, when passing Bodey in the hall or the cafeteria, to smile vaguely as if she were thinking of something else.

But in the afternoon, as she heads toward the cafeteria, Bodey Marcus stops in the hall right in front of her. "You missed class again. If you don't start showing up I'm going to have to call your parents."

He stands so close she'd have to step back to step around him. She freezes, idiotically mute. When he walks off, she drifts toward the wall and hangs there a moment in the swirl of air from his large wake. Later that day, when she sees him alone in the hall she can't resist accosting him with a pointless question. Will he be teaching in the summer? He replies without mockery. She's limp with relief. Just before she leaves she goes down to his office and chatters for ten minutes about his needing to eat well and get some exercise. "You're right. I'm a bad boy. Self-indulgent and shortsighted." He smiles, loving himself.

"A short life and a merry one?"

He puts his arms half-out, as if struggling not to embrace her.

That night, to disentangle from the odd pull of him, she describes him to Eileen over the phone. "He sounds like Jack Nicholson," Eileen says.

"Yes. But fatter and uglier."

"So what's the attraction? Is there attraction?"

"Not physical. Well, maybe. I don't think it's healthy." Her face flames, thinking about it—her fascination with an egocentric man who probably doesn't even like her. "Of all the men I know," she tells Eileen, "he comes the closest to *seeming* single-celled without actually *being*."

"That's deep, Claire."

It's too deep for Claire. Too something. But after class for the next three weeks in a row she goes down to his office, and sometimes the things he says make her feel larger than she is. He mocks the work of famous contemporary artists as if he and she inhabit their own superior world above them. At the hospital, with Nancy, she avoids personal chats. But the anxious tedium of her life is relieved by the proximity of Bodey Marcus, his sharp pale-eyed gaze that seems open to just about everything. His voice that goes deeply nasal at times, as if he found some aspect of humanity or something she said absurd or ignorant. Could he be genuinely interested in her? Sometimes it seems so. In the light of his slightly mocking attention she appears more interesting to herself.

She talks to him as she talks to her close girlfriends, that's how it is now. She's as voluble with him about her past as she is with Eileen (and more than with Leo). Then she notices that, although she's describing the same situations—the tyranny of her brilliant brother and her overprotective, stifling mother—the stories come out different. With Bodey, impulses and intentions come to light that challenge her long-running history of herself. She's fragile, isn't she, and harmless and pure of heart? Well, maybe. But Bodey reminds her that she always gets her own back. Yes, Eric tossed her stuffed fishie out the window into the rain, and he led her to a hole in the ground to be stung by thirty bees, and he got into an Ivy League college that later rejected her. (Why did she even apply?) But when her bike disappeared from the driveway in front of their house, she told her mother Eric had lent it to his girlfriend, and maintained the story throughout Eric's outrage. No doubt, Bodey says, she felt herself to be the victim of a cosmic inequity that the deception served to set aright. "But, Claire, come on! Your poor brother had to use his bar mitzvah money to buy you a new bike and he was grounded for lying!" He laughs as if he were not applauding her chicanery but sincerely delighted by it, and she laughs too, so hard her stomach and chest hurt. She feels found-out. Recognized, in some way freed. Eileen, who might glimpse this side of her, would still courteously refrain from throwing it at her. And Leo, she's sure, is so bent on protecting her from herself and everything, he doesn't really see her. Bodey Marcus, however, who doesn't try to fix her, or cheer or console or protect her, is simply intrigued and amused. If she ever told Bodey her creepy visions and the mental holes she sometimes falls into, she could hear him say, "Lucky you."

One day she brings one of her pieces for him to see, a plaster skull in which she has cut a heart-shaped hole, revealing a piece of pink netting, a rose petal, a dead fly. "It gives me goose bumps," he says, looking at her straight on. She's close enough to smell his sweat. She feels his goose bumps on the roof of her mouth. If he tried to kiss her she'd kiss him back, she knows that.

———

That night the feel and smell of Leo's skin on her skin would have violated the pact she feels she has made with Bodey, and she sleeps downstairs in the den. The next night as well. The third night, just before dawn, Leo comes down to her. She's awake, as she has been all three of the past nights, in a dream dance of strength and tenderness that leaves her refreshed as sleep. "Claire?"

Her eyes are used to the dark. She sees his face. She feels sorry for him, so thin, dry and empty.

"Claire, are you awake?"

She closes her eyes, breathing evenly, silently. He walks back upstairs.

In the morning the girls go to school and Leo stays home. Outside, the air is thick and wet with moisture from the lake. His eyes are puffy. In the clear weak March sunlight streaming through the kitchen window she sees the bones of his wrists.

It's Tuesday, her day off this week. She'd planned to call Eileen, see if she wanted to have lunch. "Leo, what's your schedule? When do you have to be at the hospital?" She puts her hand on his arm as if it's the arm of an old friend. He winces. His lips are chapped.

"What's going on with you, Claire?"

She shakes her head, serene inside the fabric of her dreaming. He pulls his arm away, circles the kitchen.

"I think you should see a different therapist," he says. "I have some names."

"That's what you stayed home to tell me?" She's sitting at the table with a cup of coffee. She folds her hands in her lap. A bubble of joy is bouncing around in her; she would like to attend to it. "I'm a lot less depressed," she says. "Don't you think Kara's doing a good job?"

He looks at her hard and cold. "I don't know. Claire, listen. Have you seen Hadley's progress report?"

She stretches toward concern. There's something up on the fridge. She'd looked at it, though now she can't remember what it said.

"Hadley didn't turn in her research paper. She didn't do her research paper, were you aware of that? And Nora's getting into God."

"Nora's almost sixteen," she says. "We can't police her spiritual life." She likes the sound of that. "And Hadley's grades—she's responsible for them. Natural consequences. That's what you used to say!"

"Claire, where is your head at? What does a smart, healthy, pretty Jewish girl need with Jesus Christ?" She wraps her arms around herself. She watches him, though he seems very far away. "You used to care so much about all of us. But you've changed, Claire. You're becoming so..." He looks for a word. "Self-absorbed." He sits down beside her, takes hold of her hand. "I've been trying to handle things. Because of what happened, you know. I figured I was in somewhat better shape so I could take on more of the household stuff. Give you a break. With the girls. With your, I don't know, hobbies? But now *I'm* feeling rotten."

His words must be true, since it's obvious to her that he believes them. But for some reason she can't take them in. Can't take in the feeling of his feeling bad. In her dream last night she was closed up inside a balloon drifting away from earth. She describes it to him. She wants to cry but she can't. "I feel like I'm changing. I just don't know what I'm turning into." Did that make sense? She eyes him, hoping. "I'm waiting to see what will happen."

"Isn't that interesting. This is prime-time TV for you!" He slaps the table. Her coffee splashes up.

"Leo, you're scaring me."

He gets a paper towel and wipes the table. He lowers his voice. "I'm sorry. But I've got to tell you, I'm tired of being the only adult in this house."

He turns to walk out of the room. Her heart jumps. "Leo? Where are you going?"

She runs after him. Stands with her back to the door. She's not sure if he's right or wrong but it doesn't matter. When he returns with her to the kitchen, tears are running down her cheeks.

She tells him about the scene she'd witnessed in Bodey's class, making the teacher fatter than he really was, intriguing but on the verge of abusive. She suggests they start doing more things together. Weekend dinner dates. Lunch, even. She works to keep her teeth from chattering. There's so much they need to talk about. Nora has her head on straight, she thinks, but he might be right about Hadley. Should they send her to a private school? As for herself, she'd be glad to stop the Tegretol. Or the therapy, or art classes, or whatever's been messing her up.

His first surgery is midmorning. To maintain the resumption of warmth between them she drives him to work. Drives with her left hand, her right holding his across the gear shift.

CHAPTER SIX

"**H**e's totally in love with you," said Rachel, who had read the note. Her whisper was loud enough for people to hear. Hadley gave her sister's soft, twitchy laugh.

They edged back from their friends clustered outside the third-floor washroom, where they weren't supposed to be during lunch. "I like your bracelet," Rachel said. "Is it from—?" creating a space for the new developments to reside in their natural luminosity. "In Music he kept looking at you!"

Hadley twirled the diamond bracelet and told Rachel that when Fletcher looked at her she couldn't look straight back, a reaction of Jennifer Aniston's in *Friends*. Not looking at Rachel either but at the washroom door, which said GIRLS, blurred but readable. "He makes me feel quivery here," she breathed to Rachel, placing a hand on her stomach. Which wasn't true, but was so clear in her mind it was better than true. Then Rachel smiled her sympathetic mild envy, and all the shifting, uneasily fluttering parts of the world fell into place. Fletcher Lawson was attractive, desirable to her friends, a source of possible jealousy. "I could maybe fall in love with him," she said, looking Rachel right in the eye. Rachel gave a light, controlled scream. Hadley's legs started to shake, though it might have also come from skipping lunch or wearing the borrowed bracelet. Or from the thought of May Sun all by herself in the dark washroom.

Hadley and Rachel had rejoined the cluster of girls outside the washroom door, when it banged open. They edged back respectfully as May Sun emerged. "Tell us!" cried Felice Pinter, who liked to include herself despite Sherelle's whisperings. "Did it freak you?"

Hadley stood so close to May Sun, she could see the tiny freckles on the girl's perfectly oval, gold-colored face. She loved the smooth hairs on the golden skin of her arms, her eyes as calm as water in a glass. She was six inches shorter than Hadley but truly needed the bra she wore. "You didn't see anything," Hadley whispered hopefully.

"Yes, I did."

The rustling, the murmurs ceased. Sounds beneath it rose

86

up—the muffled roar of the lunchroom downstairs, and down the hall, a female teacher's occasional shrill directive. Hadley's stomach buzzed under her hand. She sucked it in, let it out.

"It was a little gross," May Sun said.

The group gave a collective sigh. Hadley gazed at May Sun, the bottoms of her feet growing moist.

"Was there blood?" said Sherelle, folding her thin arms across her chest. At the same time she raised her chin and lowered her eyelids, a gesture as unarguable as the hiss of a snake.

"There was blood on her forehead," said May Sun, "but it didn't touch me." Her face stayed blank and clear; only her mouth moved as she described her pleasantly ghoulish washroom vision. "Who's next?"

"Right," Sherelle said. "We have ten minutes."

The murmur from the group was like air escaping. Eyes went from face to face to face. "Who's left? Who hasn't gone yet?"

Hadley turned to Rachel, tried to find something to say about Fletcher that would affix her to her friend and to earth, but her stomach was roiling hard now, as if her words had brought on the bad feeling, and when Sherelle's gaze landed on her, and locked, there was nothing to do but shrug, "What is the *deal*," and push open the heavy door to the washroom.

Inside the long, high-ceilinged room she complied with the rule not to turn the light on. The air was a pale, mottled gray, dark-thick in the corners where the walls met the ceiling, black where the stall doors stood ajar. The glints of light were no easier to bear than the shadows, glary spots on the row of sinks where the sun seeped through the grimy, granulated window glass, and a place in the long, corroding mirror she was careful not to glance at. She leaned against a sink, squinted at the face of her watch and counted her breaths for the five minutes in which she was supposed to be gazing at her reflection and chanting *Bloody Mary*. Not that she ever would. She'd heard of a girl at a Catholic school who came out of the washroom knowing the name of the man who would be her husband. Last week Felice emerged crying, her hair parted on the wrong side; she wouldn't say what she'd seen.

Hadley wanted to cry, herself, a little. Her eyes weren't working; she could only see the numbers on her watch when it was up to her face. A voice whispered, *You are average pretty and not that smart.*

She subdued the voice by shaking her head from side to side, a gesture she camouflaged, even alone in the bathroom, with an amused smile. She watched her watch and walked out at the end of precisely five minutes, knitting her brow and loosening the set of her head on her shoulders in what she hoped was a look of confidence. "Nothing!"

The girls gazed at her, their eyes open wide. Even Sherelle was silent.

"Nothing happened," she said.

Sherelle's mouth was a straight line of unbelief.

"All right," she said. "There was a ring of fire around her head. With blood dripping down."

"That's what Rachel said yesterday," Sherelle said.

"So? It dripped down her forehead. Into her eyes!"

Sherelle remained skeptical. But Rachel was clearly thrilled. Hadley and Rachel swayed toward each other, touching shoulders in the conscious-unconscious way of girlfriends.

"Who wants to come over after school?" said May Sun. "I have the new Britney Spears."

Felice's eyes were round with eager good will. "I'll bring my Christina Aguilera!"

"Oh, that'll be super dupery duper!" Sherelle said through her pinched nose.

Felice looked at Sherelle, at the group, confused by the disjunction between the content of what was said and the tone. As if herded by the silence the other girls swayed and shifted into a clump that excluded Felice. Felice shivered in her isolation. Then her arms took hold of each other. She turned almost gracefully and went off down the hall.

Hadley felt Felice's sadness like a moth at the back of her neck. She pictured Fletcher's quick-moving mouth and nervous, questioning eyes. Nothing was good in the world, or beautiful, or even whole. She looked at the faces of the girls in her group, her eyes wide open like a baby's.

"You're crying, Had!" Sherelle peered at her like an eye doctor. To the others she said as if it were something repulsive, "Hadley's crying!"

Hadley shook out her head, stared back with eyes as hard and dry as marbles. Stronger than anything inside herself she felt Sherelle's thin body, the narrow planes of her face. There was power in the slim form, in the whole body of girls of which she, miraculously, was part. Something evolved from the act of grouping, she was suddenly aware, a mass greater than the sum of the group's individual members, too great for their cumulative size and weight like a boulder dropped from another planet.

CHAPTER SEVEN

Renunciation

It's like losing ten pounds, a goal from Claire's days as a dance student, and even now, occasionally. It can be done with the appropriate vigilance. Claire talks it over with Eileen, who worries about her losing her newly-emergent "self," but even Eileen believes in compromise (if not sacrifice) when the children are in the house. (Her only son, thank God, is away at college.) As for Nancy, she applauds Claire's change of focus and tries to be helpful. With Nancy, Claire makes up a new schedule for herself and Leo; they try to adhere to it:

Sundays they spend with the girls, sometimes together,

sometimes not. So far, Leo has taken Nora to see the Rabbi, while Claire helped Hadley write a compare and contrast essay. Hadley has opinions but has trouble organizing them. She bends so close to the page it's a wonder she can see anything. Claire has always urged her to sit up straight. Be proud of her height.

Claire buys a treadmill and starts exercising before work, thirty minutes on "Hill." As a result, or so it seems, she feels a little more clearheaded at the hospital, and at home less inclined to sink into a fog of silence. Leo, who for years has followed the same exercise regime, agrees to shift two days a week from late afternoon to early morning; when she gets home she can concentrate on dinner while he handles the carpooling. Organize, organize. After the meal, the girls clean the kitchen and she and Leo either play Scrabble or watch whatever's on TV, chatting amiably during the commercials. She sleeps better. A decided improvement.

Friday—which she asked for and obtained as her permanent day off—is dedicated in part to Leo. After her tennis lesson, and sometimes a game with Eileen, she returns home to prepare a multicourse Shabbat dinner, candles and all, a ritual that wasn't performed in her own household. Leo sits at the head of the table, thinking of his grandfather.

Saturdays are hard. Leo has no problem with her taking the sculpture class, and in truth the idea of her life without the class fills her with a watery terror. But all through Sculpture, even as she kneads the clay, and pinches and pokes it into a grotesque female head, her attention is fixed on the hall beyond the door. When class is over she races out of the building, as if, if she let it, her body in spite of her would descend the fuchsia stairs. *Wanting* is a bird in her breast, pecking and pecking.

She changes Kara to Saturday at four-thirty, giving herself just enough time to jog the four blocks up Michigan to her therapist's office. At night she and Leo go out to dinner, either alone or with friends, and if they have the energy when they get home they make love. He is sensitive and appreciative and grateful for her renewed interest. He didn't require a complete transformation in her. Just a few key changes, a "redirection of energy" toward the family. Which is what she wants, too. They can live like that more or less indefinitely.

The third Saturday of this new regimen, a clear evening in February with splotches of melting snow on the ground, they have theater tickets. Free tickets, the gift of a friend. Claire doesn't usually like the plays at this theater, full of snappy lines that make you feel there's something you don't get. That, compared to these characters, you're a plodder, at best naïve. But the seats are on the main floor, fifth row center. The play is supposed to be "dazzling." Leo is exuberant because they found parking on the street. She tries to float on the lapping waves of his lightheartedness.

Then halfway through the first act the female lead rises from her stage-prop desk, faces the audience, and takes her shirt off.

Her breasts swing bare. The couple directly behind them burst into a simultaneous *ha!* as if they're halves of the same person. Claire looks at Leo who seems to be working at nonchalance. She takes his hand. He kisses the top of her head. Her face feels warm and larger than usual.

During intermission she turns around and starts talking with the amused couple, both of whom teach theater at DePaul. He acts; she directs. She looks gauntly beautiful. Usually it's Leo who draws strangers into their world. He's interested in other people and he has ready commentary on a wide range of topics. This time, though, Claire can't stop talking. She and they agree this is the best thing they've seen in a while. They have season tickets here and to two other local theater companies. It's their second marriage. They have no children and no desire for children.

After the play she and Leo walk up Halsted to their car, discussing their mutual pity for the couple who—despite the romance of having only each other and the riches of an unencumbered cultural life (not to mention being able to set an object down on the counter and find it later in the same place)— lack life's deeper pleasures. She holds Leo's hand and imagines them traveling with the girls in Europe. She imagines later, the two of them old together. She's about to interrupt him, though he hates to be interrupted, to discuss possibly taking the girls to France or Italy this summer, before they've lost all vestige of interest in being with their parents, when she sees the gun glinting in light from a distant streetlight.

She halts without the sense of having ceased moving. Rather, it seems to her that the whole busy street has stopped, turned to face her, and is now bowing backward away. Her gaze travels from the gun to a denim sleeve to a narrow, outraged young face. Leo, though, is in the dreamland of his self-analysis. "There was a time when I'd have envied them. But now, I probably shouldn't say this, but I really love our life." Looking at her, gesturing fervently, he steps into the gun barrel. It pushes him back with a poke in the chest.

"Turn around, buddy," says the young man. Leo makes a garbled sound.

The man is tall but slouches like someone ashamed of his height. Oh, Hadley. This she'll remember for a long time, along with the fact that the store across from them (closed) says "Occult Books." Parked at the curb is a small rust-spotted car of a make no longer in production, an Omni? Its passenger door yawns open with a purpose she doesn't care to fathom.

"Did you hear?" The voice is high, and not particularly authoritative. "Turn around and start walking!"

She turns like an obedient schoolgirl, but the man grabs her arm. His hand is surprisingly large, or else her body has shrunk— she reels with the loss of perspective. The gun itself is as small as a toy. Even pointed at Leo it looks like a bad joke. "Run," the man says to Leo. "Scram! Get the fuck out of here!"

For a moment Leo looks at him with the slightly mocking amiability he proffers to all strangers. Then he steps to her side with his hand out, as if the two of them have simply been advised of an alternate route. Later, she'll remember; she'll appreciate this. But now before she can take his arm, and stroll with him down the sidewalk and back to their life, the gunman prods her in the direction of his car. Gently, as if Leo has danced with her long enough, tonight, and now it's his turn.

"You don't know her, George," he says to Leo. "You never saw her before." And Leo, who knows her very well, better than anybody else knows her, she has always believed, begins a slow walk, and then a stupid little trot down the sidewalk.

Of course, as she'll tell Nora the next day (but not Hadley), nothing terrible happened. A Volvo station wagon pulled up next to the Omni, a window rolled down, a woman called out, "Excuse me! Might you people be leaving?" She sounded English. The gunman vanished into the darkness of his own car, and she ran after Leo, catching up with him in the middle of busy Halsted trying to flag down a police car. His voice shook like an old man's. Frightened at last, she made herself put her arms around him. She told herself he had done right to retreat: The man had a gun. The worst that would have happened to her was rape, probably, while Leo might very well have been killed. People were nuts these days. In the taxi back to their car, she told him how glad she was that he was alive, that they were free to continue their good, sweet life together.

Several times that night Leo brought the subject up, trying to explain. He didn't mean to desert her. He was completely unprepared. He wasn't thinking clearly. He had to get help. She told him to forget all about it because that's what she was going to do.

But she can't get out of her mind the image of that trot of his, a little bouncing walk-run like a small dog loping across a lawn.

The next day Claire took the girls to Borders and bought *Let's Go Italy* and some Italian tapes. But on Monday she wakes too anguished and furious to brush her teeth. She thinks of the pretty farm scene painted on the wall outside the fourth-floor elevator at Children's, the country road curving through farmland and into the woods beyond, and she sees her life stretched before her, a straight, paved, narrowing road to obviously nowhere. Panting as if she can never in her life get enough air, she calls in sick.

She dials Leo's pager, leaves a message of thin-voiced urgency, and lies utterly still on the couch till he calls back. "Leo," she murmurs, "I am so angry with you."

A pause. "You were fine when I left this morning. Weren't you?"

She can't speak for a minute. Hears his sharp, exasperated expulsion of breath. Can't speak at all. Her heart beats painfully.

"I'm sorry. I don't have a lot of time. What is it, Claire?"

She swallows around the lump in her throat. "I know it's not your fault. But I don't— I just don't feel—"

"What, Claire?"

She'd have said "protected by you" if it didn't sound so naïve, as if she were helpless and needed protection. And it wasn't exactly protection she needed that night on Halsted. With all those cars going by, people on the street, she hadn't felt so much endangered as simply abandoned, like property, a set of golf clubs handed over to a buddy who wanted to borrow them. Her fury feels too primitive to express. "I'm a mess," she says.

"Honey, let's talk about it when I get home. Okay?"

"Okay." She's glad to set the phone down.

She goes down to the basement, recently converted into a workroom for her. Ripping the cellophane from one of the blocks of soft, moist clay, she pulls it apart clump by clump, digging her nails in as if it's flesh. She prods the clumps into a human face, pinches the nose into the hooked beak of a crone, jabs fingers into the nostrils. She heaves the dead mass at the wall. It thucks to the floor.

Breathing in hard gasps she walks to the workbench in the furnace room, Leo's province, though all he does here is glue the handles back onto coffee mugs. The rough pine work surface is bare except for a vise and a Skil-saw, blade shining with oil. She plugs in the saw, squeezes the trigger; the vibration climbs her arm. She raises the shield, presses the swirling blade to the pine skirt. Watches the bite deepen, virgin white in the grimy wood.

Her breath comes slower. Something is improving.

She finds an old footstool from a house sale, and with precise, unhurried fingers, screws it into the vise. She aligns the saw so that the blade will pass through the length of two of the bowed legs and about an inch of frame. She hums to herself. Is this a worthwhile activity? It's surely absorbing.

Kara has been nudging her toward these moments of absorption that mean freedom. Toward "mastery" (note, said Kara, the root of the word), a sense of one's power (beneficent, well-intentioned) that Kara finds lacking in many women of Claire's generation. In the realm of art there are no limits to the voyaging; one is free and powerful. But if art is to be the source of her bliss she should do it more than once a week. Kara read her a poem by Robert Bly. If art is her mistress (or lover) she will devote herself, create a space in her life free of responsibility toward anything but her art and herself. She has to quit being a leaf in a stream, Kara said. There is such a thing as *will*.

Nancy's advice is just as fervent but her values are different. For Nancy, the focus on *self* almost instantly becomes *selfish*. Your devotion should center on other people and on God, the duties for which your choices obligate you. This too requires will at times. Nancy and Kara agree on the power of will.

But Claire is starting to have doubts about will. If choice were possible she'd have chosen to be like Kara, who was not only fearless and intelligent but kind and funny. Sometimes in conversation at work, or over coffee with friends, she says what she thinks Kara would have said. But Kara is ten years younger, as different from her, it seems, as a fox from a lemming. Kara's instincts aren't at odds with society's expectations of her. Kara grew up with Margaret Thatcher and Madonna and not Jackie Kennedy.

When Kara gets tired of living solo she'll marry her intellectual and personal equal, and move from career to home and children and back as smoothly as swimming. If she gets divorced, no biggie, another experience to learn from. The electric saw in Claire's hands whines and roars for Kara. Claire applauds Kara.

The whirling blade has begun to fray the stool's upholstery when Claire pulls back. She isn't a leaf in a stream. That's an oversimplification, a source of the easy assurance of people like Kara and Nancy. How pleasantly confidence-inspiring, if your will instigated action like a wheel steered a car, no neurotic driver mumbling to herself, *Half a turn to the left, why dontcha? Drive us into this here oncoming lane.*

The saw is thrumming though, vibrating through her arms and back; the dilemma retreats in her mind to a less prominent spot. Her hands are dry and steady against the ongoing shudder of the blade. Sawdust beats against her closed mouth. She is neither happy nor unhappy, just intensely present. She breathes as in a sandstorm, small, cautious sniffs that remain constant in depth and interval as the blade passes through the last splinters of footstool. It falls into her outstretched hand

It's an upside-down U. The yoke of a miniature ox. She gazes upon the newborn artifact. A slice of frayed needlepoint, orangey stuffing, the pale nude flesh of the interior wood. She's riveted, like an apprentice surgeon who has just exposed a heart to the light of the operating room. When Eric was young he'd pull flowers apart, plucking out the tufts of their soft golden centers. Her stomach would squeeze at the sight of petals and stems on the grass, her brother's pollen-yellow mouth, the part of him that did this thing, so pointlessly, unredeemably destructive. But in the face of this piece of "work," if she dares to call it that, the shimmer of revulsion is overcome by pleasure. Or whatever it is that originated in her arms holding the footstool against the saw.

Moments later she calls the School of the Art Institute, her voice high, studentlike. "Bodey Marcus, please?" When he answers she realizes she hadn't expected to reach him. She says the first thing that comes to mind, spacing the words, loving how hard it is to utter them. (Though she isn't sure what Kara would say.) "It's Claire. Winger, do you remember me?" She holds back a nervous laugh. "Just kidding. But I need to talk to you. Could you handle a quickie visit today?"

There's a good chance she'll humiliate herself, but it doesn't slow her down, descending the Day-Glo fuchsia cement stairs to his office. Several young women pass without glancing at her, multi-earringed and pierced, their pants loose and paint-spattered. A skinny, bald man climbs the other way in the embrace of a store mannikin with papier-mâché wings and no feet. Her jeans, she thinks, are too tight, too blue, too clean and sharp-seamed, pressing on her thighs as she pushes open the door to the performance area.

Bodey's office, in a corner of the large, haphazardly differentiated space, is a plywood enclosure whose walls end a foot or so short of the ceiling. The door is opened by an Asian boy with a pretty face and black hair with so little luster it sucks up some of the light around it. Bodey introduces David Kakutani, his new and highly talented graduate student. He introduces her to David as a student-at-large on the brink of learning how brilliant she is. She emits a giddy, stupid laughing sound; quickly tamps it down. "Can you wait a few minutes?" Bodey says. "We're just finishing up."

David doesn't mind her presence in the room, so she is invited to sit during the critique. She moves the one vacant chair to a corner of the room where the student and teacher are in profile. His compliment—a lie, but such a pretty, kind lie—burns like sun on her face. She takes off her coat. Stares at the backs of her hands. Stares at a print laid out on the table, a lithograph, in profile, of an elderly nude man in a rocking chair, his oversized penis in the hands on his lap. Ordinarily it might have disturbed her, but her mind won't stay still. It flitters from the print to Bodey's reddish hair, thick like a rug.

From the conference she gathers that David's performance piece emblemizes the Japanese-American experience in World War II. The audience is asked to write their answers to the question, *Which color do you prefer, blue or yellow?* Their answers determine whether they will be locked together in a tiny room or seated in comfort to watch a video of the less-fortunate members. Bodey says, "This might be brilliant!" Claire fixes on the print on the table, the lines of the chairback and the aroused male organ, which, if extended backward, make a right angle. Above the man's head in pistol-gray letters are the words, "Whistler had a father too." She feels a familiar mounting euphoria.

"How's it going, Claire?"

Bodey is speaking. To her.

"Hey. What's on our mind, Claire?"

She tries to answer, but her tongue is too thick and weak to shape words, even if her diaphragm had the energy to send them out into the world. Bodey sends David for water. He helps her to a chair. She's afraid to move even her eyes.

The student gone, Bodey's hands take hold of the twin triangles of muscle between her neck and shoulder. Pleasure and pain begin to circle around each other. She tries to sit upright, to breathe deeply and evenly as his hands pry her striations apart, band by band, till her back is a chorus of distinct, separate voices, each calling for her attention so insistently that he might have been touching the top of her breast for some seconds—not the whole, just the skin along the top of her bra!—before she noticed.

She holds her breath against what might be an oncoming seizure as well as the pleasure she wants to go on and on. Here it is again, seizure and pleasure, rising as one. She stands up, steps back, turns to face him. In a hoarse whisper, "Who said you could do that?"

"Your skin. The way you breathe."

She gives a small outraged cry.

"Do you want me to stop?"

103

"I wanted to talk to you."

"Talk," he says.

She folds her arms. Although taller than Leo, he is soft in the middle; he doesn't play tennis or work the Stairmaster at the club. But his gaze is so direct it's hard for her to look back. "I think I'm afraid of you."

"Is that why you called me today?"

"I'm starting to be sorry I called you."

She feels like crying. He continues, though, to amuse himself. "Do you know about Marcella? I should maybe have mentioned her. Marcella is a fact."

"Why are you telling me that?"

"And you have a husband."

"Stop, please."

He laughs. "So it comes out even, in a way."

"A sick way."

He's delighted by the fact of their having partners, as if his live-in girlfriend and her husband make two of the four walls of a room in which they can play together. It makes no sense to her. What have their partners to do with what's happening now, the immediate fact of smell and touch and possibility? He walks to the door, peers out. "Where the fuck are you, David?"

Then it occurs to her. He is frightened, too. She grows comfortable with contempt and pity for him, this thick, loose, soft man who doesn't exercise. He could be her uncle. Her balding older brother. She stands up. Puts her coat on.

"Are you leaving?"

"You shouldn't make fun of me. Of *this*," she says, with a circle of the arm indicating God knows what.

"Was I? Hey, learn about tone, Claire."

"Tone? Fuck *tone!*"

He laughs. Puts a hand on her shoulder. Looks, quizzically, at her face. She makes herself look straight back, although his gaze seems somehow painful. She hates the jokey, almost nasty, part of him. He kicks the door shut, rattling the plywood walls. Reaches back to throw the latch. They thump against the table. A print floats to the floor. He takes her head in his hands. Looks at her. She kisses him, out of the way of his looking.

There's a faint, polite knock on the door. "Nobody home!" Bodey calls out. She kisses him with her whole mouth, running her tongue along his teeth, the tip of his tongue.

"Mind-fuck!" cries David Kakutani. She holds onto the table, caught by her jeans, which are bunched now between her knees and ankles. And by the thought of the eyes of the talented David Kakutani, of all the gifted young art students roaming the floor. Courtesy, though, is ingrained in her. "He has the water," she says, and pulls her jeans back up. "His glass of water for me!"

"You crazy lady you."

Still, he opens the door a crack and takes the water. There's a conversation, brief and electric, which either has nothing to do with her or everything to do with her in a way that horrifies and shames her. She thinks of Leo in their bed, gentle-fingered, painstaking in his preparation of her. Cassandra purrs between their pillows. Sex is tender and unfrightening.

But with Bodey her body needs no preparation. He sets the glass on the floor. She trembles, waiting. He kisses the back of her neck, turns her toward the long table, presses her down upon it. She feels his chest on her back, and against her cheek the smooth surface of a lithograph.

She and Leo tried this position a couple of times but it had frustrated her. Her hands felt bereft, all her tender parts unattended. Now, though, she feels enwrapped over and under by the beating of wings, and she fixes on the figure in the print under her face. *Whistler had a father.* She thinks of hang gliding, wafting from gust to gust. Doing battle with gravity. She hangs for a dizzying span on the edge of a knife, holding firm against the letting go. Then his hand slides beneath her belly, his penis nudges the ring of hard curls between her legs. Her moan startles her so much she bites down on the next one and cuts her tongue.

TWO

CHAPTER EIGHT

Bodey

A t first she is either frightened or on the brink of rapture. Either way it's dizzying, as if she has been awarded a prize meant for someone else. The third week, they lie on the floor of his office, her head on his chest. He says, "You know, I know you."

He has just come but remains hard. She smiles nervously down at him. "I'm glad someone does."

"No. I really know you. I know what you want. And I can give it to you."

"That sounds dangerous."

"Why?"

He says it unsmiling. It sounds like a dare. His eyes are colorless like water. She doesn't come, but she almost came. In the car on the way home she decides it's better than coming. Thinking about him is sometimes better than being with him, another thing she doesn't completely understand. But in the car on the way home she knows she doesn't have to see him again. If they meet again, ever, it's up to her. And a week will have to pass—Sunday, then Monday through Thursday at Children's, and Friday tennis, and, all along, shopping and driving and dinner to make before seeing him is a possibility—during which time she'll have shored up the reservoir of herself for him to dip from. Why she needs to shore up anything, she doesn't want to investigate. But the ordinary week enables the hours with Bodey, which in turn enable the ordinary week. With these options in place, she has a real, it seems, life.

She tells him things about herself, at each encounter something new. In fourth grade she was good at jacks, best in the neighborhood. In middle school she was turned down for admission to a girls' club; three for, four against. She was not popular. For an entire year in her early teens she thought she had breast cancer. Now, sometimes, she fantasizes about sex on a restaurant table or the dentist's chair or the cement lip of a crowded swimming pool, the locus of multiple hands and eyes. In his office in the basement of the Art Institute she offers him these stories like gourmet fruit.

Sex with him is a more ambiguous transaction. His hands are

large and hard, his fingers thick; he touches her so roughly or abruptly that part of her shrinks back. While another part just beneath the surface regards him eager and trembling, even when he's rough. Once he let up just a little. She gave an embarrassing cry, smothering it, thinking: If she can hear talk in the hall she can be heard too. Thinking: How boring she is beside the charged, gifted, whimsical people who teach and study with him. Any minute he'll turn to her, "I'm sorry. I can't imagine what I was thinking," and kiss her apologetically, absent-mindedly goodbye.

One Friday in early March, after her tennis lesson, she decides to drive downtown to see him. Until now they've met on Saturdays, with an hour or so borrowed from the afternoon session of her class. Today at half past two it's relatively early. He turns off his desk lamp, puts on an old Leonard Cohen tape, latches the flimsy door. She makes a nest of their clothes. There's just enough room for her between his desk and the wall, and for him crouching over her. He's on the verge of too forceful; as usual she's moved simultaneously toward and away from him, just out of reach of being taken out of herself. He stops, elbows on either side of her on the thin hard carpet. Leonard Cohen sings, "She feeds you tea and oranges that come all the way from China." He says, "I'll bet you have no idea how beautiful you are."

"How beautiful?" Impishly. An uncharacteristic mode.

His eyes open wide. She feels again the intoxicating sensation of being closely examined. He whispers, "I think I love you."

"No, you don't."

"Don't you want me to?"

He raises himself on his arms. There's a little cool space between their bodies. Her face burns.

"Do you want me to?"

She can't look at his face. It's too large and too close. Her bones are so soft she no longer feels her limbs as segmented, but something between her belly and her heart pushes toward him. She wraps her legs around him. Through the high narrow basement window the afternoon light pours down like honey.

It's late. En route to the parking garage, the cold wind whips through her light spring jacket. But she drives home through rush-hour traffic as if on a chaise on an ocean liner, viscerally moved by the shimmer of the lake and even by the shimmer of light on the roofs of the cars clogging Lake Shore Drive. If something was ever wrong with her, she can't remember it. What used to frighten her? Fear is unreal, she thinks, the product of mistaken or limited perception.

At home, she finds Leo in the kitchen making a salad. He cuts the lettuce with a knife. She has been taught to use her hands "so as not to bruise the tender greens." Where did she read that? She kisses his cheek, quickly, so as not to inhale his familiarity. "Hi. Sorry I'm late. I have this crazy project. You've got to come down to school and see it, a new clay head! Filled with worms and feathers!" She sees it in her mind complete. Tomorrow she'll start on it. She tries to take the knife out of his hand. "Go sit down. I'll finish. God, traffic was disgusting!" He continues chopping, dumps the leaves into the bowl. "Come on, Leo."

He doesn't respond. His back is stiff against her.

"I know I should have called. I lost track of time. I've been a ditz lately." Her voice is giddy, a Lucy act, or is it a Marilyn Monroe act? Something Fifties. "All right, I'll make the dressing!"

"It's made, Mom." Nora walks in, takes plates down from the cupboard. "I did it. *C'est fini.*"

"Ooh la la!" says Claire. "*Sacre bleu!*" She pushes her hair out of her eyes, although it wasn't in her eyes. "I screwed up. I know it. I apologize. Don't I get to screw up every once in a while?"

"You were supposed to get Nora from school," Leo says.

"I waited an hour," Nora says. "Outside. In my sweats."

Her heart squeezes. She doesn't usually forget things like that. The thought assaults her like a crazy bird. "Oh honey. I feel terrible." She feels, for a moment, terrified. She follows Nora into the dining room, helps her set the table. "Did you take a hot shower? How can I make it up to you?"

With the cold stare of an aggrieved mother Nora hands her a pile of cloth napkins. Claire folds them, distributes them around the table. Her hands are shaking. She takes out Sabbath candles, and Leo's grandmother's brass candlesticks. She lights the candles, says the blessing. She feels her mouth smiling, bites the side of her hand. The price of a virtuous woman is beyond rubies? The tremor in her stomach might be guilt but might also be a memory of pleasure. She bites harder. "So where's Hadley?"

"Up in her room. Doing her homework, I hope," says Leo.

"On Friday night? Hadley?"

Nora and Leo eye each other. She looks from one to the other. "What am I not getting?"

"Let's discuss it after dinner," says Leo.

He calls Hadley, who comes down with red eyes. She looks thinner, Claire thinks, although she just saw her this morning at breakfast. Or had she slept through breakfast? She stares at Hadley, who seems, also, to be taller than she remembers. Almost as tall as Nora.

Hadley doesn't look at her, or anyone. She seats herself. Accepts food in silence. Stares at it on her plate. Claire would tell her to eat but she has lost some prerogative, so it seems. She observes the family drama like a member of the audience.

After the meal is over but before the dishes are cleared, Leo asks Hadley to explain to her mother the little scheme she and her friends cooked up, as a result of which the highest grade she can get in World Studies is a C. Hadley picks up a green bean, squeezes out a small white seed. Her chin quivers. "Why is everyone making such a big deal about this?"

"That's true," Nora says reasonably. "She isn't in high school. Even if she flunks, it won't go on her college record."

"I won't flunk!" Hadley cries, and explains to the tabletop: World Studies has too much busy work, study questions to answer every night. It was logical for people to share it. People:

her and Rachel and Sherelle and May Sun. One of them did the assignment, then at lunch the others wrote it out.

"As in *copied*," says Nora, helpfully.

Hadley ignores her, her forehead shining with righteous anger. "We took turns! It was just homework! But for some reason the bitch decides to read the stuff which she was too lazy to, before..."

"Watch your mouth," says Leo.

"Why? It doesn't hurt anyone."

"It hurts my ears," says Nora.

"Mom swears."

Claire turns to Hadley, a little startled to hear her name mentioned. "Rarely," she says. "Only under provocation."

"Your mother has privileges you haven't earned yet," Leo says.

Claire smiles at Hadley. "I'll stop. I'll watch myself. It really does sound ugly."

"Mom," Hadley says, "are you on my side?"

"Look at me, Hadley. You are my darling girl. I'm crazy about you. Don't you know that?"

Hadley is sobbing now. Claire puts her arms around her, her cheek to the top of her head. The sobs get louder. Hadley cleaves to her, holding tight.

Claire holds her, kisses her forehead, waiting for the room or her mind to start humming or melting. Objects remain intact. Stranger still, right now she notices in herself a new power with regard to her family. As if her former predictability or integrity had in some way enfeebled her. When they don't know what will come out of her mouth they have to listen harder. "Leave the dishes," she says, "Let's play Cranium. The four of us. No TV, no reading." She smiles at Leo, who smiles back.

"Who'll do the dishes then?" says Hadley.

"Elves!"

Hadley rolls her eyes but runs to get the game. Leo clears off the coffee table. Nora is heading for the stairs. Claire calls to her.

"May God have mercy on your soul," Nora says.

"Excuse me? Nora, what did say?"

"*Je suis occupé,*" floats down the stairs, but Claire runs up after her, too full of self-love not to prevail.

Like a kite in an updraft, there's no telling how high she'll fly. At Midtown Tennis Club she advances to the next level. At Children's her patients' faces relax when they see her, and most of them are doing well. Josh Potrero came back a couple of times with fevers but she hasn't seen him since his central line was replaced with a port. She takes it as a good sign.

At the end of her Thursday shift she says to Nancy, "You know, I've been so happy lately." It's break time. They stand together in Nourishment waiting for their popcorn to pop. Nancy is an outstanding nurse, competent and supernaturally even-tempered. Claire wants to tell her how it feels to let go of oneself, to give oneself over to whatever is in charge, good or bad.

116

She restricts herself to an account of her new giddy optimism. She touches her arm. "Even my girls have stopped sassing me. I don't understand it."

Nancy smiles. When Nancy smiles her face looks almost beautiful. Claire voices the observation, without the "almost."

"What a nice thing to say!" Nancy says, and blushes. She retrieves the popcorn, opens the bag. Some of it is charred. "We need a new microwave."

"We need a lot of things."

Nancy laughs. "What are you on, Claire? I could use some."

Claire's ebullience flags for a second: Not even Eileen knows she's taking an anti-convulsant.

But Nancy is joking of course. They pour off the burnt kernels, take the rest to the lounge, make a new pot of coffee. Claire doesn't even like to think about the Tegretol, but she'd like to confess Bodey. She has told Eileen, and basked in the warmth of Eileen's giddy approval, but Eileen isn't here now. The story dances around her mind. She takes a handful of popcorn, stuffs it in her mouth, weighing Nancy's possible moral repugnance against the pleasure of telling.

She tells her the story of a fictional girlfriend who has fallen in love with her fictional boss. Embarrassed, excited she describes the friend's unfurling potential, inspired by her kind, charismatic boss. Nancy sips her coffee, nodding from time to time. But when the imaginary friend's imaginary husband enters the story, Nancy's face shuts down. Claire mentions the imaginary friend's imaginary children. Nancy takes a piece of popcorn, examines it, puts it back in the bag. "Your friend should give some thought to other people, don't you think?"

Claire is obliged to defend her imaginary friend. "The situation's complicated. She doesn't want to get divorced, it might screw up the kids, you know. And I think she really loves her husband. But she has the need, you know, to fulfill herself." It sounds trite. A feminist cliché. Her cheeks start to ache. "It was a crazy thing. The way she describes it makes it sound almost, you know, pure." She describes something that happened to her with Bodey at school in the cafeteria line. As she reached for a tray, he took hold of two of her fingers; she had felt an actual jolt. "Electricity between people isn't a cliché, it's a phenomenon. An authentic experience. That's what she told me," she says, looking Nancy straight in the eye. "I kind of envy her. To connect like that."

Nancy shrugs.

"Even so," says Claire almost desperately, "isn't it better than the same old same old?"

"It doesn't last," Nancy says.

Claire sees the switchboard light go on. Room 432. She hopes the desk will take care of it. "Maybe it can last, at this age. Since we're all more experienced now. And wiser and braver." She's moved by her own words, but Nancy is looking at her strangely.

Her name sounds over the intercom.

"That's how we thought in our twenties," says Nancy. "Everything was feelings. We tried to be honest with our *feelings*.

Men should respect our *feelings*. Don't you think by now we should be past that?"

Claire changes the bedding in 432, and comforts the girl who messed herself, all the while thinking, Should she be past that? There's a pinch of old terror. She once heard Dr. Laura telling an unhappily married man who'd fallen all over again for his high school prom date that he was a moral idiot. Claire can't stand Dr. Laura, but for the rest of the shift she argues with her in her mind. What do we listen to, if not our feelings? Which make us our unique selves? And, really, what does Dr. Laura know? Or Nancy, who's married to a shy, silent, evasive man whose inability to communicate would give Claire a nervous breakdown.

The following Saturday she's struck by how heavy Bodey looks. She averts her eyes from the overhang of his belly.

Bodey, however, seems more genuinely affectionate. He looks at her hand on the formica table in the cafeteria. Her left hand, adorned with watch and wedding band. "I like your veins," he says. It's lunch hour, a jam-packed room. She likes how students hover respectfully on their borders. And how pretty her hand feels under his gaze. But part of her watches them together. Who is this man who thinks he knows me? Who is this woman, who laughs with an ache in her stomach, fiddling nervously with her hair? She wants to give him a hard time all of a sudden. She wants to make messes.

She makes a fist of her hand. The veins flatten out. "A medical miracle."

119

He draws his chair nearer. "You're a woman with the mind of a gifted child. You haven't been hardened. You're still *open*." He pauses at the word. She twists the ring on her finger, picturing the red open throat of a baby bird. A slimy gray oyster on the half shell.

"I'm naïve, you mean," she says. "Simple-minded."

They walk down to the basement together, continuing the discussion. "All the women I know are prima donnas. Even Marcella. Especially Marcella."

The name echoes in the empty stairwell. He isn't lauding Marcella; if anything, he's complimenting *her*. But something jabs. "And you too?" she says, snide and clever, as she imagines Marcella to be.

"Don't make fun of me."

He says it like an order. Not as if he's hurt, but as if he's laying down a law. She hardens herself.

Back in his office, he's still fierce about something. "I'll bet you don't know what it's like to be depressed," he says. "You're afraid to get into your car because driving you just might turn into the oncoming lane. Did you ever dream a train is bearing down on you and you can't move? The world, the air on top of you, all around you, feels, literally, heavy." He speaks into her palm against his lips. But now he doesn't mind getting out of bed, at least on Friday and Saturday when there's a chance to see her. He's working on a new installation, something he's really excited about. It's been a long time since he felt that way. "I love you," he says, without qualifiers, not snide or ironic or self-conscious.

120

She looks at him. There's a mole on his cheek, brownish black and not quite round. "You should get that checked," she says. His red hair is fading. His desk is a mess, papers all over the floor. "You need a maid." She stands up, ready to go. Surprised how easy it is. "You should go on a diet. Will you? You'll live longer." She puts her arms around him, kisses the fabric of his shirt, sees her jacket hanging on the back of his chair. She puts it on.

"Do you love me?"

She's caught with her fingers in a buttonhole. No one ever asked her that before. Leo is content with or else oblivious to whatever she projects toward him. If Leo asked, of course, she'd have assented no matter how she felt. As if there were no choice. But with Bodey she can tell the truth, or refuse to answer, or lie, even; it's up to her. She buttons her jacket. Thinking, suddenly, that it's only when you have the power to choose to lie that honesty means anything. "I don't," she says. "I'm sorry, I really don't."

She buttons her jacket. His face has stiffened. There's a twitch in his cheek. She kisses the soft temple of his head, feeling more sharply defined than she has ever felt in her life.

Now she can try to know him—now, the first time she has ever been able to look at a man with any degree of clarity. In high school her vision was blurred by the anxiety of picking boys that significant girls would approve of. In college she went out a lot, but still huddled inside herself, unable to see past the face she put on to be attractive. If it worked and she was asked out again she felt obliged to resume the pose, and if it didn't work, she forgave herself by resolving to be cleverer next time. Then she met Leo. Twenty years passed. Reasonably good, unreflecting years. Though for a while it has seemed that her love for Leo is just fervent gratitude; it's so indefinite and reasonable compared to her feeling for Bodey.

She summons whatever reserves she has of objectivity. In many ways, compared to Leo, Bodey falls short. Physically he's an odd specimen. And at times he's irrationally, even morbidly sensitive, to the opinions of people he shouldn't have to worry about—a department secretary who refuses to xerox something for him, an eyeball-rolling grad student. She has seen him exaggerate it into comedy for the numerous students who hang around him, then afterward sit in scorched silence. His ego continually swells and shrinks, depending on who has treated him well or badly lately. And sometimes even when they're alone together, he's obsessed with Marcella. "When I met her she had flash but that's all. Do you know how much her pieces sell for now?" Claire wonders if he's drawn to her merely because she's no competition.

But he loves her. Or so he says.

With Eileen at Starbucks she submits to the pleasure of talking about it. "I'm not sure how I feel. But I think about him all the time."

Eileen's boyfriend is still in town, but with another woman. Younger. Dumber. Eileen vents her disgust, that she acknowledges as a cover for pain; it turns wry. "Men are pigs," she concludes. Claire politely refrains from excluding Bodey from the generalization. After a while, Eileen can enter into her friend's more agreeable dilemma. "I won't say be careful. Just enjoy it."

"I do. I don't even feel guilty. Is there something wrong with me?"

"If so, it looks good on you."

Claire hugs her. Something feels good, inside her. She walks with assurance and speaks without first checking her remarks for signs of incapacity. It's how she felt after her wisdom teeth were removed. On Percocet every four hours, not to exceed four tablets in twenty-four.

Bodey's installation, entitled, according to the poster in the window, "The Final Solution," opens at a gallery in Pilsen, which is set up to look like a concentration camp extermination facility. The audience, come to view a "performance," file into a small room, empty and unadorned except for a row of fake shower heads. Bodey, wearing a German military cap and Hitler mustache, orders them to remove their jewelry, wallets and handbags and place them in a box by the door. When the door shuts, the room goes black. A recorded hiss of gas fills the closed dark space, along with recorded augmenting screams. At the end of twenty minutes, the time it took the prisoners in a gas chamber to breathe Zyklon B and die, the door opens. Playing softly, but easy to hear in the sudden silence, is Israel's national anthem, "Hatikva."

People walk out shaking and sobbing. Claire too, ambling along with Leo but a little behind like a teenage girl with a potentially embarrassing parent.

In the anteroom the department head Rosemary Smith-Jones, a middle-aged woman with a salt-and-pepper afro, is passing out flyers with directions to her loft. "You better come," she warns the viewers, mostly grad students and faculty from the School. "Or else what am I going to do with my three cases of wine? Not to mention my twelve-foot-long sub sandwich?" Claire, eyeing a tall slender woman with short dead-black hair whom she thinks is Marcella, hurries out the door, but Leo gets into a conversation with Rosemary and accepts the invitation.

"Let's go," he tells Claire. "You can introduce me to your new friends."

They stand outside in a pool of light from the gallery window. It's cold and windy, a good night to be home. "I know exactly three people in the department," Claire says. "I'm not even a BFA candidate, I'm a 'student-at-large.' Lowest of the low."

"So let's social climb!"

"But it's Thursday. Don't you have to get up early?"

"We'll stay an hour, that's all. I can operate with my eyes closed!"

"Oh God." She touches her head. "I'm starting to get a headache."

"All right. We'll go home. Would you like a foot massage?"

Her toes curl inside her shoes, against even the prospect of touch. "Okay, we'll go for an hour." Her heart starts to thud. "Maybe I'm just hungry." She studies the flyer in the street-lamplight, checks the address. It's close to the gallery.

At the party she stays at Leo's side sipping wine, while he navigates from group to group fueled by a seemingly inexhaustible fund of small talk. "I'm taking Sculpture," she says when asked. "It's my first class." Or, in response to a reference to the performance, "It was highly disturbing!" Out of the corner of her eye at times she sees Bodey, at other times the black-haired woman, but always in opposite corners, as if they have nothing to say to each other or else they just had a fight. Not that Marcella should be a problem for her. He doesn't plan to leave Marcella, nor she, Leo. There's a tenuous symmetry.

She tries to relax. She admires the loft, its fourteen-foot ceilings, exposed pipes, varnished old floors. Tries to imagine herself living in such a place. On her second, or is it her third trip to the wine table, Bodey is standing beside her. Her heart stops but her voice, bred to be mannerly, says, "Your show was very strong." He beams, jovial and exuberant at this party in his honor. His red hair curls past his collar. "Wrenching," she says. It had felt exactly that.

He bends to her ear, whispers, "I want to fuck you."

She drops her her plastic cup, which was, thank God, almost empty. She stoops to retrieve it. He kneels beside her, emitting actual heat. "Do you know what I love about you, Claire? You

125

can't hide anything." He presses her arm with the back of his hand, then moves off.

When Leo is ready to go she looks at her watch. It's ten o'clock. "Honey," she says, "I'd like to stay. I don't have work tomorrow."

"I thought you had a headache."

"It's better."

"You just want to flirt without my distracting presence."

"Exactly!" She takes a long drink from the cup in her hand, not caring whether he or anyone else sees her blushing.

"Seriously. I feel weird leaving you with all these crazy artists."

"They're all your best friends now. They'll take care of me." She pats his arm. "One of them will drop me off. Or I'll take a cab." She promises to be home by midnight. He'll be in bed, reading, waiting for her. She manages a totally deceptive flirtatious wink.

With Leo gone, however, her timidity returns. Bodey is seated on the kitchen counter, center of a good-sized group who laugh at his stories on cue. She drinks more wine but her discomfort, without abating, becomes merely hard to think about. Professor Ko was here earlier, but he must have left. She walks toward a woman sitting alone on the couch but can't remember her name. She approaches a small group, thinking of the boy in Bodey's class whose nightmare initiation she'd witnessed. None of the people, two men and two women, look familiar, although she's pretty sure they didn't just walk in. The taller man is nice-looking except for an oddly diminished chin. As she gazes, his chin elongates. His cheeks swell like a cartoon character's. She smells coffee emanating from the sleeve of his blue shirt, or is it figs? Something delicious.

Half aware of trouble looming, she heads toward the bedroom where she left her coat. Quickly now. Cinderella out-running her curfew. She has on jeans and a black silk blouse. Will they turn, at twelve, into a matching pants suit? Outside the room there is Bodey talking to the black-haired woman with florid sweeps of the hand. The woman has unusual dark blue eyes rimmed in violet. The hall isn't a hall but continuous space in the loft that hasn't been segmented into rooms.

"Claire? Come over here, I want you to meet someone."

She fixes on the mole on his cheek but it doesn't hold her. It flies up, up, out of reach, then gone.

She must be home because she's lying on a bed. But it's smaller than her own king-size and full of coats. Her legs ache as if she has been running. Her head throbs all the way down her spine. There's a hand on her forehead, large and warm. She likes the hand.

"She's waking up."

She? Voices circle like a swarm of bugs.

"What happened? Did you see what happened?"

"I think she was unconscious."

"She must have passed out."

"Which means unconscious, right!"

Someone bends toward her. Sour breath, sweet perfume. "Should we call a doctor?"

At that remark, some clarity returns. Beyond the arm attached to the hand is a cluster of people looking down at her with the concerned confusion of medical students. And the hostess, department head, what was her name? The hand is heavy on her face; she pushes it away.

"I'm all right."

The hostess looks doubtful.

She blinks rapidly. "I'm fine, really." She sees Bodey hovering. For some reason she feels like crying. She sits up, addresses the hostess, Rosemary. "That was good wine. Too good. I'm sorry. I'm really sorry." She tugs at her blouse, which has ridden up under her. She stands, adjusts herself. People are staring, or trying not to stare. It doesn't matter. She can't even fake politeness.

Bodey offers her a ride home. "Thank you," she breathes. "Thank you," in the tone with which she'd have said, I love you.

CHAPTER NINE

Stories and Lies

An Artist-in-Education had come every week for the past month to help the seventh grade write creative stories, and now everyone had brought their stories, even Bobby Molina who smoked and only came to school three days out of five.

But Hadley didn't have her story. She'd tried to write it. Not as Nora would have, a week ahead of time, but the whole night last night. She'd turned on her computer and written her name, the date, the room number, and she had a copy of the myth she'd been assigned, about Persephone, who ate six pomegranate seeds and had to stay in the Underworld for six months out of every year, but no matter how many times she reread it, she had no idea how to make it "real for today." Nora wouldn't help. "Use your imagination," she said, as if Hadley didn't know that. She'd even gone down to ask her mother for help, but her mother and dad were busy arguing, as they had been doing lately. The problem was, Hadley could picture Hades with its clammy stone furniture, and the electric light that was always on in that otherwise dark world, but in the "world of today" the closest she could come was the basement of her grandmother's old house, its painted cinder-block walls and dusty ping-pong table, and nobody would ever live there. She had stayed up late looking for a way around it.

Now, dead tired, she shrank down in her seat as the artist-teacher, Ms. G ("Call me Ms. G!" she'd said as if conferring a favor) asked for volunteers. With Boltz out of the room there were no volunteers. "Be brave," said Ms. G. "You know we all love you."

There was a room-wide light snicker, which Ms. G joined in, though it was almost wholly at her expense. Ms. G was her mother's age but dressed younger, in a long loose skirt and droopy earrings. Her hair hung down her back. The silence that followed was charged, awaiting the woman's embarrassment.

"Does *she* love *me*?" Darnell whispered, cocking his head in the woman's direction. The snickers gathered confidence.

"Anybody?" Ms. G turned from one side of the room to the other, swinging her earrings. "Or should I just call on people?"

Felice raised her volunteering hand. The frustrated classroom sigh was dangerously audible, but Felice read in her clear, loud voice her modern version of Theseus slaying the Minotaur.

Theodore (Theseus) was a college freshman pledging a fraternity called Gamma Epsilon Epsilon Kappa (GEEK). The last day of pledge week, Theodore was given a laundry bag and driven blindfolded to a haunted house on the edge of town. To earn entry into GEEK, he had to capture a possibly rabid cat that lived in the attic, place it in the laundry bag, and transport it back to the fraternity house, a task complicated by the fact that a senior in the fraternity had cut a hole in the bag. Luckily, however, the senior's girlfriend Adrienne (Ariadne) gave him a ball of string and a needle to sew up the hole through which the cat could have escaped and bitten him, as a result of which he'd have had twelve rabies shots in his stomach and missed the rest of the basketball season. In the end Theodore decided he didn't care about basketball, or fraternities, which were mean-spirited and undemocratic. Adrienne and he drove away to live in San Francisco.

As Felice concluded, Hadley saw her hands shaking on her typed pages; they continued to shake as she returned to her seat. But the boys beat their feet on the floor, roaring unironic applause; even the girls clapped with some enthusiasm. Ms. G said, "That was extraordinary," and looked as if she wanted to hug her. Hadley leaned her chin on her fists and tried to figure out how Felice had invented such a long, detailed story when she herself had trouble making anything up. It was hard to think of something that wasn't in the world already in front of her eyes. When she couldn't *see* it.

131

There were five minutes left in the period—one more story offering, and she was home free. She prayed for someone to raise a hand. Then Ms. G was standing at the foot of her row, beaming in her direction. "The young lady, third seat back? Yes, you. Could we hear what you've written?"

Ms. G beckoned joyfully. Hadley stared down at her desk, full of books and papers but not what had been asked for, while heat throbbed in the back of her neck. She hoped ridiculously that her silence would discourage the woman's interest in her.

"Don't be shy. We're all rooting for you."

Hadley closed her eyes. Normally, it was easy to lie. When her safety or desires were threatened, she'd say the first thing that came to mind regardless of truth, and usually it was the right thing. She avoided punishment, pleased her friends. And Ms. G. Airhead, who didn't even know her name, would not close-question her.

But for some reason now, the matter seemed complicated. Sometimes lately when she said something to Rachel or to one of their other friends that wasn't completely true, the kind of thing she used to say a million times without thinking, the expression on her friend's face or maybe something in her own voice would make her nervous. It didn't happen often, but it happened. As if she were in a play she knew, saying lines she knew by heart, and they were the wrong lines. As if she were trying to be funny and no one laughed. As if in the world there was no truth capital T, just things you created as you described them. Ms. G was still looking at her. Something was required.

She looked hard into Ms. G's eyes, then turned away as if embarrassed. "I don't feel comfortable reading mine aloud," she said. "It's too personal."

Ms. G nodded sympathetically and turned to someone else.

When the period was up Hadley tried to merge with the group rushing out the door, but Ms. G put a hand on her arm. "Are you all right?"

The woman's eyes were so sympathetic, Hadley couldn't speak. A place low in her stomach was starting to hurt. She wanted to ask what the G stood for but felt she didn't have the right. She nodded, then shrugged, wanting to cry. Out in the hall she stood alone by the wall for several minutes, till her stomach stopped hurting.

When the bell signaled the end of the school day, it was drizzling outside, a March rain, not warm, not cold, and instead of getting on her bus, Hadley walked with Fletcher to his townhouse. It was her third visit, the second this week. He'd been hanging around her at recess, and after school he waited with her for the bus, and every night for the past seven he had called her on the phone and told her his views on capital punishment (for), gun control (against), and how you stay seated on a bucking horse (squeeze your knees together), and when he hung up he always said, I love you, Hadley. It made her feel sorry for him, as if he'd confessed a secret deformity, like six toes on one foot. Now he was telling her about Communism being bad not just for people's freedom but for economic production. She did not say, Everybody knows that, though she knew or thought she knew that Communism was dead. She did not say she wanted to go home, although her stomach still ached. "Yes," she said, "right," following him through his living room, through his kitchen to the garage out back. If Communism was dead, how did it die, she wondered but didn't say. She felt meek, subdued, sliding into the passenger seat of his mother's SUV. He climbed in on the other side.

He left the garage door up. It wasn't raining anymore, but the cloud mist was thick. Inside, the light was so dim all she could see, really, was the tiny silver horse on a chain around Fletcher's neck. He had a lighter and a pack of Kools, and he offered her one. She declined as usual; she had never smoked and didn't ever intend to. Besides, none of her friends smoked. He put a hand on the side of her face and kissed her.

She kissed him back. It was the first time. He had kissed her before and although she hadn't pushed away, all she did was keep her head still. But in this new meek mode her lips did what his seemed to want hers to. He was shorter than she, but you couldn't tell sitting down. He had long eyelashes and smelled of Dentyne. Where he came from boys raised prize hogs and wore plaid flannel shirts, and he was the kind of slim that could be called skinny, but he was already on the Edison Magnet basketball team and he'd started a club called The Trojans that most boys wanted to be in but only some were.

When the kiss concluded, he leaned back against the leather seat and lit his cigarette.

"Why do you smoke?" she said. "It mucks up your lungs."

"I like muck in my lungs." He laughed his usual laugh, three loud crisp beats, and blew a smoke ring. "And I like the head rush."

The cigarette looked odd between his first and second fingers, how sleazy men held it in old TV movies. "You could get cancer," she said, then with a flash of her old easiness, "Y'all must think you're mighty brave or something."

She'd borrowed his Texas drawl. She waited for him to acknowledge her sass, but he started talking about some rich old guy who paid to go up in space, and how with money you could do whatever you wanted. Generally, she didn't think he heard her when she talked. He'd wait for her to finish but what he said in reply would make her forget what she'd said in the first place. Mostly it didn't bother her. She saw other girls with their boyfriends. No reason to think there was any difference. But now he started in on what it was like to take off in a space shuttle (which he had never done), and her stomach burned. She began counting to a hundred, to see how high she'd get before he stopped talking. She said, though it didn't connect to his subject (sometimes things came out like this although usually she tried to make more sense), "Was there a queen of England called Bloody Mary?"

"The Virgin Mary?"

"Don't be stupid, Fletcher."

135

"Not," he said. "How about Mary Magdalene? Or Mary, Queen of Scots? Or Mary Ellen Turner?"

"Who's Mary Ellen Turner?"

"My cousin in Dallas!"

His voice was triumphant. She let him put his hands on her shoulders and kiss her again, mouth open, and busy avoiding his tongue, she missed the arrival of his hand under her shirt on the small of her back, and when the sensation knocked at last on the door of her consciousness, there was a very slight uneasiness but still no reason to move the hand away or move out of reach of the hand, which seemed to believe in what it was doing. The hand was triumphant like his voice, and the small of her back was just that, small, and anyway her back was public domain, exposed to the world when she went to the beach. Then his finger callus scratched her. She jerked away. Felt her back for torn skin.

"Really, Fletcher. What about Queen Mary? Did she do something terrible? Did something terrible happen to her?"

He gave her a look of utterly fake authority that boys knew how to do from birth. "She murdered a lot of people."

She tried to laugh but hard nubs had risen on the lining of her stomach. "You jujube."

"She executed them. Chopped their heads off. You don't have to be a genius. That's what they did, all those Queens of England."

His lit cigarette sat in the ashtray. Her throat burned. She swallowed hard on the cough, while he told her about an English queen who'd killed her sister for believing in a different religion, and a king who murdered eight wives because they had daughters instead of sons. "In those days," he said, "boys were more highly valued."

She nodded, understanding. In the present world, it seemed to her that girls were more valued, or at least everything that mattered came from the world of girls. Fletcher himself was most appealing to her *after* she'd seen him, in the discussions with Rachel and her friends. Now Fletcher's hand was rubbing her back. She overlooked its widening field till it stopped smack-dab on the hook of her bra. "Hey!" she said.

"Hey what?"

She was upset now. Though maybe it was only that she was supposed to be upset. Either way, she reached behind her. He'd unhooked it with one hand; did they practice that? He puffed on his cigarette but she couldn't tell if he inhaled or not. Her lips felt larger than usual and a little chapped. Her stomach growled. She felt overly full, but empty at the same time. She couldn't remember the last time she'd eaten anything, today or yesterday. It might have been yesterday. Unable to rehook without taking off her bra and turning it around, she adjusted her shirt. Wishing it were still winter and she had a thick sweater on. A down parka.

The cigarette was out, but he didn't move toward her again. He told her about the story he'd turned in to the Artist-in-Education. It was based on Icarus and Daedalus, a son and father who flew with wings they made out of wax till Icarus got too close to the sun and his wings melted. In Fletcher's story, son Eric races his Porsche too fast in the Indy 500, his tires burn up, and in front of his dad in the stands he dies in a tangle of exploded metal and rubber. Normally she'd have snorted with disgust. Death and violence. What all boys wrote about. But she just wrapped her arms around herself.

"What was yours about?" Fletcher said, obviously proud of his.

"I'm kind of hungry," she said. "Is there anything to eat in your house?"

Inside the kitchen he sliced bananas over cornflakes for them both, and poured milk. When she was done, he'd hardly started. She ate his, too, thinking about the story she hadn't written and would never write even if she flunked Language Arts, just as she would never look in the mirror and say *Bloody Mary, Bloody Mary.* Would she say to him that she wasn't his girlfriend? People saw them as boyfriend and girlfriend and she didn't like to disillusion them. It felt wrong, for some reason.

He went up to his room and came back with the book of myths he'd found his story in. "Which one did you pick? Is it in here?"

She opened the book, more pictures than words. There was a color illustration of a boy falling through the sky. He looked a little like Fletcher, the same brown curly hair. Fletcher looked at her gravely. "I'm not asking to see your story. But there's no reason not to tell me your myth, is there? Or is that too personal?"

Her mind moved slowly now, picking its way as if through briars. Her myth wasn't the least bit personal, having been chosen for her by Ms. G. But Fletcher had absorbed the image of her as shy or private or something; she felt obliged to maintain it now, no matter how tired she was. She produced an indifferent shrug. "What made you choose death to write about?" she said, as if she were fascinated.

He smiled, thinking, liking to think. "Because of the flying. When I'm sixteen I'm going to take flying lessons. At Palwaukee Airport."

"But your character died, didn't he?"

He laughed, liking himself, the way his mind worked. Not needing to explore discrepancies. "After dinner tonight do you want to see a movie?"

"I'm sleeping at Rachel's tonight. May Sun, too, and some other girls. You can probably come for part of it."

"I love you, Hadley."

He looked at her, his face so blank and empty all of a sudden she had to touch the counter to orient herself. Her stomach was hurting again. "Okay. Well, bye now!"

She grabbed her pack and ran out of the house, out of sight of his empty face. It was raining but not hard. She ran for the El.

Home, the stomachache remained. It was a new kind of pain, low in the abdomen, dull and burny at the same time. Hadley went down to the basement studio that her mother had set up for herself. Knock, knock. Anyone there? No, per usual.

Nora's shoes were in the hall. Nora was home. Nora walked

around everywhere barefoot now. But it was too far up to Nora's room.

She sat on the bottom stair, opened Fletcher's book to a picture of a sun-speckled meadow in which a girl with flowers in her hands fell into a hole in the earth that, according to the caption, was supposed to have opened just for her. The girl's hair floated prettily upward. But Hadley didn't like much to read, and it was twice as hard with her stomach like this. She went to her room, got in bed, pulled up the covers.

A couple of years ago she had taken two of her mother's crystal wine goblets out of the china cabinet for her and Rachel to drink from, Sprite, that looked like champagne through the Florentine glass, and afterward she was careful washing it but still one broke on the side of the sink. A week later when her mother missed it, Hadley denied all knowledge, keeping a blank face while her mother questioned Nora and her father. When her mother concluded that the culprit had to have been the cleaning lady, Hadley got a stomachache so bad she had stayed in bed all day. It felt something like this one, as if some mud in her stomach was seeping out into her other organs. As if there were no truth in the world, not even facts mutually agreed on, no way of knowing at a given time what really had happened. Her mother never directly accused the cleaning lady, but a couple of months later there was a new person to clean, and afterward when Hadley thought about the broken goblet she had trouble remembering it. Maybe the cleaning lady had broken it. Maybe there had never been a goblet. The word goblet sounded strange in her ears.

In bed now, her palpable, familiar bed, under her familiar flowered poly-filled comforter, she brought her knees to her chest and squeezed. Her stomach felt hot, like when the shampoo girl says, Is it too hot, sweetie? and it almost isn't, but it is. She put a pillow over her stomach and turned over, pressing down. She could almost forget it, watching the stripes of light from the lowering sun beyond the window shift with the slow sway of the mini-blinds. But what could she focus on tonight at Rachel's?

With the late afternoon sun bleaching a diamond onto the white oak surface of her dresser, she looked in the mirror, on the spot where the reflection of her upper body dissolved in glare. Her eyes began to tear. "Bloody Mary," she said fiercely, meeting the source of fear, beckoning, taunting it. Nothing happened.

She put on her mother's bracelet and held it up to her face, leaned toward the glare. There was a gap between her front teeth that would be closed by orthodontia when her bones stopped growing, the dentist had said. "Bloody Mary," she hissed. Leaning closer still, she could see tiny pencil-point pores in the end of her nose. She listened for her mother's car in the driveway, the garage door purring up. "Bloody Mary!" Her room looked odd, its silence a hole to fall into. Her stomach continued to burn.

She called Rachel. She hated to talk about things that upset her but she said to Rachel, "I have a horrible stomachache."

"How sucky," Rachel said.

"I don't know if I can come tonight."

Hadley heard Rachel's breath going into and out of the receiver. Rachel sounded like she had a stomachache herself. "Did you tell your mom?"

"She's not home."

"You could call your dad at work."

"He won't know anything."

"He's a doctor!"

"An *eye* doctor!"

"Do you want me to ask my mom?"

"Well, actually, it's starting to feel better now."

"I hope you don't have stomach cancer," Rachel said.

"I don't!" Hadley said, hanging up.

Her mother's cat poked her head into the room, then turned and padded down the hall. She heard it clicking up the stairs to the third floor. The phone rang but she didn't pick up. Down from Nora's room came radio music like a sweet-voiced boy crying though she knew it was a violin. Nora played first violin in her high school orchestra. Nora had just been inducted into her high school honor society, an organization Hadley would never in a million years be asked to join. Nora had a letter in track and dark wavy hair like their mother's that she cut close to her head as if she didn't even care. The only thing Hadley had that Nora didn't was a decent boyfriend, an ascendancy she kept in mind as she climbed up to Nora's room. The door was open, the radio music loud, swelling. On the floor by the bed lay a small open

142

suitcase, with track shoes nestled in a plastic bag beside a pile of neatly folded underwear. Nora sat on her bed in a T-shirt and jogging shorts, a book propped against her thighs, Cassandra curled under the tent of her knees. "Are you going somewhere?" she said to Nora.

"God," Nora said, "don't you pay attention to anything outside your own little world?"

"Where's Mom?" Hadley said.

Nora scratched Cassandra's head. "I'm not our mother's keeper."

"What?"

Nora looked apologetic. The delicate swell and contraction of Nora's calves into her white socks induced a small ache under Hadley's breastbone. "I have a meet tomorrow. In Springfield. It's kind of a big deal. What's going on, Had?"

Hadley shrugged. The radio played long sticky violin sweeps, wrapping her head around and around. The words in Nora's book were small and close together. "Kids don't get stomach cancer," Hadley said, her voice against the swell of violin louder than she wanted it to be.

Nora turned the radio down. "What are you talking about?"

"I just said."

"No, I mean, who has stomach cancer? Do you think you have stomach cancer?"

Hadley shook her head vehemently. "Was she here when you got home?"

143

"No, but she'll come soon. After her art class."

"Her art class is Saturday."

"She goes down sometimes to do extra work. She's dedicated."

"Just like you," Hadley said.

Face down on Nora's bed lay *The New Testament*, for people who weren't Jewish, centered on one extremely gory event Hadley had no reason to think about. There was nothing in Nora's book that would have compelled her to take it off a shelf. She said to Nora, "I hate our mom."

"Me too, sometimes," Nora said, "but then I think—"

"No," Hadley said. "I really hate her."

Her sister looked at her. Hadley let her look. It was one of those days. Nothing terrible had happened today but everything seemed a mess. More and more days were getting like that. "She's very unhappy," Nora said. "Hadley, what's the matter with you?"

Hadley picked up *The New Testament*. "Do you read this for fun?"

"I'll tell you a secret," Nora said, "if you promise to keep your mouth shut."

Hadley rolled her eyes.

"Last fall, you know, Mom—"

"When she fell down the stairs? And had to go to the hospital?"

"She tried to kill herself."

Hadley had been about to sit down on the bed. She remained standing. "Do you think I believe you?"

"I don't care if you do or not."

"Did Dad tell you?"

Nora shrugged. "He didn't have to tell me."

"So how do you know? Did you just figure it out with your brilliant brain?"

"Hadley, I found her. I got home before Dad and saw her on the floor. I shook her but she wouldn't wake up."

"That doesn't mean she tried to kill herself!"

"There was a bottle of sleeping pills in her hand. Empty. Put two and two together."

"Shut up, shut up, shut up, shut up!"

"You used to cry at the drop of a hat," Nora said. "Now you're just pissed all the time."

"You're the one who *cries!*"

Nora shook her head. "You expect everything to center on you. Things don't center on any one person."

"I know that."

"How are you and Fletcher?" Nora said. "Did something happen with Fletcher today?"

"Fletcher's great."

"The way you talk to him on the phone, it's like you can't stand him."

"I love Fletcher! When we graduate college we're going to get married." She put a hand on her stomach. "He makes me feel quivery right *here!*"

She told Nora about something funny that Fletcher had said

145

to her and something expensive that Fletcher bought her, but her sister didn't absorb her words the way her friends did. But lying was like eating potato chips, fun at first, then no taste. "Forget it, Sister Saintly. You wouldn't know what I'm talking about."

"Neither do you," Nora said, and yawned. She made a show of returning to her book, then seized up at the sight of Hadley's arm. "Hey, where did you get that bracelet?"

"Fletcher—" she started to say.

"It's Mom's," Nora said.

"I hate your guts."

"You should pray," Nora said like the Queen of England. "It helps to focus on something greater than yourself." She picked up Cassandra, kissed her nose like you'd kiss a baby. She looked stupidly happy with everything.

Hadley went into her mother's bathroom, sat down on the toilet and tried to focus on anything beside the pain in her gut. She was tracing in her mind a line that zigzagged across the bathroom floor connecting the first two rows of tiny black hexagons, when she saw on the crotch of her underpants a small brownish stain. For a second she wondered if this was her period. Half the girls in her class had started, even Rachel, who was shorter than she and flat as a board. But it was brownish like you know what. Feeling humiliated although there was no one to see, she balled up the pants and stashed them under the debris in her mother's wastebasket. Then in the medicine chest Hadley found a bottle of something marked "for pain." Take one or two capsules every six hours or as needed. She swallowed a plump white Percocet, counted sixty waiting for the pain to stop. She took another.

At the sound of her mother's feet on the stairs she tried to rise from the bed. Outside her window the light had turned black purple. She closed her eyes, pulling the corners of her mouth into the faint, pretty, dead smile of Snow White in her glass coffin as her mother wafted toward her. "Hadley," she said, "what's the matter, honey?"

Hadley tightened her closed eyes but increased very slightly the arc of her smile.

"I hope you're not getting sick." Her mother bent over the bed. She smelled of clay and the heavily sweet chemical soap she used to wash the clay off her hands. "Hadley, talk to me." She put a dry, fragrant hand to her forehead. "You're cool."

"Yes," Hadley whispered. "I'm really cool."

The hand lifted. "Hadley, I want you to get up now. It's almost dinnertime."

Hadley wanted to cry. To open her arms to her mother and put her face into the sweet-smelling niche under her chin and sob like a baby. Instead she opened her eyes wide and hard and dry. She imagined her eyes saying to her mother, you don't deserve to be alive standing in front of me on this planet.

"Nora's gone. There's just the two of us tonight," her mother said. "Let's go downstairs. Would you mind setting the table?"

"Where's Dad?"

"He's driving her. And some of the team, actually. A carful of fast girls!"

"He didn't say goodbye to me."

"You were asleep. What's going on, Hadley? You're acting strange."

Hadley put her thumb in her mouth like a baby. She giggled. "I am strange."

Her mother laughed. "I wouldn't brag about it."

"I'm eating at Rachel's," Hadley said. "I'm sleeping at Rachel's."

"You are? I don't recall being asked."

Hadley stretched. Tried to wake up. Her mother bent over and kissed her forehead. "So you're going to leave me completely alone tonight? What will I do all by myself?"

Hadley looked at her with an odd gap where her reactions were supposed to be. Her stomach felt light and airy, as if nothing could ever have been wrong with it and could never be. Maybe she didn't even have a stomach down there. She groped for words that sounded like normal words. "You can call up one of your girlfriends?"

Her mother smiled. "That's all right. Get your things together. I guess you want me to drive you."

"You can call Eileen," Hadley said.

"That's okay. Thanks, dear."

As her mother left the room, it occurred to Hadley that her

mother sounded a little strange. She was at least in a strangely good mood.

Half an hour later Hadley walked down to the kitchen with her sleeping bag and her overnight case. Her mother was talking on the phone. Hadley brought her gear over to the front door, transfixed by her mother, the tilt of her head, the low, amused purr of her voice, her shining black hair. Hadley walked into the downstairs washroom and looked at her own face in the vanity mirror. Her hair looked flat, mousy. She fluffed it with the fingers of both hands, then leaned over, let it fall down to the floor and fluffed it out again.

When she opened the bathroom door, the house held a silence more potent than speech. A little nervous, but for no good reason, she tiptoed toward the kitchen. Her mother hung up the phone but didn't turn around. Hadley stared at her back, wondering if the sound she thought she heard from her mother was a small intake of breath.

In the bustle of moving gear from house to car Hadley let go of the apprehension, which she hadn't been able to fathom. She sat in the passenger seat, hands in her lap. Then on her wrist she felt the sharp smooth stones of her mother's bracelet, which had been there all day and her mother hadn't noticed, and she thought of her mother on the kitchen phone, her quick turn and hunch, the curling tight around her conversation. Pressing the bracelet into her wrist, Hadley rewound the tape in her mind, traced the moment back in time, then played it and heard what her mother had breathed into the phone, the laser beam of her whisper, meant to be heard but not overheard: "I want you."

CHAPTER TEN

Last Night

Hadley exits the car with her overnight case and sleeping bag. Doesn't say goodbye.

"Did you forget something?" Claire calls through the door. Hadley seems not to hear, trudging up the short flight of stairs to the Mosses' front porch. Suddenly Claire feels the pang of loss. She rolls down the window. "Had, come back for a minute." Hadley pauses, a bag in each hand, but she doesn't turn around. "Please, honey! I forgot to give you something!"

Hadley sets the bags down on the top step, her slow movements and bent head declaring her irritation. Claire is sick of it actually, this studied discourtesy from both her daughters. If she dared to treat her own mother like this, her father would have belted her. But by the time Hadley arrives at the car Claire is grateful for the privilege of leaning out the window to kiss her. "Do me a favor," she says fiercely, "don't grow up so fast." She regards her daughter's beautiful face. Her eyes sting. But there's also confused joy in her heart at the thought of the night's projected freedom. At the thought, even, of her duplicity. In her car on the Moss's driveway the world seems limitless, possibilities endless. As Hadley feels it, shifting impatiently from foot to foot in front of the car. Hadley, glorious and frightening in her ascent from childhood. "Have fun! I love you!" she cries. "Call me tomorrow when you want to get picked up!" Fleeing her duplicitous mother-voice she backs out quickly. A horn blares. "Sorry," she whispers to the driver she frightened or angered, to Hadley, Leo, God above. She'll take Hadley out to lunch tomorrow, if she doesn't object too strenuously. She'll call Nora before the meet. Her hands shake on the steering wheel.

At home her hands continue to shake as she throws away newspapers, centers plants and knickknacks, not that Bodey will value or even notice her housekeeping. Upstairs, she tears the three-day sheets off the bed and remakes it with fresh ones. She's nuts. All right, so she's nuts! But rituals don't have to make sense. They soothe, that's all. You relax in the simple movements of the unfolding, the soap-smell of the laundered cotton. In the bathroom mirror she regards her forty-year-old face, decides she looks a lot younger than forty.

Decides she looks her age.

She pulls the too-relaxed skin back from her temples, watches twenty years drop away. But whatever she looks like, she's more charged than your average forty-year-old woman. She laughs the laugh of a crazy person, claps a hand to her mouth, laughs into her fingers. By tomorrow, or tonight, even, she'll have made love in the same bed to two different men. Her virtue worth rhinestones now. Broken-bottle glass. But at least she's *alive*. At least she hasn't done them at the same time! The laugh boils up again. The hour till Bodey is due gapes like a mouth.

Downstairs on the kitchen counter is the name and telephone number of the Springfield Sheraton where the track team is staying. They're driving, and it's too early for them to have arrived, but she dials the number.

"Could you leave a message for Nora Winger? *Good luck, Darling.*" She speaks slowly so the clerk can write it down. "Say *Run for your life. I love you. Mom.* Sorry. No, don't write *Sorry.*" She's about to hang up when her heart starts thudding. "Or, what do you think?" she asks the clerk. "Does it sound too, I don't know, ominous, the 'run for your life' part?" The clerk reassures her. Though maybe he just wants to get this ridiculous woman off the phone. "Give the same thing to Leo Winger. Except the 'run for your life' part." A small giggle leaks into the mouthpiece. A new silliness is coming out of her. A new tendril on the ordinary little stem of her personality. "And the 'mom' part. Sign Leo's *Love, Claire*. I'm Claire. But I'm so unClaire! Thanks and have a good evening!" She holds the phone out from her ear till she hears the click. Her cheeks feel hot.

She has to keep moving.

She descends another flight to the basement and the shelves that hold the work from sculpture class. There are several lifesize clay heads, handsome and grotesque as if someone else has made them. But she has made them. She turns away so as not to worship them. She sweeps the basement floor with mild satisfaction, gone the moment she empties the dustpan. Back upstairs she opens several books but can't take in written words. The kitchen counters are clean but she scours them again, dries them with paper towels. She sits down, stands up, puts on music. It annoys her. She has two men and she needs both of them. Which sounds at best self-indulgent and most likely (probably) morally wrong. But right and wrong are as flimsy as thin old T-shirts beside the fear that squeezes her chest at the thought of losing either of them. To stay alive, it seems, a person requires two mates, the first for safety and the second for love, the first to maintain life and the second to give it a point, make it worth the trouble. On National Public Radio she heard of an Indian tribe whose conjugal practices addressed these needs, for men at least. A man married four wives, the first to keep the house and bear and rear children, the next three for erotic love. Apparently all got along well. Like sisters. She tries to imagine

Bodey in her Lakeview household. She, Nora, Hadley, Leo, and Bodey makes five. Her laugh rises crazily.

She runs upstairs, brushes her teeth, flosses, gargles, showers in the hottest water she can stand, steaming away what doesn't belong to the event to come. Separating, insofar as she can, her two essential lives, Leo and Bodey, Lakeview and the Loop, home and school. But—how can she deny it?—by inviting Bodey to her house she is blurring boundaries, merging compartments, and she has no desire to stop what she started. No; to phrase it more precisely—to stop what *has started*. What began last night through no will of hers, or Bodey's either.

His car was icy cold even with the heat all the way up. She was blasted with cold air and noise. Why had she stayed at the damn party? Why did she drink so much? He said, "You didn't just pass out, you know."

"What are you talking about?"

"Your body was twitching. Your hands and feet. Your toes curled up."

"What!"

"Your shoes fell off. Your feet looked like they were turning into fists. Like you were being electrocuted."

"Oh God." She hated the phoney sound of her voice and how loud she had to talk over the heater fan. On Lake Shore Drive the noise compounded, tires on asphalt. Her teeth would not stop chattering.

"I'm no doctor, Claire. But my baby brother had fever seizures. I think you had a seizure."

She wanted to cry. "You sound weird. Like I lost it, and you're glad or something."

"Why would I be glad?" He turned from the road to look at her. "Did you ever have a seizure before?"

"Bodey! Why are you making such a deal of this?"

Her throat hurt. His face glowed like the face of Moses coming down the mountain. "Jesus, something is wrong with you."

Weakly she shook her head. But something was wrong with her, it was clear. She was crazy in a way no one would ever be able to fathom. When she was four years old she ran across the street and her father spanked her. Right there on the opposite sidewalk. Grabbed her by the arm and whacked her bottom four times, one two three four. She had no idea why. It was a cool, beautiful, sun-flecked day. She was too obliterated to cry. When he died she was thirty and still afraid of him, though she knew by then he had meant to disincline her from running into traffic. Now her body ached as if she'd been hit by a car. Her teeth clacked together. *You don't have to hurt me to teach me something*, she wanted to tell Bodey, shivering. She rather liked shivering.

He pulled into a closed gas station, put his arms around her, rubbed her back to warm her, but she wasn't ready for warmth. "I'm sorry, Bodey. But I need you to tell me the truth. Is there a tiny, barely conscious part of you that wants to maybe humiliate me? Is there, or am I nuts?"

"Claire, you're nuts."

"How am I nuts?"

"De Nile is a river in Egypt."

"That's really funny."

"Claire," he said, "what's so shameful about having had a seizure? You're in good company."

She pushed his arm off of her. She couldn't make one more teeth-gritted remark.

He turned off the lights, the motor. They turned to each other in the adjacent front seats, and he told her what he saw as their shared inheritance. Shame. He was a spaz compared to his athletic older brother and a retard compared to his brilliant younger brother. Add a tendency to overeat and you got a nightmare child-hood, his family the exact wrong family for someone like him to be born into. In eighth grade he got so heavy, even Huskies didn't fit; the pants he could zip all the way up were too long and his mother wouldn't shorten them. As a joke. "It'll slow him down," she'd say, "on the way to the fridge." If he went for seconds at a meal his father would pretend to gag or back his chair out from the table, making room for his imaginarily ballooning stomach. "They were comedians. And I was material. At the dinner table I'd imagine myself in Treblinka in line for a *Selection*. If I showed my hurt feelings or said a word in protest I would be gassed."

His face was pink with rage but she felt only tenderness. If he was a hurt child, so was she, just as sensitive. And more cowardly, more inclined to twist herself out of shape to avoid trouble.

157

"Bodey, the woman with the punk haircut, was that your Marcella?"

He smiled grimly. "Marcella's in New York. Marcella's working her way to the top. Even as we speak. Is that what's bothering you?"

She shook her head no. "Well, maybe a little." She closed her eyes, said to the darkness under her lids. "I have epilepsy. I've had it since I can remember."

It's almost nine and the house is clean and she has on silk pants and a chenille sweater, inviting to soft touch. And she's glad Bodey knows about her. Knows this about her. But sweat is dripping down the sides of her face and down her sides inside her sweater and he isn't here, the asshole.

She turns on the TV, remotes through the channels. The shows seem complicated. Gestures, expressions hard to decipher. She stares at the flickering screen and thinks of hands on her back, thumbs on her instep, the flame traveling up her leg, and she wants Bodey, who knows her. Though he's almost an hour late, she'd rather be waiting for Bodey than eating a fancy dinner or even flying to Paris with someone else.

CHAPTER ELEVEN

Bloody Mary

Mr. and Mrs. Moss had gone to temple with Rachel's younger brother, whose Bar Mitzvah was coming up next year and who had to attend a minimum of ten Friday-night services. Now, in the living room window, the Shabbat candles had almost burned down, and in the final throes of the Percocet, Hadley was wilder than usual. Under her guidance, the girls dialed a multi-consonanted phonebook name and uttered incorrectly targeted ethnic slurs (remembering to block caller-ID). They ordered Cantonese dinner for eight to be delivered to Felice Pinter's address. When May Sun wandered off to the den to read the book she'd brought, they took a bra from her overnight case, soaked it and put it in the freezer.

Winston and Fletcher came over with Winston's cousin, a quiet, pretty-faced boy a year younger than the group. They sat on the Oriental rug in the nest of the sectional sofa in the large family room and played spin-the-bottle, three boys and five girls including Rachel's younger sister, who had promised not to tell (if they let her play). Kissing was required regardless of gender, with the kisser deciding lips or cheek, and patterns were quickly laid down. May Sun kissed Winston's lips but everyone else's cheek. Sherelle was experimental, at times kissing even girls on the lips. Rachel offered her lips only when the bottle pointed at her and the kisser insisted. Her sister Tova, who wouldn't play (and might tell) unless she was allowed to override the bottle's decision, kissed only Hadley's lips. She had a crush on Hadley.

Other nights with this game Hadley had imitated Rachel's modesty, but now it felt too restrictive. Her stomach no longer bothered her. When Fletcher's lips touched hers, she stuck her tongue in his mouth. She whispered, "I want you."

He lost his balance, fell on his wrist. "Ouch! Sorry, what did you say?"

"Nothing." She laughed ferociously.

Later Rachel took her sister upstairs, promising her money if she stayed in her room. May Sun and Winston went out to the screened porch. Sherelle and Winston's cousin played a video game he'd brought with the most lifelike fighters Hadley had ever seen; even their blood looked real. Hadley took Fletcher's hand and led him to the closet, which had been converted from a coat receptacle to a sort of pantry for art supplies and board games. The floor was strewn with cards, markers, and green, sharp-edged Monopoly hotels. Shelves started at neck level; comfort was minimal. "There'll be more room if you sit on my lap," he said, and showed her how to sit facing him, with her legs around him. Light was a crack under the door, the music muffled. In the room outside, only fifteen feet away, Sherelle, Rachel, and Winston's cousin danced and laughed, but parental eyes were gone till at least ten-thirty, and in the game pantry Hadley sat straddling Fletcher's hips and played the game she'd started, with lips and tongue and hard breathing, and then the soft air in her head from the pills was gone. She was used to kissing Fletcher, used to their tongues together, and she didn't even mind his slightly sour taste, but she didn't like her legs around him, especially not the lumpy center part of him that every once in a while, softly, as if he hoped she wouldn't notice, pressed against the seam of her crotch.

For many minutes Hadley felt without feeling the silent approach and withdrawal of his torso. Beyond the door Rachel and the others danced, and Rachel sang along with the music, sweet and familiar, but they could have been in another country. Hadley sat on Fletcher's lap, trying to decide if she wasn't getting up because she didn't want to hurt his feelings or because she was frozen-paralyzed like an alligator she had seen in Florida once.

An Indian had rubbed its belly, and it went into a trance and let the Indian open its toothy mouth and put his whole head inside.

For some minutes she sat, paralyzed-open like the alligator. Then he sighed, breathing out the breath she'd gotten used to. "I love you, Hadley."

"I love you too, Fletcher."

Saying it only added to the terrible pressure of uncertainty; she had no idea how she felt about him. He couldn't tell, though. Her words made him happier than ever. "I looked up your Bloody Mary," he said. "On the Internet. She was a real person. Queen Mary the First of England." He paused a moment for her appreciation, then forged on without it. "In the fifteen hundreds. She really killed a lot of people, a better word is executed, but only the ones who weren't Catholic. They were burned at the stake."

"She'd have killed me," Hadley said.

"Me too."

She gazed at his shadowy face in the closet dark and said, despairingly, "I really love you."

At ten, as agreed, the boys departed. Shortly afterward Rachel's parents returned, jovial, kissing not just Rachel but all the friends. "Are you guys having fun? How come no one's burned the house down? Is Tova sleeping?" Rachel's brother Simon went up to the computer in his room. The parents went up to check on Tova. Hadley had no opinion of Simon, who was a year younger than her and Rachel, and hadn't said a word to her in the three years of her being best friends with his sister. But she loved Mrs. Moss, who yelled instead of talked and treated all girls including her daughters as if she knew exactly what they were thinking, the vixens, and it was all right with her.

Soon all was quiet on the parental front, Tova asleep, Simon under the spell of his chatroom; it was time for Bloody Mary. But while people were arguing about which of the two possible bathrooms to use, the pretty one or the one down in the basement, Hadley pushed open the Lazy Susan cabinet full of Mr. Moss's liquor and took out a bottle with the pleasantly shivery name of Absolut. Once before, she and Rachel had snuck something from here, sweet and bitter orange; it had made them laugh at things that weren't normally funny and fall asleep early. But this time she did it alone, a clear drink that poured thinner than water and gave a peppery underside to her Diet Coke. She sipped, murmuring to herself or someone, *I want you.*

When she rejoined the group outside the powder room, it was her turn. She walked in calmly, almost beyond things mattering, and shut the door. This was the prettier of the two rooms, newly retiled and papered. The mauve and rose of the abstract flowers in the wallpaper repeated the mauve of the gleaming hand soap and tissue dispensers and the rose of the gleaming sink and toilet bowl. The air was clean with the sweetness of lily of the valley. She sat down on the toilet and checked her pants for a return of the nasty brown spot; the pants looked clean. In the light from the tiny night light, she felt almost buoyant, loving the flower smell, the rosy ceramic glow. She said almost contemptuously, "Bloody Mary."

Nothing happened.

She turned off the little light, looked in the mirror over the sink at the vague shape of her head and shoulders. On the wall behind her the thick folded towel in Rachel's mother's rack felt warm to the small of her back. She said, husky-thick like her mother, "Bloody Mary." Her reflected forehead blended into the reflection of her hair, a grayness barely paler than the wall behind her. Her mouth was a smudge, hardly there. She opened wide, bared her teeth: "Come. I want you!"

Slowly her eyes got used to the dark. Her nose appeared, neat and unobtrusive, a feature she'd never worried about. *Bloody Mary.* Her eyes, large and gray, she'd never minded either, though they were less beautiful than her mother's. She leaned forward, steeling herself for the evil face behind her face, her secret soul staring back at her, inner and outer joined at last—*I want you*—but from her chin to the crown of her head there was one face only.

She leaned in over the sink. Above the line of her nose the swatch of gray spread to the tendrils of lightened hair. She turned to one side, then the other. On her ears the segmented silver triangles Rachel had given her for her last birthday made pretty, jangly sounds and glimmered where an edge caught the light. At the same time the pain that had been gone the past few hours grabbed the bottom of her stomach. Some heavy liquid found its form and its gravity and fell out of her body, wet and warm in the crotch of her pants. She tried to keep her gaze on the face in the mirror, but her breath gathered what felt like bits of sand and spiderwebby hairs till they clotted into a scream.

"Ha-ad?" Rachel's voice outside the door was hesitant, tender. Hadley struggled out of her jeans and underpants, toed the mess behind the toilet.

"Hadley?"

Hadley opened, pulling her shirt down over her legs. Rachel stood with the other girls, their eyes stripped bare of their seventh-grade cynicism. "The lady with the burning hair," Hadley cried, "she tried to take me!"

Another clot or whatever it was began its descent. She drew her legs together. But the girls stared at a dime-size spot of red on the floor at her feet. "Get your mother," May Sun whispered to Rachel.

Mrs. Moss brought maxi-pads and clean underpants and Tylenol. "Mazel tov!" she cried, hugging Hadley as if she had just accomplished something.

Simon appeared on the stairs, leering, "What's happening, girls? Somebody see a Peeping Tom?"

"Back to your lair, Grendel," his mother told him. She kissed Hadley's forehead. "Go call your mom. Come on! This is something she'll want to know."

Hadley dialed, but no one picked up. She was glad, or as glad as she could be under the circumstances. While her uterine lining dripped from her body she listened to Mrs. Moss's story of her own first period, an event she remembered with extraordinary clarity. She and her friends from those days called it their "visitor." "I can't take gym, I have my visitor!" Hadley sat on the floor on the slim, flat, carefully situated pad, liking Mrs. Moss's round motherly shape in her old flannel bathrobe, laughing from time to time in gusts that threatened to divide her from the bottom of her body. None of the girls seemed surprised by her laughter or at all put off by what had just happened to her. It meant, simply, membership in a new club, whose existence she hadn't appreciated till she was invited to join. May Sun had been getting her period for over a year. Sherelle had just started. Sherelle's sister in eighth grade was pissed that hers hadn't come yet. Rachel, in fact, was the only girl who hadn't started. She felt left out, and her mother worked to reassure her. Everything in its time.

When Mrs. Moss departed, the conversation moved to more general topics: movies that sucked or were awesome, boys in their class who sucked or were kind of nice, whether or not when they got old and wrinkled they would have plastic surgery (Sherelle's Mom had had a chemical peel), whether or not, when they were in high school or college, they would ever take drugs. A couple of them had friends whose cousins or older brothers had snorted coke (they snickered at the word) or taken ecstasy. May Sun said that Aaron Rappaport said that he saw his parents smoking weed, but then he took it back. Hadley said her mother said her Uncle Eric, who lived in the woods with his friends like a Sixties hippie, smoked weed all the time. Rachel posed a question that Sherelle thought was stupid, but it gave Hadley goose bumps: If she had to choose between death and shooting up heroin, which would she pick?

Hadley was surprised how closely her friends listened now to her opinions, no matter how tentative. They gave her extra space in their circle to fill as she wished, aligned themselves on the rug for a view of her face, access to the flickerings of new knowledge her own "visitor" had bestowed on her. So, occasionally doubled over with private laughter and speechless for minutes at a time, she told them truths. She was not and never had been in love with Fletcher Lawson. She was afraid of Sherelle. She liked Felice Pinter. (Sorry; she did.) There was a central truth toward which she was straining, and she kept on. She had lied about Bloody Mary, she'd never seen Bloody Mary. She told them everything that came to her mind regardless of whether they'd like her tomorrow. But it didn't help. The pad was damp, and between her legs it felt as big as a log, and she clung to a log drifting out to sea, and her girlfriends were blurry shapes in the dark farther and farther away. Still she kept on talking, till there was only Rachel at her side. She told Rachel that the bracelet on her wrist came not from Fletcher but her mother's jewelry box. Rachel shrugged. Then with Rachel's ear sharing the earpiece she called Fletcher Lawson. "I'm sorry," she said, "but I don't love you."

"I know that." His voice was rough from sleep. "Okay."

"Okay," she said. Not knowing what to say now. "I'm sorry," she repeated.

"Is that what you called up to tell me?"

"Yes."

"I'll live," he said, and hung up.

She turned away from Rachel, picturing his face round and babyish. She swallowed back the lump in her throat, though she didn't know if it was for him or herself. She held the phone till it started to beep.

Rachel whispered, "I love you, Hadley. You're my best friend in the world, ever, ever."

Hadley wanted to return Rachel's declaration. She wanted to give Rachel one more confession, a last nugget of truth. But all she said was "I know," for fear the look on Rachel's face—whether pity or disgust or incomprehension—would ban her for all time from the world of girlfriends. "Did you know," she said to herself, "that my mother tried to kill herself?" She fell asleep in the sleeping bag next to Rachel, dreamed of an eyeless face, dreamed herself curled on the rug at the foot of her mother's bed like a dog, woke in the dark holding Rachel's hand and wanting her mother.

She called for a ride, but when no one answered she wasn't upset. Her mother was sleeping. This time of night almost everyone was sleeping. And it wasn't a long walk, fifteen minutes, maybe. She put on the clean jeans from her overnight case, and her socks and sneakers. She opened the heavy front door and closed it softly behind her.

CHAPTER TWELVE

Sex and Death

I t's nine-fifteen according to her watch and NPR. Bodey's here at last, on the front landing, explaining: He has trouble leaving work he's begun. People he's involved with. He's contrite. She puts her hands on her hips, trying not to look as happy as she feels.

"Who were you flirting with?"

"I don't flirt." He puts his hands up, mock shielding his face. "You're the only woman I flirt with."

"You made me feel bad. Weren't you looking forward to this?"

"I'm an asshole."

"You are. Just don't exult in it," she says, although she's so glad to see him she feels like crying. She had begun to think he'd changed his mind about coming. Now, at the second mention of his contrition she lets him embrace her. She likes the cool slippery fabric of his khaki coat under her hands and the fact that her hands barely meet around his chest. She and her family are slender people, while he's so large in the gilt-edged mirror across from the coat closet, she can't see all of him.

Carefully, as if the garment is rare and precious, she hangs his coat on a wooden hanger over her own winter coat (deciding against the hanger with Leo's). She makes him tea, which they drink at the polished walnut table that used to sit in her mother's kitchen. The chairs have needlepoint seats her mother made the year she almost died—the year she lived expecting, daily, to die, not expecting ever to sit on her newly-covered chairs—her mother, who lives for other people. Then, after the bone marrow transplant, in the quarantine room in the hospital where she breathed supplemental oxygen behind plastic and waited for an everyday microbe to kill her, she raised the head of the hospital bed and having finished the needlepoints, knitted bright red sweaters for the girls, ages eight and four. Nora and Hadley loved the soft wool of the sweaters (though Nora would have preferred a more muted color) and their grandmother loved their loving it. If the Jews had saints, she'd be a saint, people said so often Claire was tired of it. But her mother had only the gentlest antipathy toward death, and only because it meant the end of what she could do for people, and when she got out of the hospital and moved to Florida she didn't remarry and work on her golf and tennis game, she opened a gift shop in a mall and put away half the money she earned for Israeli orphans and the girls' college education.

People used to tell Claire she was just like her mother, and she had believed it, but now she knows it's not true. She accepted the gift of her mother's beautiful old Victorian furniture, allowing her mother to believe she believed that the humidity in Florida would warp the wood. Now she and her lover sit on these chairs at this table, and if she feels any guilt, it's a drop of water that turns to steam in the blaze of what she feels for him and makes it all hotter still. She's essentially selfish, that's clear, which should appall her, but doesn't. She sips tea and holds Bodey's hand, distinctly too large for the curved arm of her mother's chair.

But now, what to do with him? Now there's too much unstructured time. She takes him around the house as if he's about to move in with her. In the basement there's "Medusa I," a female head coiffed in green and salmon-pink phone cord, with giant eyes and no mouth. He suggests titles: "Should Women Be Heard?" Or "Marilyn in Iraq." He seems restless, though. Is he uneasy on her turf, or bored already? Eluding a spurt of anxiety, she runs upstairs for a play she'd bought for them to read aloud together sometime. He's willing, as long as they do so without their clothing. They sit on the basement couch, bare thighs touching.

She and Leo saw the play in New York a couple of years ago, Stoppard's *The Real Thing*, about love in and out of marriage. On the old, worn velvet couch, once the living room couch, soon to be picked up by the Salvation Army, she and Bodey read the characters' intelligent, witty lines, pausing every few minutes to kiss or caress. The play is interesting, and so is what they're doing, the moments when pleasure stops the brain, and so is their reading, accentuated by irregular, sharp breaths, the starts and squeaks neither can keep out of their voices. Soon they read without comprehension, their speeches serving only to delay and concentrate pleasure. Laughing, she straddles him, and they continue reading, turning the book for each other in the small space between them. His British accent is terrible, though he's possibly making a joke of it. Or maybe he just can't read anymore? She can. Her awareness of their bodies only heightens her enjoyment of the play and his skin, inducing vocal tremors that bely her character's breathy archness, a complexity she doesn't remember in the professional actress's portrayal. The phone rings, the three and a half rings until voicemail kicks in. Toward the end of the first act he presses his face to her neck and comes.

"Shame on me," he says.

She looks at the creases at the corner of his mouth where he doesn't quite smile. "You are a beautiful man."

"Tell me I'm fat and ugly."

"You're not! Is that how you see yourself?"

"Tell me you loathe me," he says.

A finger of muscle under one of his eyebrows jerks back and forth. The whites of his eyes are faintly yellow. "I don't loathe you at all. I may *love* you." It's a reckless thing to say. She looks for more reckless things, sex with him a trip she might not return from. She closes her eyes. Then she calls him by the wrong name. "Charlie," she says.

"Who's Charlie?"

She starts, like a child waking in a strange house, then starts to laugh. She tries to stop, puts her hand in her mouth, bites down, saying to herself, Bodey. Bodey. But the laughter leaks out, heaving past the tightness of her diaphragm, hysterical almost. "I'm sorry," she manages to say, then laughs again. "I'll stop, I'm trying to stop!"

But as the laughter slows she thinks about this Charlie, Charlie Axelrod, whom she'd gone out with four times as a freshman in college. She thought he was brilliant, then she didn't. He was a junior, an AE Pi. He was no one that mattered. Soon she'd cry out Louis, for Louis Newman, who sat in front of her in Algebra I at Roosevelt Junior High School. Louis was lost in Algebra I, an inability that had charmed her in 1969, along with the ribbon of uncut pale hair at the nape of his neck. She's laughing so hard her legs begin to shake, and she wraps them around him again till the laughter fades away. She wipes her eyes. He says, in that same bad British accent, "And who, pray, is Charlie?"

She tells him. He looks at her face, as if for something she hasn't said.

"I have to go," he says.

"This is a joke, right? Bodey?"

173

"I don't like what's happening here."

"What's happening? What is happening?" Her voice sails up. She tries to hang onto it. "Is this really about Charlie?" she ventures. "Because, Bodey, everything I told you was total truth. It's crazy, it's almost flattering, but—"

"So something is funny again?"

"What? Bodey, now you're acting crazy." Without looking at her he's getting back into his clothes. She does likewise, hands shaking on the zipper of her silk pants. "Where are you going, Bodey?"

He heads upstairs, and she trails after him, angry that he doesn't turn around. The phone rings again. She lets it ring, though now she wants to answer it. She wipes her eyes. All right, go, she tells him in her mind. Then she's ready for him to go, for the world to simplify. She's angry but containing it. She takes his coat out of the closet, holds it out to him a little impatiently, like a bag of groceries she wants to set down. She'll call Springfield again, then get in bed and finish the play by herself, or maybe she'll just turn jazz on low and fall asleep. He bends to tie his shoe. She opens the front door. But stooped over his foot, he exposes a white vulnerable span between his collar and pale red frizzy curls. With a pulse of tenderness she kisses the back of his neck. He takes hold of her ankle. His hand moves up her calf. She presses her legs together, allowing herself this last moment of pleasure, ready to detach at any intensification. But his hand stays where it is, between the smooth sleeves of silk covering her thighs. She

174

begins to stir again, something that rarely happens more than once in a session of lovemaking. Hugging his coat to her chest, she kisses the thinning hair on top of his head. "Don't," he says.

"What?"

"Keep stiff when I try to touch you. Push my hands away."

"Is this a game?" She speaks as if merely, vaguely curious. She doesn't want another struggle.

"You're sixteen years old. You're a virgin. I'm going to seduce you." He takes his coat out of her hands and tosses it in the corner. His fingertips strokes her throat. She works to regulate her breathing.

"Bodey, I don't know about this."

He turns her around, one hand around her waist, the other inside the collar of her blouse. He murmurs against the side of her face, "No one has ever touched you before, not even yourself. You have no point of comparison. You're scared to death. What will your high-school friends think?"

"Stop," she says, not sure if her response is authentic or part of the game. Trying to eject the hand. But her own hands feel limp. He runs a finger along the base of her neck.

"You want this."

"Not the least bit."

"You do. You said you were a virgin but I've talked to guys. Remember Howard?"

"Cut it out!" She doesn't move though. Was there a Howard? She remembers several Howards, one as far back as first grade.

She doesn't care about these Howards. "You said I was innocent!" she says, trying to be playful.

"And what do you think Howard said? What did Howard say?"

Her first Howard was a quiet fat boy who sat across from her in Miss Hurley's class. Later, she heard, he went to military school. She pulls back and turns to face him. "Could we please stop this?"

"Stop what?" He undoes her buttons, one, two, three, his voice so mocking and light, she no longer knows him.

She pictures herself waltzing with Leo around a ferny, high-ceilinged ballroom. He moves lightly, turns her adroitly. Doesn't step on her feet.

The other night in the middle of the night she woke him up, wanting for the first time in weeks to lose herself in the kindness of his touch, but she could barely feel it. It was as if some central nerve line had been severed, leaving only the shallow, peripheral connectors.

"Is there something you want me to do?" he said.

She rolled back onto Cassandra, who clawed her halfheartedly. She let the cat out, closed the door, sat down on the edge of the bed. "I'm sorry, I keep thinking of other things."

"The mortgage? Your first exhibit?"

"Don't be mean."

"It doesn't have to work every time," he said. "There's nothing in the marriage manual. Though we seem to be rewriting the marriage manual."

She looked at him, feeling the confused anger under his irony. It heated her skin. There might be something he could say to break the spell she was under. She prayed for him to discover it.

"Claire," he said, "I love you so much."

"Yes."

"Sometimes I feel sorry for other men. The ones who don't have you."

"Stop, Leo."

Outside the door Cassandra yowled like a baby.

"You know," he said, "when we got married I was so full of love I thought I'd burst. But the funny thing is, it's grown. You're more beautiful to me now than you were then. When I think how I love you it hurts sometimes." His eyes were wide open looking into her eyes. She smoothed the soft springy hairs on the back of his arm.

"I love you too, Leo. Like crazy!"

But the things she used to like in him put her off now. Since their near-mugging she seems to have rewritten in her mind the story of their life together. Comfortable only in superficial exchanges, emotionally unfledged, he married the first pretty-enough woman who was as fearful as he. He's afraid to ask why she spends so much time at the School, and why she no longer wants to kiss him. She'll fuck him but she won't kiss him. Isn't that creepy, Leo? She's sorry but without the will to make amends. Leo, forgive me.

But how can she forgive him? He left her on the street to face

177

what chance and the gunman had in mind for her. In a pinch, she's on her own. Sometimes now she just wants to tell him straight out that with him her body is numb as death, while with Bodey her senses are so keen it's almost like illness. After fierce, prolonged pleasure, the molecules of her brain, facets of her personality, even the facts of her personal history refuse to coalesce. It's hard to drive home, let alone make dinner. She wants to tell Leo and watch his face shut down, as it shut down on Halsted Street in the face of the gunman. She wants to say that last night at dinner with her ordinary, decent family, her mind was filled with Bodey. It was adolescent, aesthetically *gross*, like an old woman in a miniskirt, but all through the meal some distillation of the man pulsed in her. How could Leo not have felt it? At one point in the half hour ritual—she didn't know what had just been said or not said—she was coming back to the table with the boiled rice, and Nora said, "Mom, stop smiling like that!" and she stood, pot in hand, lips trembling, unable to fashion even a lame excuse.

If you measure love by the intensity of the ache of the fear of its loss, she loves this man as she has never loved anyone.

To retrieve Bodey from the nasty place he has gone to, she reminds him of what he told her about himself. "You're afraid of shame so you want to shame me, Bodey. That's what this is about."

"It's pretty to think so."

She disregards the tone. Tries to touch his face. He pulls his head back, lips just beyond reach. "Fucking is dangerous," he says.

"That's so—" she watches him smile with one side of his mouth. "So melodramatic!" His eyes are pale like milky ice. Outside, wind rattles the storm door. "This is like a bad movie."

"Is it?" He holds her loosely. She could back off, herself, if she wanted to. "You have to let loose. Let go completely. Be ready to die, even."

"Sorry. Not me." She tries to smile. "Not my job description!" He rubs his thumb along the edge of her lower lip. She shivers like a dog not petted enough. She stiffens her back, tries to speak coolly, though his face is so close all she can do is murmur, "You can go. Bodey. Goodbye. Get out of here."

He murmurs back, "You say goodbye. And I say hello."

"What does that mean?" His smile looks softer now. She labors to resist it. "You have a cruel streak, Bodey."

"Do I?" His eyes are looking straight into hers. His voice is free, it seems, of irony. "I think I get carried away sometimes. The line is fine between what's cruel and what's thrilling. I try to stay in bounds."

"Well, you don't try hard enough."

"I'm sorry." He swallows. She hears the sound in his throat. "I'm really sorry."

Now it's her turn to back away. She leans against the wall, folds her arms. "I don't know whether to believe you or not." His eyes are clear but she can't read them. "I want to believe you. No, I'm not even sure that's true. I hate this game!"

"Claire," he said, "you're going to be a very important person in my life. You're already an important person."

She forces herself to shrug.

"Should I go? Do you never want to see me again? I'll go if you want me to. What's the matter, Claire?"

He reaches out and she shrinks away. His face looks swollen. She presses two fingers to a spot on her forehead that houses a mild but augmenting pain.

"Claire, I love you."

"I don't believe you." She thinks about what she just said. "It's true. I'm sorry," she says.

She's afraid to look at him now. For a few minutes she holds herself while the world goes away and comes back. There is too much saliva in her mouth. She tries to swallow. Tries to retreat further inside herself. But now he is touching his forehead to hers. He seems to have tears in his eyes. Does he? She can't tell. Pain beats at the ridge of her brow.

Then he puts his hand on her shoulder, and her shoulder is the only part of her body that doesn't hurt. His hand moves down her back; everywhere he touches softens and warms. She leans part of her weight against him, breathing his smell of sweat and cologne, as his hands move up the sides of her legs, over her hips, along the corrugations of her ribs. Now touch and smell is all; she feels pressed like a flower between the pages of a book, in this moment that will last forever if she can only tell him about it. Into the hard curly tuft of hair over his ear she says what has been tapping at her mind all evening, "I could glue myself to your skin. Bodey. I could burrow in like a chigger. If I had to choose, torture or the pain of never touching you again, I would choose torture."

"I want to sleep with you tonight," he whispers. "I want to go to sleep with you in my arms and wake up next to you, is that okay with you?" She doesn't say no. He picks her up, carries her upstairs.

She imagines her life without Leo. In a small high-rise apartment with a balcony if she's lucky, waiting for someone who might or might not come home, she'll sip a vodka martini, after half of which she'll once again accept the fact that her daughters will never completely forgive her, not just for leaving their father but for living as she does now, with a view but a tiny kitchen and no dining room, no place for serving. If you get what you want it's only in snippets, and you still have to pay.

Bodey carries her as if she's light as a cotton dress. He smells of sweat and aftershave, gardenias and something like fertilizer, a man who can save a woman from a burning house. Gently he settles her in her bed. The phone rings again, and it seems to her the phone has been ringing incessantly tonight, so strange, since she has no intention of answering; don't they all know that? He curls around her. She weeps the sweet tears of a child about to be comforted.

CHAPTER THIRTEEN

Nearsighted

At two A.M., in spring, Chicago was friendly and safe, it seemed to Hadley. Police cars sped by with their pulsing blue lights. Along the main streets celebratory groups and couples or solitary walkers smiled or gazed benignly like aunts and uncles, keeping pace, it seemed, with the almost silent crunch of her sneakers. In the parking lot of the Dunkin' Donuts at Clark and Belmont she passed a group of teenagers in studded jean jackets and heads of spiked hair that glimmered crayon blue or purple in the street-lamplight. Skateboarding across the asphalt, a boy bent his knees, leapt three feet into the air and landed with a soft clat, the board stuck magically to his feet. He looked barely older than the kids in her class. A girl with a round button of a face and hair shaved to the tops of her ears held a cigarette between chubby fingers and gave her a kind of military salute; at least Hadley thought it was directed at her. Just below her bottom lip three wires protruded like the whiskers of a fish. Smoke from her mouth tendriled upward. Then the girl beckoned her over. Normally Hadley would have marched on, looking carefully forward. Now, though, she let herself drift toward the girl as if it was no big deal. Nothing was a big deal. "Hey."

"Hey yourself," said the girl. "Do you want to go to a party?"

"Where is it?"

The girl gestured across the street. At a spread of storefronts, doorways.

"Maybe later." Hadley smiled her thank-you and resumed her journey. With normal hair, the girl would have been pretty, she thought, surprised and pleased as if a locked door had suddenly opened for her. Through the exhaust-and-cigarette air of the city she smelled the lake wind and things swelling in the ground and bursting out and up. Good things starting to happen. Her sanitary pad kept riding back, and she had to make an occasional adjustment (whenever it seemed she wasn't being looked at). But mostly she wafted up and down curbs, over cracks in sidewalks, in a bubble of clear-eyed serenity.

It was almost three when she let herself into her house. Dark, not a light on. She almost tripped in the front hall, then picked up the heavy cloth of a coat. Whose coat? Probably (obviously!) her father's. His old coat, left out by her mother for the rummage (maybe). She hung it on a hook in the closet and closed the door, careful not to rattle hangers. Overlooking this violation of the house's usual tidiness.

Continuing quiet, she removed her shoes and climbed the bare wood stairs, avoiding the one that creaked. The house smelled clammy with the breath of people sleeping, though it might be the new odor of brass exuding from her pores. Outside, she hadn't minded the brisk wind. Inside, the heat was on. It was too warm. She set her bag down at the top of the stairs and tiptoed down the hall to her parents' room. The door was slightly ajar, with music coming through the crack, opera music, that her father liked, proclaiming enraged or grief-stricken love, too loud for anyone to sleep through. She opened the door a careful inch.

The room was dark, and Hadley couldn't see distances, so that even afterward she wasn't sure exactly what she saw. Faint light from the street lamp at the end of the block edged through the mini-blinds onto what might have been a stretch of her mother's bare thigh, the rise of her kneecap, but maybe it was a fold of quilt pushed by a sleeping foot to the end of the bed. Out of the corner of her eye Hadley thought she saw someone kneeling there. But her father was with Nora at a hotel five hours away, so it was maybe a blanket or a robe slung over a chair. She peered closely at the form that seemed joined to the place where her mother's legs came together (or else it was the juncture of two long folds of the

185

quilt). The blacks and grays shifted, signaling movement. Then the singing voice broke loose from the musical web and started swimming around the room, up and down, back and forth, and the orchestra followed, drums and cymbals; the music thrashing and the covers on the bed swirling and thrashing, and Hadley's eyes began to tear. She turned half-away, glancing sideways to see more clearly. She squinted till her face hurt. Under the music she heard what seemed to be her heart beating or her mother breathing, then came a sharp outbreath—aaah!—rising to a squeal. It reminded her of pain, worse than what she had felt under her stomach (it was gone now), but from which no one seemed to want to be saved. She stepped back, waiting for the image to explain itself or vanish. It hovered at the edge of her awareness like girlfriends talking about her in a corner of the room.

Part of her wanted just to go to bed now. To sleep. In the morning, like other mornings after nightmares, things would be normal. But tonight everything was so crazy, it was crazy to expect normal. She tiptoed back down the hall to the bathroom, shut the door, faced the mirror and forced her eyes open to whatever hid in the reflected dark. "Bloody Mary?" A ribbon of light from a passing car crossed a corner of the sink, dipped into the basin and climbed out. The oval of her face floated to the surface of the mirror, framed by the paleness of her lightened hair. "I want you." Her mouth twitched with her pronounce-ment; her chin elongated, the bones swelling, sharpening to form the face she would have fifteen years from now. "Bloody Mary."

There was a sound. She froze, half closed her eyes, afraid to turn around, but just as afraid to look harder into the mirror. The sound continued, a murmur just below the level of understanding. Then she heard, *Hey yourself.*

It wasn't her own voice, or the voice of the girl in the parking lot. But it sounded real. Female. It spoke distinctly.

She's not your real mother.

It was Nora, she told herself, who had driven home with their father in the middle of the night and was trying to freak her. "Do you think this is funny?" Hadley tried to fill her voice with indignation but her whisper was too frail to contain it. "It *isn't* funny!" Keeping her shoulders square to the mirror she flicked a glance toward the door. She walked halfway down the hall, then stopped, and listened for whatever there was in her mother's room. But aside from the radio, behind her mother's door there was silence. No voices, no breathing other than her own.

They are not your parents. This is not your home.

"Who are you?" she almost cried, to the voice that wasn't herself but wasn't anyone else either, existing at the point or line or boundary where her mind met the world of sound. *Go,* said the voice. "Where?" she replied.

There was no more advice for her. But the walls and ceiling pushed out and out, thin as balloon skin, till there was no boundary between the nighttime house and the world outside. She stuffed her new, lightly-padded bra into her knapsack, and her make-up, her mousse, and hair dryer. She replaced the sodden pad with a new dry one from Nora's box under the sink. She put on a clean gray T-shirt without any message or brand name and her black Edison sweatshirt, inside out, and a pair of old, pale-black stretch jeans in which she could raise her leg over her head. She still had on the diamond bracelet. She tucked it inside her sleeve.

She wondered whether or not to leave a note. She wrote something to Rachel, about missing her, then decided it was stupid, since she wasn't planning anything crazy or permanent. She'd be back before her mother woke up, she thought with a pulse of scorn for her sleepyhead mother, and crumpled the paper and threw it in the wastebasket. It took a while to locate the two twenty-dollar bills that her grandmother had sent for her thirteenth birthday, but she finally found them inside a card in the bottom of her jewelry box. Downstairs on the kitchen counter was her mother's purse. On several occasions she'd borrowed a secret dollar or two, another thing her mother didn't notice. Now she took all the bills (fifty-seven dollars), and returned to the writhing exhilaration of the street.

THREE

CHAPTER FOURTEEN

Her New Life

One afternoon three years ago, when Hadley was ten and Nora thirteen, they had set off from home to throw themselves to the winds of random chance. It was late summer; soon school would start, but not yet. At every new intersection they flipped their new 1995 quarter; heads meant a right turn, tails meant left. Neither will nor desire would govern their destiny.

The game was Nora's idea. The same age as Hadley now, Nora hadn't yet entered the adolescent social stream. It would have accepted her; she was pretty enough and self-possessed, reserved without being arrogant. But she seemed to sense even then a more interesting world beyond their own and was continually looking to surprise it; that day she ran the first two or three blocks. For Hadley, though, after the first few coin tosses, in which she held her breath as for a revelation, the blocks stretched in front of her, tedious and leg-hurting, and if not for Nora's enthusiasm she'd have gone back. Nora was laughing with excitement. Hadley struggled not to whine as they zigzagged east, south, east, south, west, south, east, east, east out of their neighborhood through the tunnel under Lake Shore Drive to the beach. Nora threw off her shoes and ran down the damp, hard shoreline sand till she was a distant speck. Hadley used their governing quarter along with a dime from the pay phone to call their mother to drive them home.

Now, three years later, Hadley left home again, with the same plans to lose herself. But now it was the thick, dark middle of the night with Nora completely out of the picture and her mother what she had run from—her mother repelling, pushing her away like the back of a magnet.

She proceeded toward Clark and Belmont, and the friendly girl with the half-shaved head. The girl was gone, though. Across the street all the stores were dark, the doors closed. At Dunkin' Donuts she ordered a cinnamon roll and black coffee, which burned her tongue, but which she finished stoically, adding sugar, alternating sips with bites of roll. She tried to look indifferent to the people who came in, either drunk and grubby, it seemed, or high and grubby. Hardest to bear were the kids her age, who looked at her curiously and said things to each other. If Rachel were here, it would be they looking and commenting. On the verge of tears she was about to return home when a girl sat down on the next stool and started talking to her. This girl had wild brown hair like Janis Joplin's on her mother's old record album and a freckled, large-nosed ugly face, but didn't seem troubled by it. She was from Bangor, Maine, she said, where the primary cause of death for ages ten to twenty-five was boredom. She walked her across the street to a store called Ruptured Disc. In the alcove beside it, a second door led down to a place where "crazy kids hung." She was helpful and kind, the good-hearted ugly sister that you didn't have to be jealous of. She punched a code to unlock the door. "Is this where you live?" Hadley asked.

"Sort of," she said, and descended the stairs before Hadley could ask anything else.

Hadley was uncomfortable in the foyer, full of wrappers and butts and scraps of newspaper, but it seemed shameful to return home so soon. She went down five dark stairs, opened a door that throbbed with the music behind it, and felt her way along the wall till she found a place to stand. The music was so loud, it was like too much oxygen in the air. Or steam, hard to breathe in. The place was dark and packed.

She had stood there five or ten minutes, waiting for a place to open up on the carpet where most of the people were sprawled, when someone passed her a joint. "Thanks," she said, waving it away as if she'd already smoked as much as she wanted. As if she were so stoned already, there was no point getting any higher. "I'm fine!" she told the boy who offered it.

"So pass it."

Hadley looked at the boy, who wore glasses with yellow lenses, and at the half-smoked item in his hand. His eyes widened under the lenses the way hers widened when someone said something retarded. Then either he forgave her stupidity or else immediately forgot about it. He reached past her and gave the joint to someone on her other side. If the transaction had occurred at Edison Magnet, someone who knew her would be watching with respect for her that reinforced her own self-respect. She could have said something to the boy that established her social inviolability. But here, even if someone knew her, no one was paying attention, and by this time the boy had faded into the room's hazy outreaches. Where was her backpack? She squinted downward but didn't see it. She looked around for the girl who'd brought her here, though in a room this dark her nearsighted eyes could barely see. She didn't remember the girl's name, and wasn't sure if she'd learned it. I'm fine, she told herself under cover of the noise, and leaned back against the wall. Rap was playing, music for boys who wore baggy jeans that showed the waistband of their jockey shorts. She could remain standing if necessary; at this point beyond fatigue it seemed she could stay awake indefinitely.

Then someone got up from a nearby chair that turned out to be a white ceramic toilet. Hairs rose on the back of her neck. She repressed thoughts of clean and dirty. Became aware of the pad between her legs, its wetness. Started off toward an inner doorway that must lead to a bathroom. But she had no more pads. At the same time, a couple of kids got up from the carpet. Before the empty space closed in on itself she sat down. On one side of her was a couple locked in a horizontal embrace, on the other, a girl with a face so thin and beautiful that Hadley would have exchanged it for her own face.

At first all she could think to say to the girl was, *Excuse me, where's the bathroom?* What her mother would have said. "The music sucks," she ventured.

The girl's smile was wide and brilliant, what you'd expect from beauty, but her voice shook when she talked. "What's your name, I'm Cheeta. You have great hair." Cheeta touched her finger to a strand of Hadley's brown hair, which was clean but that was all you could say for it. Cheeta had wavy blonde hair, far better than hers. Her face was so thin her jaw angled out. "I'd die for straight," Cheeta went on. "Do you like The Clash? I can't get into them either but I respect them, you know. Some people here go nuts for The Clash, but mostly it's Snoop Dogg." She smiled helplessly. "I hate video games, they infantilize you, what's your take on video games?" Before Hadley could reply—though she had no strong feeling about video games—a joint came round again. Cheeta took a long drag. "You don't do weed? Me neither under most circumstances. But sometimes you have to, you know, relax?" She gave Hadley another beauty-queen smile and lay down on the rug, stretching her long legs into the throng of seated people, prodding them to make room for her. No one seemed to mind. "Different personalities respond to different drugs. I'm basically methamphetamine. I don't like to float, but for a change, you know. Hey, what did you say your name was?"

Cheeta's eyes were closed; Hadley didn't think she had to answer the question. "I'm not into drugs," she said firmly. Asserting her right to be here anyway. She explained, so as not to hurt the girl's feelings, "They don't do much for me."

"That's cool." Cheeta smiled with her eyes closed. "I'm signing off now."

Cheeta lay on the rug, her hands twitching in time with the music. Her size 0 jeans encased her hips without bulges or creases. Hadley looked down at her own stomach. At dinner tomorrow she'd skip the potatoes or rice her mother liked to heap on her plate. That is, if she wasn't banned from the table. She'd probably be grounded, but it didn't matter. Then the impression of her mother as someone she didn't know and could never know pushed away the comfort of these future minor punishments. She focused on the second piece of toast that she wouldn't eat. The bowls of ice cream. Self-denial, a rope to hold onto.

By this time the population had thinned somewhat. On the futon couch in the center of the room two Latino boys with identical buzz cuts and earnest faces aimed their controllers at a large screen. Their video skateboarders sailed along railroad tracks, high walls, down the railings of staircases, without ever losing their balance. The boys were all right except for a single repellant feature; one had what looked like peas growing under the skin of his cheeks while the other had lost a front tooth. But they were the best gamers Hadley had ever seen. Onlookers lounged over the back of their couch, rooting or giving instructions.

Cheeta wasn't watching, though. Nor were two girls in a dimly lit corner, one of whom was rubbing the other's back. Hadley imagined herself rubbing Cheeta's back. Imagined the tiny perfect bones of Cheeta's spine. Once in the dark school-auditorium Rachel had tickled up and down the inside of her arm; now the thought gave her goose bumps. There was lots of room on the rug now, a large Oriental that needed vacuuming. She brushed away the major crumbs and stretched out beside Cheeta, trying to float on the skin of the music.

Up to now Hadley had navigated skillfully any social seas she ventured upon. At Edison she had risen from grade to grade, increasingly affirmed in her sense of herself as likeable. When a new girl entered their class Hadley had, next to Sherelle, the biggest voice as to whether or not the girl would sit at their lunch table or hang out with them after school. But the kids here had shorter hair than her friends, and tighter clothes, or else their hair was wild and they tripped on their pant legs. As for the apartment, although less than ten blocks from her house, it looked like nowhere she had ever been before. The light kept shifting intensity, changing color as it emanated from an enormous TV screen on which played the flickerings of video combat. The walls, painted black, seemed to extend in all directions indefinitely. She remembered something Sherelle's real-estate mother had said, that light colors made a room seem larger. Dark colors made it hard to see even how many people there were. Counting once, she got thirteen, but the next time there were only ten. Had she counted herself? It was cold in the room. Or was it hot? It seemed both hot and cold.

The joint traveled from hand to hand but, thank God, passed her by now. She breathed shallowly, avoiding the dangerous secondhand smoke, recording in her mind, as she always did, the looks of these mismatched, oddly confident kids for Rachel's appreciation. She could see herself back at Rachel's now, lying between May Sun and Rachel on Mrs. Moss's pale green wall-to-wall. There was a reason she'd left, but here—maybe from all the pot smoke—she couldn't remember it. When the sun came up, she would go straight home, a fifteen- or twenty-minute walk, arriving so early no one would know she'd been gone, and she'd crawl into her familiar bed and wait for her father and Nora. Saturday. Sunday. She sighed with the anticipated pleasure of hearing about Nora's running times. The sweetness of the ordinariness of her envy and love for her older sister.

Then, in the brief silence of the space between songs, from one of the inner rooms came a sharp, unsettling cry, joyful and terrible, immediately submerged by the next cut. On the couch under the pair of high windows, a boy took off his shirt exposing a hairless, phosphorescent white chest, and a girl placed her hands over his nipples. Scared now, almost panicked, Hadley stood up. She looked for the door that led up the short flight of stairs to the outside door. She didn't have to wait for morning.

She was looking around for her backpack when a gust of wind blew through the room. It was as if someone had turned the music down, though in fact music was the only sound now, stripped of its underlay of laughter and talk. A man stood in the doorway surveying the scene, the remaining eight or ten people. He had black hair pulled back in a ponytail. Hadley sat back down but his eyes lighted on her, and his head nodded some sort of judgment. A shiver passed through her. A sensation she associated with sitting in temple on Yom Kippur, praying to be written up in the Book of Life. Trying to bring to the front of her mind the pure, selfless thoughts that would change God's mind in case He was deciding against her. She cast a hidden glance at the black-haired man's face. She couldn't see it clearly but he seemed older than everyone else, though with the same slouching assured walk. She thought: here was the source, the inventor of that walk.

The man said something in Spanish to one of the video players, then he spoke to Cheeta with a New York accent like Rachel's mother. Cheeta rose and followed him out of the room, and Hadley remembered the shadows in her mother's bedroom. And wondered whether, in the year to come, she would get a fatal disease or die in a car crash, a destiny God not only knew but had previously determined. She shivered a second time, so distant from Rachel and her other friends that she couldn't imagine ever seeing them again.

For a while that night Hadley lay on the Oriental rug in the living room of the basement apartment, wishing the ugly-faced girl from Maine would come back, or Cheeta. Toward morning, in increasing need of a fresh sanitary pad, she ventured deeper into the apartment. She passed a closed door she knew she shouldn't open. In the kitchen she found her guide seated at the table with another girl. Looking less ugly now, the girl hugged her like a friend back from summer vacation. She offered her vodka and orange juice—mostly vodka! she said—and when Hadley declined, gave her a Diet Coke from the fridge. The other girl was friendly too, a talker. Most likely Hadley could stay here as long as she wanted. Her name was Maria. The apartment belonged to the guy with the ponytail. Nat. Nat had money and liked people around. "Nat rules," Maria said, and sighed with what seemed like longing.

The girl from Maine crossed her eyes, which made Hadley laugh. She smiled at Hadley. "He's cool, I guess. We stay for free." Her name was Guin. Guin, not Gwen, said Guin, for Guinivere, King Arthur's unfaithful wife and Lancelot's lover.

"I think I saw the movie," said Hadley. "From the Sixties. With lots of singing?" They looked at her, and she realized more was required of her. She said the first name that came to mind. "I'm Claire." Instantly she regretted it. "Clara, that is." No one objected. But then why would anyone object? "Does someone have a sanitary napkin?"

Guin gave her a tampon.

Clara, she said to herself. She was Clara.

In the bathroom she tried to insert the tampon where she had heard it was supposed to go, but succeeded only in hurting herself. There was blood on her hands. When someone knocked on the door she cried, "Just a minute!" She peeled the soaked pad from her underpants, pressed the tampon as flat as she could, and laid it over the stain. She wound toilet paper in and out of the legholes, round and round and round the crotch.

CHAPTER FIFTEEN

Quest

Claire wakes up early. Sunlight pours through her window, warm on her cheek and neck. She thinks of Saturday mornings in Edina, Minnesota, herself five years old with nothing required and squares of bright lawn stretching in all directions. Bodey left just before dawn but her skin still feels him. Her chest expands against the remembered weight of him. Descending the stairs, she's glad he's gone. And also glad, grinding the coffee, that soon she'll see him again, but not now. Now a square of sunlight creeps over the dark wood of the kitchen table. Now is that out-of-time feeling of boundlessness.

The phone rings. Leo in Springfield. She shoulders the phone to her ear, pours coffee, asks questions, tries to listen:

"The ride? Pure joy, except for the group's musical tastes. No, Nora didn't push classical. She's all right, don't worry. She patronized me from her spiritual heights, but that's her job. At least she didn't spend the trip communing with Jesus. Except for her lips silently moving. Hey, I'm joking, honey! The other girls like her fine, they're all carbo-loading down in the hotel restaurant. Are you there, Claire?"

"I spilled coffee. I'm wiping it up. Go on."

He goes on. He's waiting for room service, then he's off to the meet. He wants a good seat. Hopes his back will hold up.

"Uh huh," she says, taking the phone to the door. Stooping to pick up the morning paper.

"The room is too big," he says. "Two queens. They make me feel lonely."

"I know what you mean," she says without thinking. Unfolding the paper.

"Oh, do you?" he says. "And where were *you* last night?"

He spoke humorously. But her heart thuds. He has her full attention. "What are you asking, did I have a hot date?" She laughs with nervous excitement. "I was out dancing! I rock when you're gone!"

"*Rock?* Where did that word come from?"

She laughs again, on the knife-edge of eluded guilt, and describes a movie-star-handsome computer magnate who flew her to London in his private plane. They went boating on the Thames and saw the Princess Di memorial. Her voice rolls on, "But I got home in time for Letterman. Didn't you get my messages?"

"Kind of you to think of us. I hope the flight was smooth."

He's drily amused. She tries to control her giddiness but manages only to speak at half-volume. "Tell me more about Nora. Was she nervous in the car? God, I wish she were over that Jesus thing!"

He concurs; her eyes water with gratitude. She talks until he responds earnestly, as if they're former spouses on good behavior a couple of years after the divorce. Why, instead of practicing real Judaism, did they go in for the lackadaisical kind? Which seems to mean either no Judaism or Jews for Jesus. Should Hadley study to become a Bat Mitzvah? There's no age limit. He's starting to think they should insist. Maybe Nora could go through the training with her. And Claire too. They could hire a tutor for all three of them. A triple ceremony. Shorter Torah portions to learn. He sounds enthusiastic. She smiles into the phone. "That's one of the things I like about you—I can't always tell if you're serious."

"Isn't that what you *don't* like about me?"

"I have mixed feelings!" she cries. "But, honey, don't turn fundamentalist on us. Promise."

He confesses an impulse in that direction. A mild impulse. But now, his continental breakfast has arrived; he'll call later with news of victory. The conversation ends with him in a palpable good mood.

205

"Tell Nora I love her," she says.

She hangs up, exhaling the rest of her anxiety. She scans the newspaper headline but has no interest in the ongoing soap opera of the President and That Woman. *Monica, c'est moi!* She goes upstairs and with moderate embarrassment, some heat in her cheeks, pulls the sheets off the marital bed and throws them in the wash. She ought to feel guilty. But she feels, actually, a light euphoria. A line comes to her, that she'd read somewhere: the solution to the problem of life lies in the disappearance of the problem. It had annoyed her, the hippie dictum, rationale for people without energy or will, but now it shimmers with subtle wisdom. She's on her way down to her basement workshop when the phone rings again. The caller has a loud voice and a strong Bronx accent. Janice Moss.

Claire knows Janice in the friendly distant way you know your children's friends' nice parents who won't eat at your non-kosher table. But she has always liked Janice's energy, at least from afar. She says, almost as forcefully as Janice, "You don't sound like someone who's been up all night with the North Side nymphets!"

Janice doesn't answer at first. Then she sounds embarrassed. "This is a weird question, Claire. But, is Hadley there?"

Claire's heart jumps. "She's not with you?" Janice says no, apologizing. Claire rubs her forehead, at some odd bleariness. "Unless she came after I went to bed. Or early this morning." She takes a deep breath. "She could be in her room. Hold on a minute."

Phone in hand she runs up the stairs, already seeing in her

mind's eye her daughter asleep under the covers. Later she'll worry about what impelled Hadley away from her friends, when normally she's central to the group. Later also she can determine the hour that Hadley arrived home, if it intersected (God forbid!) with her visitor's departure (giddily censoring her mind). She won't even hint to Janice that she should have kept better watch. Would she herself have stayed up with them?

Quietly, so as not to wake her daughter, she opens the bedroom door. The spread is wrinkled, as if previously sat on. But the room is empty.

She drops the phone, collects it. "No! Nothing!" She turns the phone around twice, seeking the mouthpiece. "What happened last night?"

The story is additionally upsetting. That Hadley started her period under someone else's care feels wrong, unnatural. "She was maybe a little freaked," Janice says, "but we cheered her up. I gave her some pads. The girls were good to her."

"Why was she scared? What was she scared of?"

"Claire, honey, I'm coming over."

Claire barely hears the statement. As a child she slept between banks of protective books and stuffed animals. In the daytime she wouldn't play alone on the upstairs floor, even with her mother below. But Hadley is sturdy and fearless. She has always been. Stupidly, Claire scans for signs. The room was cleaned and straightened Friday morning, but there's a surface rumple. A drawer open. Under the bed three shoes, a fourth near the door. Hadley's computer is on. "I'm sorry," she says toward the phone, and sets it down on the bed. "Thank you."

The phone starts to beep. She hears it, thinking about calling the police. But that would turn a possibly small and short-lived personal problem into a public event, with unknowable ramifications. She could call Leo, but he'll be gone by now. The tiny stars on the screen saver keep spreading toward her, or maybe sucking her in. She walks downstairs, then can't remember what she planned to do there. Are there plans she has to cancel?

She's scrubbing the kitchen sink and waiting for understanding, when she hears the doorbell. Janice Moss is here. She must have driven—Janice, who walks to temple on Shabbat, or stays home till sunset. Kindness flows in the act; she is aware of it.

"I feel terrible," Janice says. "I'm hoping we can all straighten this out."

With Janice is Rachel and another girl from their class, the one Leo calls the Loud Mouth. Claire should know her name. The girls bound past her uncertain greeting, up the stairs to Hadley's room. She and Janice follow, watch them roam and ogle, lifting, opening things. Claire retrieves the phone from the folds of Hadley's comforter. She turns it off, then on again, willing a message from Hadley. One from Janice is all. Then the Loud Mouth shrieks and Claire remember her name, not that it matters: Sherelle. Sherelle is waving a piece of paper she found in the wastebasket. She smoothes it onto Hadley's desk. Claire reads the crumpled sheet:

Rachel don't be mad at me, I'm not mad at you but things are completely crazy in my life. Which I will tell you about some day I promise. You're the only person I love. PS I'm sorry I left tonight I

Claire turns the sheet over, but that's all there is. The girls look at each other. Janet is glaring at Rachel. "What happened at your party? If something went on that you didn't tell us...."

"Nothing went on," Sherelle says.

Rachel shakes her head in agreement. "I'd tell, if there was something. Don't you believe me?"

Rachel and Sherelle are crying. Claire passes her eyes over Hadley's words. They say nothing and more than she wants to know. Claire, who weeps easily at distant losses, a friend's brother-in-law's child's leukemia, the death of Princess Di or a sympathetic movie character, was dry-eyed at her beloved father's funeral and she doesn't cry now. It just hurts to breathe.

Janice tries to organize the world for her. She makes tea and sits the girls down at the kitchen table to brainstorm, sending Claire into the family room to make phone calls. Claire leaves messages for Leo and Nora that signify moderate urgency. She dials 911 but hangs up, imagining all the questions she can't answer. Is it an emergency as a policeman would define it? All she knows for sure is that Hadley came home last night some time. After which she must have left again. But where she went, or if she planned to return, Claire has no way of knowing. From somewhere the memory of Bodey rises up. Her leg bones soften.

She taps her soles on the wood floor. Not that she wants to see Bodey right now. Her skin crawls at the thought.

Back in the kitchen the two girls have started a list of places Hadley could have gone although the only entry so far is Fletcher Lawson's house. Sherelle, who submitted it, raises her thick eyebrows over her expressive eyes and turns to Rachel. "Did you see how long they were inside the . . . ?"

Rachel shakes her head firmly. "Trust me. She doesn't like him that much."

"She knows everything," Janice says to Claire, her mockery of her daughter a veil that only enhances her vast and abiding approval.

"I know *some* things!" Rachel reports on Hadley's break-up with Fletcher, making clear that only the gravity of the situation justifies this breaking of a confidence. "After he left she called him. I was with her. She ended it with him."

"Ended what?" says Claire. "They were boyfriend and girlfriend?"

"Left where?" Janice cries. "Left where when? Not last night, by chance? I won't ask what they were 'inside of.'" She flashes exaggerated outrage, under which seethes a little genuine outrage. "Isn't that interesting, how we learn of the presence of gentleman callers?" She eyes Rachel, "We'll discuss this later, shall we?" then steers them back to the problem at hand. "But if they were together last night, I could easily imagine something upsetting her."

"Mother," Rachel says, "you never listen to me."

They call Fletcher's house and learn that Hadley isn't there. For a few minutes Rachel won't even look at her mother. But the discussion proceeds. Where could Hadley have gone, since her best friends were all at the sleepover? Rachel brings up Felice Pinter. Sherelle makes a face. Then she calls Felice and reports Hadley's nonpresence, trying not to seem smug. Janice inquires about teachers that Hadley is close with or looks up to. The girls smirk in unison. Relatives? No one in town. In fact, other than the two places they already called, there's nowhere in Chicago anyone can imagine Hadley between midnight and nine in the morning. What about outside of Chicago? She hopped a bus? But she has no money except her allowance; she spends all her money. Could she have met someone on the Internet?

Claire sits with her head in her hands, while each suggestion roots the problem deeper into the soil of her brain. Unnecessarily, she thinks, hopes, since any minute Hadley will come bounding into the house. Pack on her back she'll walk into the kitchen and laugh at them. *What is the deal?* Claire can almost hear her. *Is this some kind of secret club?* Reluctantly, she looks up at the sound of her name.

"Do you have the note?" Janice says. "Claire?"

She runs upstairs for it, and they pore over the knotty text like rabbis. Does "some day" indicate an indefinite and possibly lengthy span of time before Hadley conceives of seeing Rachel again? In which case she seems to have purposely run away? Or is it only the unnamed confession that is to be delayed? As far as

Claire knows, there are no things in Hadley's life she would call crazy. She tries not get stuck on, *You're the only person I love.* Holding the edge of the table as if she might fall. "I don't think," Sherelle says, "that this is helping."

Janice concurs. "Maybe if we knew what was bothering Hadley?" She looks at Claire, who doesn't look back.

Janice embarks on a tale of her own adolescence in the suburbs of New York, when she was living proof of how wild girls can get at the start of puberty. In seventh grade she and her friends were taking the train from Rockville Center to the Village to get stoned. Sorry, but it happened. She saw the Grateful Dead in Washington Square, then drove off in a VW van packed with college-age kids who weren't in college to a warehouse section of the city she didn't recognize. It was the kind of thing you did then in the name of experience. She looks at Claire. "Kids want to experience things. It's their job." She smiles with the emphatic confidence of her harmless kiddie-adventuring. "I left, but I came back." Claire feels sweat beading on her forehead. "I'm sorry, Claire, I know this is terrible—"

"Please, I hope it's not terrible!" Claire swallows, trying to be reasonable, as Janice is, though all she wants is that the discussion end. "As far as I know, nothing was bothering Hadley. She was doing fine."

In the silence that ensues, the kitchen clock strikes noon. Twelve melodious bongs. "What if she was snatched?" Sherelle says.

All three heads turn. Claire bites the inside of her cheek.

Sherelle goes on, "You know that girl in California? Who was taken from her bed?"

"She wasn't taken," Rachel cries. "She left on her own!"

"Claire," Janice says with a break in her voice, "we better call the police."

Trooping over to the Lakeview Police Station, which is literally around the corner, Claire feels a little calmer. There's energy in motion, any motion, and in being part of this respectable, law-abiding band of girls and women. She's glad that last month she wrote a check to the local Fraternal Order of Police (over Leo's objections to it as a neighborhood strong-arm tactic), seventy-five dollars to supplement the police retirement fund. Inside the large, dusty room, two men standing well behind the counter are trading Hillary Clinton jokes. A heavy woman at a desk in the back is looking at her mouth in her compact mirror and telling someone on the phone her plans for the weekend. At the counter an officer is recording numbers from the driver's licenses of two grim-faced motorists, but his left eye slides off to the side as if he's writing random digits. "Excuse me," she calls to the pair of men behind him. "We need to talk to someone!" She holds up a photo of Hadley, that the telephone dispatcher told her to bring.

She spoke with polite urgency and the most genuine smile she could manage, but the only response is a glance at her blouse. "Listen, lady," says one of the men, "you're going to have to wait your turn like everyone else." He turns back to his cohort. "What does Bill tell Hillary after sex?"

Claire doesn't hear the punch line but the men chortle loudly. Janice gives them a look of contemptuous rage, but it doesn't penetrate their good fellowship.

"So Bill's coming off Air Force One with a pig under his arm. A clean pink baby pig with a red ribbon around its neck. A Secret Service guy comes up to him, 'What's that, Mr. President?' And Bill says, 'Not to worry, I got this for Hillary.' And so what does the guy say? 'Good trade, Mr. President!' *Trade*. Get it?"

Amiably one man punches the other's arm, then at an aggressively relaxed pace approaches the counter. "So, little lady? What can we do for you today?"

"You could do your job!" Janice says. "How's that for starters?"

"Mom," says Rachel.

Soothed by Janice's ready anger, Claire starts to explain what happened, what she knows and what she doesn't know, proceeding smoothly until she arrives at the question of why. She looks down at the photo in her hand, a school photo, taken about a year ago, just after Hadley turned twelve. The face with its distinct features, high arched brows, thick brown hair swept back into a Scrungi looks like a grown woman's. The man taps the counter impatiently. "Anyway," he says, "who you need is out right now."

Claire looks at him. Her head feels thick again. She tries to read the name on his badge.

Janice hisses in her ear, "He doesn't deserve to live."

"You are *disgusting*," Sherelle shouts in his face. "We waited half an hour!"

The man says, "Someone ought to shut that kid up," then proceeds to give instructions: They should come back in an hour. They should call first. Dizzy, Claire offers him the photo. "Keep it," he says, "unless you want to get it lost."

All of a sudden Claire is screaming. People are staring, Janice is holding her, murmuring, "Hush, hush." Claire wants to hush, she shouldn't act like this in public—not in private either but especially not in public—but the word "lost" is careening through the empty chambers of her mind. "Asshole!" she shouts. "Motherfucker!"

"That was entirely appropriate," Janice tells Claire as they walk back home. "I'm serious." The girls, trekking behind them in shocked or maybe scared silence, start to giggle.

Claire is trying to remember a line from a book she read in college, that Eileen used to quote. In a mad society the appropriate response is madness? Something like that. She wants to tell Janice she's glad to be getting to know her but the declaration sounds overwrought. "Thank you," she says. Janice squeezes her arm.

Janice leaves, to drive Sherelle home and to make dinner for her family. She'll check in late, by which time—"hopefully," she says—the prodigal daughter will have returned. Clearer-headed now, Claire decides to call the station again; this time she'll ask for the police sergeant. She picks up the phone and hears the voicemail signal. There are two messages. The first, from Bodey, she saves without playing it. The second is from Leo: "Aren't you ever home? Anyone interested in a certain brilliant athlete ought to stay put. Sorry. After the awards ceremony we're going out, all the dads and daughters, for a fancy dinner. I'll try you again later tonight. If you're lucky. Be good. I love you."

She calls the hotel but Leo is gone. She leaves a more urgent message. She tries his beeper, then hears it beeping in their bedroom. She could return Bodey's call but the thought makes her queasy. She calls the police station, and this time gets through to a detective. She doesn't need to come down, he says, since he has to check out the house anyway. He and his partner will be right over.

The man is true to his word, arriving minutes later with his partner, a sweet-faced young black woman. Without examining Hadley's room, they tape a narrow yellow band across the door-frame: *Police Investigation Site*. "Good Lord. Is that absolutely necessary?" Claire asks.

The young woman explains, "Don't worry, Mrs. Winger. We'll take it down after forensics gets through."

That doesn't seem right, Claire says to herself, but here, alone, she's afraid to say it aloud. It seems, in fact, absolutely wrong, but she's afraid that any protest, even a question, will result in another event she has no control over. On automatic pilot, she produces the photograph they ask for, along with the note the girls found. After their departure, she walks upstairs, quickly past

Hadley's doorway, planning to lie down in bed and stay there till things have improved. But there are no sheets on the bed.

Almost instantly she remembers where the sheets are. And remembers with unwanted clarity the sequence of events that led to their washing. Her hands shake as she pulls them from around the agitator and puts them in the dryer. Presses High. Very Dry. Start. The damp, heavy fabric starts to rotate, galumph, galumph, all 300 lavender and fuchsia cotton threads per square inch. The water that has already effaced the damaging evidence begins to evaporate.

Now, she thinks, the time is ripe for a seizure. She sits down on the floor, presses her forehead to the heat of the throbbing machine. She has committed a terrible act. Or if not a terrible act, at least one with possibly terrible consequences. She's hunched as if for a blow. But all she feels is her head warm, then hot.

It's dark outside now. She thinks of Janice driving home, no longer violating the Sabbath. In her next life, she hopes to be more like Janice.

CHAPTER SIXTEEN

Below Ruptured Disc

The first couple of days, the other kids seemed *opaque* to her, the same underneath despite variations in attractiveness and degree of wear. That their lives before this adventure were utterly different from hers she accepted without pondering. It wasn't just that they were older. She'd told them she was eighteen, they thought she was sixteen, and didn't care either way. And it wasn't just their dark secrets. She had her own things that she could never tell. But they seemed complicated while she was simple. They were rooted to the earth and below the earth as she could never be, since she'd had drama and art lessons and played AYSO soccer and got twenty dollars a week for putting plates in the dishwasher and wiping off the table, which she'd only do with a fresh sponge.

That they regarded her as one of them, used her hair dryer, offered their recreational drugs (which she politely declined) and peanut butter crackers (which she ate, guiltily), told her their disgusting or sad secrets, was only more proof of her separateness. But they called her Clara and she could do Clara. She had a knack for mimicking a person's vocabulary and speech rhyth. Knew the amount eye contact, the tilt of head that conveyed the right blend of empathy and opinions-of-her-own.

For example, Cheeta (*Anne Gaffney,* said her ID) with her golf-ball cheekbones and narrow hips of a boy, who could earn a hundred dollars for half an hour of car sex, just wanted her to nod when she talked, comb her scalp for lice (there never were lice), and not eat in front of her. With the video game geniuses, Hadley would murmur whatever last phrase of theirs hung in the air and they'd answer back, sometimes simultaneously, in their loud, excited Spanish. One boy was Franco, the other, Narcissio. One was taller and heavier than the other; still she couldn't remember who was who. They were always together, chewing peppermint gum and cursing enthusiastically; she assumed they were brothers. "*Chinga,*" she'd say back to them, and they'd laugh and pat her arm, and she'd laugh as if this were a real conversation.

She was less sure how to handle the *patrón,* as they sometimes called the man who paid the rent. Nat had sad Jesus Christ eyes under thick lashes, wide pouty lips, and a ponytail like Uncle Eric's, though she wouldn't have dared to tease him like she teased Eric. She didn't know what to say to him. She saw him pass in and out of the living room, and she sat on the floor at his feet while he played the guitar—he was taking lessons, another strange thing!—but his image in her mind kept changing—age, ethnicity. He despised the media and wouldn't fix his TV, which was good only for computer games. He let lots of people stay in his apartment but he didn't seem to trust them. When he was out he secured his door with a padlock, and when he came home he went right to his room and closed the door. Occasionally he invited someone, usually Cheeta, to join him; it seemed to be an honor. The housemates talked about him snidely and timidly, the way you discuss a teacher you're afraid even to suck up to, but no one knew anything for sure about him. According to Cheeta, he was twenty-five, the black sheep son of millionaires, living on a trust fund. Guin said he was forty, from a Boston slum; his money came from dealing drugs. Hadley couldn't tell which view, if either, was right. Not that she needed to know. After his first unsettling glance at her, he seemed to have forgotten she was there, which was fine. She was glad to let him pass her by like a girlfriend's father, requiring nothing except attendance (not even applause) at his nightly guitar recitals.

She was most comfortable with the girl from Dunkin' Donuts—Guin Lamotta. Despite her face of a prehistoric mammal, she was unreflectingly warm, with a low laugh that sounded like wooden blocks falling on the floor. She was also an adroit shoplifter, able to pocket a steak or a tube of lipstick with an undetectable twitch of hand and wrist. For dinner the second day of Hadley's stay she brought everyone chips and turkey sandwiches from J. J. Peppers, and for Hadley her own private carton of Maxi-pads. A name brand, guaranteed not to slip. That night as they lay talking on the futon that they unrolled in a corner of the living room, Hadley wanted, for a minute, to put her head in Guin's lap and cry.

Mostly, though, in this basement apartment, eye level with the passing legs of the Belmont tourist traffic, she was not aware of sadness. When she thought of her family, she did so briefly and without regret, as if they had all died before she was old enough to know them. She slept twelve or fourteen hours at a stretch, drifting through the easy blank afternoons like a balloon that a child had accidentally let go of, wafting higher and higher over the trees and buildings and little people.

The third night of her stay beneath Ruptured Disc, the video boys walked in, one of them leaning on the other. She still didn't know who was who. The one in charge—the tall one, without the tooth—had a bruise on his cheek, but the other one, who needed a dermatologist, was hurt badly, his eye closed shut and already changing color. His nose dripped blood, and when he opened his mouth she couldn't look. His friend helped him over to the couch, then went to the kitchen for paper towels. *"Maricón,"* said the injured boy, and lay back groaning softly. The front of his shirt was red with blood. Involuntarily her legs drew together; she made them loosen.

"You look awful," she murmured. The boils were bad enough, but now? She thought of her mother, who was good with this kind of thing. She wasn't good.

He tried to smile, but the movement made him wince. He wiped his chin, shaking his head as if embarrassed to look this bad in front of her. "Am I *maricón, amiga? Dígame*, Clarita! What is your opinion about me?"

She didn't know what a *maricón* was but she didn't have to let him know. She wanted to know what had happened but felt it uncool to ask. "Who isn't?" she replied with all the certainty she could muster. "I mean, aren't we all?"

It sounded so lame she felt her cheeks burn. But the boy beamed at her; he glowed. And more brightly still when his friend returned with a roll of toweling. He cleaned off the worst of the blood and dirt, then kissed his mouth. She forced herself not to turn away. The boy on the couch kissed him back and said, "You are a faggot, my friend. Do you know this? We are a faggot!" He took the other's face in his hands and turned him to look at Hadley. "Clarita is *bonita*, no? *Muy guapa!*" Then his hands clenched. He punched the air. "*Maricón*. He talk fucking stupid, man." His friend tried to soothe him but he didn't calm down. "*Maricón! Mariposa loca!*"

He railed on. She understood the fight now, and a few other things. The boys insulted each other but there was warmth between them. Maybe even love. And it came to her that there was nothing she couldn't understand, no pit of darkness or soaring pinnacle of light. Till now she'd limited her conversation to what she thought was expected of a very pretty, fairly savvy girl just slightly better than she actually thought she was. She'd acted sure of things she wasn't sure of, but that was the limit to her self-creation. But now she saw no reason to restrict herself. Talk was play, with a loose, wonderfully mysterious connection to what lay underneath. "So did you kill the fucker?" she said to the hurt boy, "or just maim him?"

"Dude would not close fucking trap!" he shouted, angrier than before.

She plunged on, "Say it this way: The *motherfucker* wouldn't close *his* fucking trap!"

He laughed, then took her hand and kissed it. "You are my teacher."

Some of his blood was smeared on her hand but she didn't gag. She rinsed it off in the kitchen, brought back a bowl of warm water and a dish towel. Dipped the towel and gave it to him to absorb the blood that kept seeping into his mouth. "Open," she said, and looked inside, averting her gaze from a small eruption on his chin. He had a cut on the lip but his teeth were intact. She told him the good news, pleased as her mother might have been, nursing her patient. "So how did it end?" she asked. "Your fight. Did you leave them dead on the street?"

As soon as they understood her, they started to laugh. They didn't want to look like they were bragging, but after a while she learned it was Narcissio who had started the fight, with Franco's ready aid and abetment, and that it was a group of five that they attacked. *Cinco hombres.* Who ran away when the police came. "So Franco and I, we are heroes!"

Franco and I. She eyed the boy on the couch. He was Narcissio. She tried to imprint it on her memory. Franco tall, muscled. Narcissio frailer, the hurt one. Like a narcissus flower. Why was it so hard to remember?

"And we are also innocent!" said Franco. "We look like innocent because Narcissio he is lying down in blood!" They laughed louder. "One police he want to send him to hospital and Narcissio, 'No, Sir, thank you'!"

Narcissio added, "You know, and this policeman guy, he ask for runaway girl." He smiled, welcoming her into the small, bright room of the joke. "She maybe look like you, *una rubia* and tall size, but this girl she is from some rich people and just only thirteen year olds."

Hadley's mouth curved into an automatic protective smirk but a bubble of fright lofted through her. She sat still till it passed. "Thirteen *years old*," she corrected him, and leaned forward to wipe his lower lip.

"But you *gringas*," he said "you look all the same!" All three laughed again, Hadley the loudest.

She was being looked for. Hunted. How strange, like a game of hide-and-seek for real. Strange, not to be able to go outside.

And not to tell anyone, not even Guin. She was leading a fully secret life.

But she didn't feel trapped in the apartment below Ruptured Disc; in fact she was almost enjoying her life there. She'd finally stopped bleeding, which made things easier. She and Guin shared a futon in a corner of the living room. A bookcase shelf for her toiletries, earrings, and her one change of clothes she kept neater than she had ever kept her room at home. Perhaps she'd grow up, grow old and die here. There was action. Kids came and went. They smoked, played games and music, ate, slept. Maybe something else happened in Nat's room; it didn't matter. She played video games with Narcissio and Franco, and it was fun. When they smoked weed she'd light a Kool, memorizing, without any intention, the coldly threatening words of the songs they listened to, her mouth full of the nasty mentholated smoke. She'd release it slowly, careful not to inhale. Tired, she'd burrow under Guin's Mexican blanket and sleep through the afternoon, floating on the slightly sour breeze of a perpetual slumber party.

The one problem was the *patrón*—G'nat, as she called him to herself—who made her increasingly uncomfortable. It didn't help that Cheeta was in love with him. And even Guin said he had a lot of personal power. "I don't think so!" Hadley said snottily. She looked for an obliterating word. "He's *old!* What's he doing with his life?"

Cheeta laughed and called her retro.

"No offense," said Guin, "but are you like from a rich suburb or something?"

"No, I'm not from a rich suburb. Are you?"

Guin and Cheeta both laughed. Hadley's face felt hot. She could not pursue the subject.

She was upset with Guin for a while, but forgot it that evening when Guin came home with a white stretchy tank top for her, that she'd lifted from a local boutique. Hadley put it on. She stood on tiptoe to see it in the bathroom mirror—the light, pretty fabric that stopped just above her navel and revealed the small nubs of her nipples. The words *Bloody Mary* rose to her mind but she tamped them down, turning from side to side in the fluorescent light, her torso and chest glamorously slim. Despite the cold she wore the top to bed that night with nothing over it. She had it on in the depths of early morning sleep when she became aware of the smell of leather, cologne, weed. Nat was kneeling alongside her futon. He held a joint to her lips.

With a tiny, muffled protest she turned her head away. On the wall side of the bed Guin continued to snore gently. Narcissio and Franco lay as usual on the couch under the windows with their arms around each other. Cheeta lay on the couch in the middle of the room. Nat's face drew closer; she saw the skin puffed under his eyes. Sharp lines ran from his nose to the sides of his mouth. Unbound, his long black hair tickled the side of her neck. "Toke," he said, an order.

She took an obedient sip, mostly air. She gasped, trying not to cough.

"Like this, baby." He pulled hard on the roach, then fastened his mouth to hers and exhaled. Gritty, chocolatey smoke coated her tongue and the back of her throat. She was so intent on not coughing she didn't notice his hand under the blanket. He touched her with a single finger, so gently it wasn't until he'd removed it that she knew where it had been. "Yes, no?" he said.

His lips were wide, softer and pinker than they should be. Words of defense or protest fluttered feebly at the bottom of her throat. But when he tried to touch her again she found, praise God, her knees drawn up and pressed together, a shield against him. He squeezed her hip the way you feel a nectarine, and said as if reassuring her, "You are a very little girl."

Her eyes flashed him their automatic ironic refutation, not that such subtleties would manifest in the dim light. There was a raw buzzing between her legs where the flesh had turned to cantaloupe rind. As he walked down the hall to his room, she lay stiff under the coarse blanket, careful not to whine or weep or act otherwise suburban.

Afterward she acknowledged him no more than before, which meant not at all—G'nat the buzzing, biting insect—and he paid no attention to her either, but the place he'd touched, with its new thatch of straight, fine baby hairs, had been irrevocably altered. She knew from Hygiene and from discussions with friends the disconcerting acrobatics of baby making; she was sure, or almost, that Nat's hand, however intrusive, could not have made her pregnant. But it seemed that he, or something, had planted a seed in her. It swelled, put down the first tendril roots. In the dark her own hand would find its way there, to that part of her that she'd never touched before with anything thinner than a washcloth. "Yes, no?" she said to herself, pressing hard on her palm, annihilating the embryonic monsters that were starting to breed.

At the same time, though, her mind was turning over the mystery of Nat, as if he were a package addressed to someone else that had accidentally fallen into her hands. By now she had her own notion of his past, which made more sense than what she'd been told. He probably had a mother like Felice's, who thought her child was head and shoulders above everyone else. And he probably had girlfriends, being the sort of extra-confident boy that lots of girls liked. Then in her scenario, in high school he did something weird. She couldn't quite picture what, but knew how it made her feel. Maybe his girlfriend went out with someone else and he tried to kill her or himself. "You disgust me, Guh-nat," she said to herself, her tongue curling toward the roof of her mouth around the double syllable. He was pathetic, an old dude with no friends his age. Then, pressing her hips to the mattress she murmured, "I love you," to no one in particular. Knowing it wasn't love she felt, just a generalized, breathless longing.

Her sleep became ultra-light. She woke, not to the intermittent bleat of sirens, but to the night sounds of the apartment—the computer tones of the security system, the click of a key turning a latch, suck of a door opening or shutting, the rasp of clothing or skin sliding under covers. When Cheeta rose from her couch,

Hadley quieted her breath, following as clearly as if her eyes were open Cheeta's path to the bathroom. The toilet flushed. Water did not run in the sink, Hadley noted with disapproval, an involuntary response she had yet to dismantle. She heard a scratching sound, like a cat sharpening its claws or asking to be let in.

Quiet as a burglar she tiptoed to the hallway in time to see Cheeta slipping into Nat's room. Her heart was pounding so loud she couldn't hear anything, but the overhead light was on in his room, and through the closing crack of the door the picture was so fluorescent bright she saw almost sharply. Nat lay on his bed, his chest hairless and blue-white like skim milk. His stomach protruded slightly. Below, against a swatch of black lay what she was obliged to recognize as his penis, thick as her wrist and angled unaccountably toward the ceiling.

She lay down on her side of the futon and tried to delete the image from her brain. She tried to stuff it into her mental locker. According to Nora, hell was a lake of fire in which you burned and burned but did not burn up. She took off her shirt. Under the scratchy wool blanket her skin was on fire everywhere, from the back of her neck under her hair to the soles of her feet.

The following night Guin baked two chickens with a can of Campbell's cheddar cheese soup and invited the housemates to dine at the kitchen table like the Brady Bunch. The sauce was bright orange; people made fun of it but ate with gusto. Hadley watched. Watched also the joint that passed. Narcissio sucked the roach down to nothing and consumed all four drumsticks. Cheeta took the skin off her piece and took several bites; it was the first time Hadley had seen her eat. Hadley didn't eat, and no one asked her to eat, or even to put food on her plate. She didn't talk either, or look at Nat but was aware of the large chicken breast on his plate. His fingers deft with the knife and fork. Wiping sauce from his chin. When the meat was gone, he wrapped his belt around his leg and poked a syringe through a hole in his pants. His light shriek sank into a groan of pleasure.

Cheeta stopped eating and stared at him.

"Got any more, man?" Narcissio said.

"Fuck you," he said tenderly.

Goose bumps rose on her arms but she maintained her pose of amused indifference. Nat, in a dirty white cable knit sweater, looked like an off-brand Brad Pitt, sleazily handsome. She felt older than everyone but Nat. Than her mother, even. She wouldn't have minded her mother being there at that moment, just to see her.

After dinner Nat plugged his guitar into the living room sound system. Till now he'd performed mostly Seventies songs, Cat Stevens and John Denver, but tonight he was doing a song he'd written himself. He handed Cheeta a sheet with the lyrics.

This was Nat's big moment. Cheeta, though, didn't seem to care. She lay her head back on the couch and closed her eyes, aglow with her increasing skinniness. Beside her, Hadley sat as she did at school when she wasn't prepared, willing herself invisible. It was Guin, finally, who took the sheet from Cheeta's lap and sang with Nat.

At first Hadley only half-listened. The song was disturbing in a boring way. "Eat the poison hamster," kept repeating, though maybe she had heard it wrong. Guin had a beautiful voice. Nat sang the way he sometimes talked, nasal and raspy like people clearing their throats, while the clear, golden thread of Guin's voice wound around him. Then Hadley felt a pang of longing for something to be good at. In choral presentations with her class at school, she'd been told to "mouth" the words. She looked at the sheet in Guin's hands, which read, *Eat the poison, master. Let's embrace disaster*, and sang out, "Eat the poison, master!" daring Nat to look at her. He was fixed on Cheeta. *Eat the poison hamster.* Rachel had a hamster that they sometimes let out to stumble over the chenille spread of her bed, and you could feel its bones through its thin fur.

"Come on, dance," Nat said to Cheeta, who lolled in Neverland. "Dance with me." He put on a CD. Cheeta slumped deeper into the couch.

"I'm wasted."

He pulled at her hand, but she lay limp. "Wake up, gorgeous baby. You move like water over stones." He tried to pull her upright. He shook her. "Come on. Please. For me." She hung like a sack in his arms.

"I am so . . . so. . . ."

Hadley looked at Cheeta. Her blonde hair smelled of shampoo and surrounded her face like an aura, but her skin was paper white. Her cheeks were drawn in, her cheekbones like the small, round heads of hammers. "She might be sick," Hadley said.

Nat kissed Cheeta on the cheek, deposited her on the couch, and turned to Hadley. "How about you?" he said. "Are you sick?"

Hadley shrugged, although she was starting to want his attention. The music made her want to dance; she liked to dance. She and her friends would turn on Britney Spears or Whitney Houston and shimmy and slam into each other. But here, it seemed, the prevailing mode was Fatigued. Blasé. A little dizzy from hunger, she lay back against the couch beside Cheeta, gazing at Nat through closing eyelids. "I am *so* high!"

"You are so full of shit."

Her eyes jerked open. In order not to cry she fixed on the flower pattern in the Oriental rug. She heard but didn't see him put his guitar back in its case, carry it to his room, lock the door.

It was what she had been, all along, afraid of. As if she'd pulled up her shirt to show the toilet paper balled inside the cups of her bra. She'd screwed up the system of older-kid etiquette and was banned from the game.

CHAPTER SEVENTEEN

Claire's Week

By the time Janice calls back after her dinner, Claire can barely speak. Two hours have passed since the detectives left, and the phone hasn't stopped ringing, and every time it rang she jumped with the same surge of idiot hope, but it wasn't Hadley and it wasn't Leo, and she wanted to talk to the detectives again but was afraid to hold up the line (Leo hated Call-Waiting), and she couldn't even leave the house to look for Hadley, because Hadley might take that moment to call or return, and all she accomplished, those two empty hours, was to bring the laundered sheets into the bedroom and set them in a pile on the chair by the bed, and now her heart's racing like a horse with a too-heavy load; it flinches at the lash, then stands shuddering.

Still, Janice's voice calms her a little. Over the phone they devise The Hadley Circuit, a car relay of their many friends, in which at all hours of the day or night at least one vehicle will search Lakeview and environs for the runaway girl. Then Eileen comes by. Claire hasn't been seeing Eileen as much as she used to, Claire's fault, her lovecraziness. She apologizes. "You're amazing," Eileen says with a roll of her eyes. "You are so you." They hug, Claire laughing painfully. Irrationally joyful now in Eileen's company, she brings her upstairs to view the yellow tape across Hadley's door. Eileen is satisfyingly horrified and amused. "Lordy," she says, "we're in *NYPD Blue*."

"I know. It's weird to think I can't go in."

"It's your house," Eileen says. "If you want to go in, go in!"

Hadley's door opens inward. All Claire has to do is turn the knob and push. They duck under the tape, Claire careful not to catch her hair on it. Inside, Claire checks Hadley's e-mail. There's correspondence with a number of people including barff 2 and *happypsychotic* but it sheds no new light. In *My Documents* she finds two short book reports full of typos and run-ons. There's also a long paper headed with Hadley's name and the name and room number of her social studies teacher, advocating the restoration of diplomatic relations between America and Cuba. The paper, "Sugar or Sour Grapes: A Neo-Marxist Analysis of the Last Cold Battleground," Hadley couldn't have written if she were thirty years old with a PhD. A fourth file, "Persephone," sounds more like Hadley. It's a story about Sophie, a teenager in Boulder, Colorado, where Hadley went last year to overnight camp. *One sunny afternoon Sophie was in a meadow picking flowers when an earthquake cracked the ground open at her feet. Down, down, down she fell, the green grass dissapeared [sic] and the blue sky was just a tiny crack overhead and she kept falling. "Oh dear," thought Sophie, "I will never see my parents and my baby sister again.* It stopped there. It was dated two weeks ago. Did Hadley finish it at school? *Down, down, down.*

Then Eileen gives a short scream. She shows her what she found behind the wastebasket that the girls missed, a torn envelope addressed to Hadley from her grandmother. Inside is a birthday card with the message, "Don't spend it all in one place." The card is empty. Claire checks her wallet, finds it empty too. She didn't have much, maybe fifty dollars. And her mother never sent more than fifty. Claire's imagination opens out: Hadley on a bus to Florida where her mother lives. Could she get there on a hundred dollars? She could probably make it to Tennessee and Eric's commune. Claire pictures Hadley and Eric in the fields. Planting broccoli. No. But Claire feels better. Maybe it's Eileen's sturdy company. Or the feeling of action. Or the idea of these two plausible benign destinations for her daughter. She calls the number the detectives gave her and leaves a message. She calls her mother and manages not to cry, although her mother is crying. She calls Eric, leaves a message on his cell phone, though he rarely turns it on. She calls Bodey at school now that he's unlikely to be there and tells the bald facts to his machine. "If something breaks, I'll be in touch."

"This is Claire," she adds, in case he wondered who was calling, so reserved and cold.

Eileen is gone, and Claire has just finished a letter to Eric, when Leo calls. Apologetic, a little soused. The team was *sterling*, their daughter *golden*, he even met a few dads he could stand— She tells him what happened and she has to calm him down. "She'll come back." Her voice sounds weak in her ears; she speaks louder. "When she gets tired of her adventures. I have to believe that." He isn't soothed. "Honey," she says, "lie down and try to sleep. Really. I don't want you to have an accident. You can drive home in the morning. Maybe Nora wants to finish her meet. There's nothing to do here but wait."

He's shouting. If he wasn't 100% sober before, he surely is now! How can she imagine Nora wanting to finish the meet, doesn't she know what Nora's like? And how can she expect him to sleep? They'll be home as fast as the car will drive them. "Besides," he says more tenderly, "I hate sleeping alone!"

Now she's anxious in a way she hates. She remakes the bed with the clean sheets, hating her deliberation, her lucidity. She feels like a criminal. A whore. She drives to the Mosses' house, turns around in their driveway, and heads home slowly, scanning the streets Hadley must have traveled. There are signs, if she can read them. She creeps along, checking by the street-lamplight the faces of any Saturday night revelers. At five A.M., she's back on the sofa, trying to sleep, when the phone rings. It's Bodey, whom she has no desire whatever to speak to. She says, "Didn't you get my message?"

"Yes."

His pause annoys her. "Yes?"

"I thought—" He stops. She doesn't help him out. "I thought we had—I thought we were more than—I can't say this right."

She swallows her sigh, trying to work up some empathy. "There's a lot on my mind. As you can probably guess."

"What can I do, Claire? Tell me what I can do for you."

"I wish there was something."

"I'm sorry. But everything I say seems to irritate you."

"I know!" He sounds too concerned or not concerned enough. Gratuitously, helplessly concerned. She yawns, waking herself completely up, and tells him so. "I'm a bitch," she says, aware again, for a moment, of what she loves in him.

"Do you love me?" he says.

"I don't want to think about it now. I'm sorry." He hangs up during her apology. Which is a good thing, as Leo and Nora are pulling in the drive.

The next morning the detectives return. No one has slept. Silently all five mount the stairs to Hadley's room. The detectives start with Hadley's computer. Claire watches, knowing the nothing they'll find. She shows them the birthday card, tells them about the small theft, urging them to check buses and trains, as

Hadley may have the money to purchase a ticket somewhere. Against the backdrop of her husband and daughter's exhausted confusion Claire is tired but calm. She has had, after all, a twenty-four-hour head start on panic.

When the pair has gone, Leo asks her what to do—asks *her*, the boss, the queen of chaos. She smiles grimly. "We wait for the phone to ring." The friends involved in the Hadley Circuit call at the beginning and end of their two-hour shifts, sometimes just to convey encouragement. Meanwhile, she gets Nora and Leo working around the house, soaking the burners of the stove in dishwasher soap, dusting the high moldings. At the end of day two without Hadley the house is cleaner than after the cleaning team. The three make dinner together, a more elaborate meal than when Hadley was around.

That night she sleeps hard, and the next day, Monday, she's still in bed when new detectives arrive, two middle-aged white men. Nora is up in her room, Leo at the hospital with unpostponable surgeries. She ought to call Children's, it occurs to her. But Children's, she thinks goofily, could just as well call her. She puts on a robe, answers the door.

She wishes Leo were home with her now. She hates these detectives who seem to have had no communication with the other detectives and ask the same questions. Repeated again and again, the facts she proffers sound either made up or so trite that the event starts to blur. "I have no idea why she took off," she says again and again, and feels like a liar. When they go upstairs, she waits at the kitchen table, her teeth chattering. Then they come down with Hadley's computer, her bedclothes, and carpet fuzz from all the rooms, and she thinks: They think I killed her. Nora and Leo have their airtight alibis, but, ladies and gentlemen of the jury, where was Claire Winger the night of the disappearance? It's crazy, but it spews out. Only Bodey can vouch for her and there's no one to vouch for Bodey, who was either her accomplice or did the deed himself. "Bye now," she calls out to the men as they go out the door, picturing a pale red curl of Bodey's hair among the lint in their Ziploc Bag. "Thank you!" But she's stuck, it seems, in a crime show. Rationally, she knows she hasn't done anything criminal, and she certainly doesn't *want* to blame herself, but if it wasn't her fault there's nothing to be learned from it and, worse, nothing she can do to get Hadley back. She tries to bite off one of her nails but it's too hard and healthy. With a clippers she cuts her nails down to the ends of her fingers. Her hands feel lighter but Hadley remains gone.

That evening she and Leo are drinking wine at the kitchen table, in silence as they have done since he came home. From the third floor comes the faint sound of Nora's violin. "I've been having an affair," she says. "With a teacher from the School."

"That's really funny, Claire."

"Leo," she says.

He gives her a long look. "I don't believe you." He looks out the window. "Claire, don't mess with me."

She holds the roiling sides of her head. *Don't make this harder*

241

than it has to be. She wants to leave the room, get into bed under the covers, but forces herself to stay in her chair. "I feel bad. Terrible. That is, I'd feel terrible if there was anything inside me." She folds her hands in her lap, waiting for things to be different now. For the doorbell to ring, the door to open upon Hadley, disheveled, apologetic, surly, tearful.

"Leo," she says, "I am so, so sorry."

He seems to believe her now. At least he listens carefully, not speaking, looking right into her eyes like a good physician. What seems to be the trouble, Mrs. Winger? What sort of pain? What happens when I press here? But when it's over, he goes to the closet and puts on his jacket. "You've got great timing, I'll say that for you."

"Where are you going?"

He shrugs. "You just dropped a bomb on me, don't you know that?" He stops in the doorway. "I'm not sure what I'm doing, Claire. But I have to get out."

"I don't want you to leave."

"That might be true. But I'd say for the moment that you've lost some of your, I don't know, prerogative?"

"Oh, stop! Don't you want to know whether I'm still seeing him? Whether I love him or not?"

"Sometime, maybe. Not now."

"What do I tell Nora?" she asks, trying to keep from whining.

"Tell her the truth. Unless you can think up a good lie."

Now she's angry. "I think you should wait, at least until—"

She makes herself say it, though it might be bad luck, "Till Hadley gets back. I mean how can you leave in the middle of all this?"

He steps toward her, not touching but so close to her she feels the heat from his body. She can hear his Adam's apple. "Did you ever think, Claire—?"

She wants to step back but she doesn't. "What? Say it!"

"That this choice of yours. This betrayal. Might have something to do with—" He swallows. She feels him hating her. "You know."

She knows. It's what she has been thinking herself, and she hates him. He says less harshly, "Maybe I'm not being fair. I don't want to be overdramatic. I'll call you tomorrow."

"Stay, Leo." It sounds like she's talking to a dog but it's her only voice. "You've got to *stay*."

He returns an hour later, and goes upstairs for a talk with Nora. Then he comes down with bedding, goes into the den and shuts the door. She has been crying and knows her eyes are red but he didn't look at her face. She feels him not looking.

The next morning after the radio weathercasters proclaim the coldest April in fifty years, she puts on her winter coat, drives to the Greyhound Station, and shows Hadley's picture to all the ticket sellers. No one remembers her. On the way home she double-parks in front of the School and runs down to Bodey's office where, standing in the doorway, she tells him she doesn't plan to see him anymore. It doesn't hurt. She looks at his cynical, intelligent, fleshy face and isn't moved, not for a second. Not excited, not regretful, not anything. He puts his hand on her arm, and she feels its weight and warmth, but not the shiver that till now traveled the length of her arm to her heart. He tries to hold her but she pushes away with the strength of not caring.

He says, "I know why you're doing this."

"It doesn't take a wizard." His self-assurance repels her. "Of course, I expect miracles. I'm an irrational person, I admit it."

"Maybe you don't love me," he says. "But you need me."

"Then it's my tough luck."

"This isn't you talking, Claire. You have a secret you can't tell anyone but me. What do you make of that?"

She remembers but can't retrieve the feeling. When his hand grazes her neck she steps out of reach, remembering sex with him a long time ago when she was younger and capable of passion. If she never has sex with anyone ever again, she won't miss it. She's back in the car before it gets a ticket.

This is her final offering to the gods who reward duty and punish indulgence, and it's all she has. It's probably equivalent to promising to go to temple every Friday night for the rest of her life or burying a toad at the base of the oak tree, but she must not have used up her full quantity of hopefulness because, looking out the window at the gray-green froth of the lake, she feels quasi-euphoric. All she mulls, concerning Bodey, is the ease with which she has given him up, which she hopes won't count against her.

CHAPTER EIGHTEEN

Contact

In the morning before anyone else was up, she dialed home from the phone in the kitchen. It had been three days. Or was it five days? The old-fashioned wall phone gave her three feet to pace. She was thirsty but couldn't reach the sink. She was about to hang up when Nora answered. "Hadley! Oh, I was praying for you!"

"Chill, N."

"Hadley, we thought you were *dead*."

"No such luck," Hadley said, and listened to her sister squeak with annoyance. "What's the matter, Nora?"

Nora groaned. "Just imagine what's gone on here! Imagine what the house is like!"

She didn't want to imagine but pictures came easily: of her mother sprawled on the floor with a bottle of pills in her hand, as Nora had described her. Her mother's shadow writhing on the bed in the master bedroom. "I'm sorry," she said.

"You should be. If you wanted attention, well, you've got it now, because you are all we talk about. 'What did we say to the poor *baby?* What did we do *wrong?*'"

Nora sounded like her normal self. Hadley felt warmed. "I miss you. It's so weird here sometimes."

"If you're into drugs," Nora said, "God can help you."

"I'm not into drugs! Not like that!"

"Like what then?"

"Shut up!"

"Don't give up. Trust in a higher power. When are you coming home?"

"I don't know."

"You don't know? Hadley, the police are looking for you. Your face is on television, haven't you seen it?"

"Our set doesn't work."

"Where are you, Hadley? What's going on with you?"

"There are some crazy kids here. And I need to figure a few things out."

Nora gave a short scream. "Dad's right. You are totally, totally selfish."

"Do you think I care?"

"You should care. Daddy sleeps on the sofa now. He hardly talks to Mom. I think she's losing it."

"Losing it? Did she try, again, you know. . . ."

"You've got to talk to her. Mom," she called out. "Mom, it's Hadley!"

"Dad sleeps on the sofa? Why won't he talk to Mom?"

"Get the phone, Mom!" Nora cried. "Hold on, Had, I'll get her."

"That's all right," Hadley said, hanging up.

For the next twenty-four hours she sat in her corner of the living room with the words to Nat's song on her lap. In the margin, with a mechanical pencil she drew a picture of a beautiful woman in a flowing gown. Trying to remember what Cassandra looked like, she drew a cat padding down a hallway. She wrote, *lost lose lone zone*, pressing into the inner sheets of the pad. *I wanna zone.* When the lead ran out, her heart ached, because now how could she hide the fact she didn't know how to talk or act anymore? When someone sat down by her futon and said, "What's the matter?" or "Come outside with me," all her cells shrank away from each other, leaving, in the place where her body was, a little pile of dry sand. She chewed the eraser. It came off in her mouth. *WHO AM I?* she scratched on the back of the sheet with the plastic point, *Who am eye*, her depression so sticky-thick in her throat, she poked a hole in the paper and she didn't care. She crumpled the page.

It was bad outside, too, more like February than April. The apartment had only space heaters, and a chill rose from the Oriental rug laid over the thin indoor-outdoor carpeting laid over the shell of poured concrete over the cold earth. Had the gas bill been paid? None of them had anything to do with the gas bill. On Guin's advice they put blankets over the windows, but the cold, stale air scratched their throats. Nat had a heater in his room, but only Cheeta went in there. During the day, most of the people hung in stores and coffee shops. Back home under Ruptured Disc, they stayed up till dawn playing music and complaining about the endless winter and their lives. They slept under coats or in sleeping bags. Guin's leg twitched as if she were kicking someone in her dream.

Despite her respites in Nat's room, Cheeta developed a cough so deep it sounded like a ringing bell. Or maybe she'd always had this cough. Cheeta went to Urgent Care and brought back pills she took three times a day, which turned her cheeks salmon pink like the cheeks of children in books, but Hadley sometimes woke in the early morning to sounds of her crying. Hadley would lie on her back, pressing her hands between her thighs, naming all the kids in her homeroom in their seating-chart order from the desk by the door at the front to the last row by the windows. If she fell short of twenty-nine she would start over from scratch. She couldn't remember her last shower but it was too cold in the bathroom to take her clothes off. She washed her face in the sink, and used deodorant. Would it ever warm up?

Of all the people in the garden apartment, only Guin managed to maintain her sense of personal order. A pickpocket with the hands of a brain surgeon, she sometimes came home with gourmet goodies. That evening Guin brought her a carton of pesto pasta. "Don't eat too much on an empty stomach." She patted the top of Hadley's head and left the room.

The food looked beautiful to Hadley, the tangle of glistening noodles flecked with bright green, but she couldn't put a single strand into her mouth. They shimmered palely. The steam subsided. The shimmer clouded over. There were things she would never experience again or in the same way again. She felt vague dread. Then the dread subsided too.

Later, after dark, Guin sat down with her. She didn't remark on the uneaten food or Hadley's stillness. She smelled of garlic. Hadley sat with her hand on her flat, tight stomach. Guin lit a pipe. Hadley drummed on her stomach. She eyed the pipe Guin held out to her. Narcissio, who had just come in, was drawn to the small drama. "Hey girlie girl," he said, and started singing "Happy Birthday."

Except for the one choiceless moment with Nat, Hadley hadn't ever smoked weed. If someone asked and she chose to tell the truth, she'd have said she had no interest in it. Tonight, though, she felt stuck in a byway of childhood, an eddy she was determined to swim out of. She drew on the mouthpiece, tasting metal, then looked sharply around. No one's face had changed. The room was the room. She tried again. She didn't expect colors, or music from rocks, but she expected *something*. She drew a third time, holding it in till she was gasping. She knew what she was seeking, the sense of personal, knowing rightness, strong as carbon steel. "I want to get higher and higher and higher," she said breathily. "I want to see what's up there."

"Up where?" said Narcissio. Guin laughed.

Hadley tried to explain. There was a luminous, happy place somewhere. If she could describe it she could get there, and bring them too. But although words were coming out of her mouth, and maybe the right words, she was stumbling as she said them, or speaking too softly, for Guin and Narcissio so far away. She could see them, but tiny and blurred, as if through the wrong end of a telescope. Which was, she thought, exactly how it was for her and her mother and Nora and everyone—seeing each other but dim and far away, moving their mouths in sequences that only occasionally pertained to what the other was saying, and then only accidentally. And suddenly it was funny, these accidental intimacies that seemed real. Between the V of her legs the flowers woven into the rug swirled out and out like a Disney cartoon, and she started laughing. Guin and Narcissio were laughing too. Guin's hair gave off green and gold lights, ten thousand writhing strands like ferns in water, how could she ever have thought Guin was homely? Narcissio's eyes had dark thick lashes. She held her arms out and embraced them, pressed her face to their two faces—her dear friends who loved this strong wild thing she was becoming. "Mom and Dad!" she said, laughing and crying at the same time. "Mommy, Daddy." They smiled at her, their adorable child. She said, "That's some fine weed!"

Guin laughed harder. "Weed? I'm out of weed!" She laughed again.

Hadley laughed because laughing was called for. Then it ceased. Shut off. Just like that. She fixed on Guin, trying to see her without the laughter. "You are or you were?"

"Were what, hon?"

Hadley thought for a moment, a process that took longer than usual. Her mind limped from the weed she thought she had just been smoking, to Nat breathing it into her mouth, to Nat shooting something into his thigh, to her own thighs, which jigged up and down on the rug in front of her. Her knees shook; she pressed them into the floor, then looked up to see Guin with a question in her eyes. She remembered her own question. "What was in that smoke, Guin? Was it crack or ecstasy or something?"

"Oh, dear!" said Guin. "I'm sorry, I thought you'd like...."

Guin paused expressively as if to fill in the blank. Then Cheeta walked in, her white blonde hair a beautiful cape over her shoulders. Guin rose, hand out, to draw Cheeta into the family group, but Cheeta didn't seem to see her, or anyone. She passed into the hallway, vanished behind the bathroom door. A voice droned in Hadley's ear: *To drown in the river of Hell.*

Hadley looked around the room. "Excuse me?"

The words came again, whispered but insistent. They wrote themselves out in her mind in black on white as if typed onto a page, *To drown in the river of Hell,* letters one at a time forming words the way her thoughts had turned into typescript words at night in bed in third grade when she was learning to type. Now more thoughts assailed her, typing themselves out before her eyes, the letters at first black and crisp, only to fragment as they were pushed aside or buried under new thoughts. She tried not to think, she mustn't, because every thought in her head became a sentence on the page of her mind. And as more thoughts flooded in, they piled heavily around her, breaking to bits the older sequences, some of which blew around her head and got into her mouth and nose like dust or feathers. "This is awful," she said to Guin, but Guin wasn't there now. Narcissio was gone too. "Cheeta?" It was hard to breathe without coughing. She walked to the bathroom, jiggled the knob. Sounds of retching came from within. She ran to the kitchen where she thought Guin had gone; it was empty. She banged on Nat's door. "Help me!" She gasped for air. "I'm drowning!"

"It isn't locked!" he called from behind the door. She turned the knob, peered inside. A gust of air assailed her, warm and dry. "I'm drowning too," he said with a little smile. "You get used to it."

Goose bumps rose on her upper arms, crept over her shoulders, down her back, but his nasal, insinuating voice was soothing. She stood across from his armchair. "Nat," she said, trying not to whine, "where is everyone?"

He shook his head. "That's how it is, sweet thing. They come, they go."

A sob rose in her throat. He was so right. People came and went. Her thoughts came more slowly, and then dissipated, as she was used to. The only light came from his reading lamp. He was beautiful, she thought, like a woman is beautiful, and she wondered why she had just noticed it. Maybe because of the book on his lap. With the book, his long hair, his loose cableknit sweater he looked like a beautiful high-school girl. "Nat," she said, "my mother tried to kill herself."

"That's tough, baby." He stared down so long she wondered if he were reading the book, but then he looked at her, and his eyes were bright. "My daddy tried, too, and he got it right. That was the sort of guy he was. He got things right." He smiled at her confusion. "Couldn't stand mistakes, incompetence. He said that. Smart dude. V.P. and moving up. In a giant corporation, household name. Cereals, refrigerators, dinners for Mom to pop in the oven when she comes home from work. One night he came home from work, parked the car in the garage and blew his brains out. Closed the garage door. As if that would keep it private. Shortsighted in the end, I guess. Well, we can't be all perfect."

If she had been able to speak, she'd have asked what her mother would have asked. When did it happen? How old were you? Stupid questions. She was glad, when she opened her mouth, that nothing came out. He closed his book, set it on the floor, then leaned back in his chair. The sweater was all he had on; hadn't she known that? Of course, she knew. She had seen his bare legs, their curls of dark hair. Still she was careful now not to look at them. She looked at his face above the neckhole of his cable-knit sweater, the ring of thick white wool.

"I know all about drowning," he said and put an arm out.

She was terrified but also ecstatic. She was flying across a stage, her net skirt lifting. Outside the room she was one of many, part of an audience, but inside, now, here, Nat was talking to her as he maybe talked to Cheeta, "Close your eyes, honey baby. I'll be good to you," as tender as a lullaby. "You're so beautiful, baby. You're a tight, beautiful bud, and spring is coming." She stood before his armchair and he talked while his hand stroked her hips over her jeans, unsnapped, pulled them down, touching her skin like fragile silk. "God, you're sweet. Come sit on my lap. That's a good girl." He had a husky, musical voice and hands light as insect wings. "Relax, baby girl. Nothing's going to happen that you don't want, you can trust me. Open to me." And it seemed to her that on Nat's lips, at least, words were magic—"trust," uttered, driving away fear, and "open," creating itself, the *O* the very image of the word's meaning. Open, sesame! And his hands were magic, not strong but the opposite of strong that was much more powerful, so light, so almost absent that she had to let herself open in order to feel them. Knowing for a fraction of a moment that she didn't care what happened, what she opened to, a frame of mind in which she could jump out a high open window to her death, serene and eager.

The ending was bad, though. She opened her eyes as if to end a bad dream. She hurt but didn't want to mention it, sitting in his upholstered armchair with her T-shirt around her neck. On the seat cushion was a smear of blood. "I think I have my period again," she said, blinking back tears of shame. "Do you have a paper towel?" She thrust her arms through her shirt sleeves, stretched the hem over her knees.

He gave her a tissue. She wiped as best she could. She put her jeans back on but continued to shiver. She hugged herself. She started jogging in place, a repetitive motion that slowed her thinking.

"Easy there," he said, rummaging in a drawer. "Are you cold? Try this." He tossed her a man's long-sleeved shirt. It hit her, fell in a heap. She maintained her jig. "You came to me, girl. Don't forget that."

She stared at him, hopping up and down. She liked this up-down, up-down thing. She increased her pace.

"Don't go looney on me, Clara. Nothing happened that hasn't happened before. To millions of folks every day."

The words did not compute. What had happened to her had never happened to anyone even on the outreaches of her imagination. Hopping still, she found her bra, but didn't want to put it on in front of him. She balled it up, put it in her pocket. He observed her, shaking his head in nearly reverent wonder.

"You were so tight. So warm. Like you were lined in velvet."

CHAPTER NINETEEN

The End of the Week

When Hadley called, Claire was upstairs napping, and by the time she picked up the phone Hadley was gone, but at least she's alive, she says to Nora. She embraces her older daughter. "Damn her, damn her," she says while tears of relief pour down her cheeks. It feels like a sign from on high. The first softening. She calls Leo at work. She calls a detective and yells at him for not having bugged the phone. "What is wrong with you people!" She calls her local phone service and orders Call-Waiting and Caller ID, then drives to the closest outlet and purchases a digital box that records the last fifty incoming numbers. She sits down by the phone. Leo joins her. They live there for twenty-four hopeful hours on vanilla wafers and the cups of coffee that Nora brings.

Toward the end of the week, though, it takes all her strength not to break down. From the knocking radiator. From the fridge whose compressor clanks off like a bag of forks falling on the floor. Claire is not a person that people call helpless. She is more than competent, she is good in emergencies—at Children's, after Nancy, the best nurse in a code blue, hands and mind in synch. But regarding her personal disaster, she can barely think. The mind is a terrible thing to waste, she says to herself again and again, a stupid joke, but all she is capable of. She worries about the energy lost through appliances that aren't on but simply plugged in, and unplugs the toaster, the Cuisinart, and the three TVs, and she'd have unplugged the boombox in Hadley's room if not for her fear of symbols. She's superstitious like an old woman. She cringes at the sound of the phone. If it isn't Hadley, or news about Hadley—and it's never Hadley, or any useful news—she can barely hide her disgust with the caller.

Other people are no good to her. At dinner Leo speaks to Nora but not to her. They sit at the table, three separate, terrified, waiting people. As for Bodey, she hardly thinks about him. Men are almost useless to women, she has come to believe, required only for making children. That men are crucial to women's happiness is a grand deception. What women care about are children, primarily, solely, the fledgling bearers of their values and their genes, of their selves.

When she reaches this point in the train of her thought, and the train keeps chugging around to this point, she'll brush her teeth, counting ten on each tooth down from the gum, as she brushed for an entire month after the dentist warned her about gum disease. She makes the bed in slow motion, pulling the sheet smooth, smoothing it again before starting on the comforter. But then Hadley comes to mind in stinging, clear, fluorescent bits: How, after the bottle, she went loose like a puppy and fell asleep on her shoulder. The first day of kindergarten, bounding onto the bus, her arms out to the blasé big kids without a thought of not being welcomed. How deftly she unwrapped a Choco Taco. How she refused to take even one violin lesson—just to try it, see if she liked it, they had a violin the right size—screaming, "Do you think I'm *Nora*?" She is definitely not Nora, she's no one but Hadley—so forcefully, palpably herself that right now, this moment, how can she not be standing here?

On Friday, late in the morning, the seventh day of this dream that won't quit, Claire is murmuring pointless, terrified incantations and gazing at a framed photo on her dresser of Hadley holding a soccer ball. It was taken last year, one of the perks that came with participation in A.Y.S.O. Hadley wasn't a star player but for three years she went to practice happily, probably because Rachel went. In the picture she's smiling down at the ball like a kitten in her arms, her face rounder and sweeter than Claire remembers. The phone rings.

By the time she gets there, the caller has hung up. But on the new Caller ID is a local number she hasn't seen before. There's no message, it's probably a misdial but who knows? She calls back and on the first ring gets a man who sounds as if he just got up. Thirty years old maybe. He never heard of Hadley.

She hangs up apologizing. Then sees in her mind's eye the thirty-year-old man tearing the phone from Hadley's grip, and holding onto it through Claire's return call while Hadley screams, pulling at his arm. For a moment Claire thinks of calling the police. Instead she sits down at Leo's computer, plugs the ten-digit number into Reverse Anywho—it's terrifyingly simple—and gets Nathaniel B. Hale on Belmont, with a house number between Clark Street and Sheffield.

Nora is out with the car right now, but Claire doesn't wait. She puts on her bright-blue running suit and tennis shoes, puts Hadley's picture in her purse. She runs down Kenmore, along Waveland to Sheffield, whispering with each breath: *Hadley, come home. Hadley, I'm sorry. We'll go to Italy, this summer, as a family, I promise.* Her feet pound, her heart pounds, her purse bangs against her side. The air is frosty and hurts her lungs, but her muscles warm as she runs, her throat loosens. She can almost smell her daughter's hair and skin in the breeze from the lake. At Addison and Sheffield, taped to the south wall of the ballpark is a poster of Hadley with the markered addition of a beard and mustache. She has no time for annoyance though. She stops a young woman in a business suit and shows her the framed photo. "Have you seen anyone who looks like this?" The woman shakes her head but not impatiently. At the next light Claire accosts a couple of senior citizens.

"I'll keep my eyes open," one of them says. "Hey, isn't that the girl on the news?"

She blinks back tears. The woman embraces her. "Good luck to you."

Claire turns onto Clark, where Hadley's face shines back from every other post. Feeling the redundancy, still she questions anyone who seems lucid. There are a lot of kids Hadley's age or just a little older, skateboarding, rollerblading, or just hanging out. Sometimes a head of long brown hair on tall narrow shoulders makes her heart jump, but then the head turns, showing an unfamiliar face. Sometimes a style of walk brings Hadley so sharply to mind that Claire stops and stares, trying to see if she missed something—if Hadley has changed so much in the past week her own mother wouldn't know her. If Hadley is in plain sight but disguised, like the Goose Girl or Florinda who was turned into a bird, waiting for someone who loves her who is brave and clever enough to break the spell.

CHAPTER TWENTY

The Other Side of the Mirror

Hadley locked the bathroom door and turned on the shower, feeling a sad laugh trapped in her chest. There was hot water and good water pressure today, and she stood under it till the laugh died down. She washed herself evenly all over, rinsing, then soaping up again. Dried off with a beach towel, courtesy of Linens 'N' Things. "There," she said aloud. It was early morning, but what day she didn't know. She walked down the hall with her legs slightly apart, which was not how she used to walk, but maybe she had? At any rate, with this looser walk she could almost ignore the oddly insistent buzz where her legs came together. She tucked her shirt inside her jeans. The waistband was loose and she could do it without unsnapping.

She retrieved her notepad and pencil and sat down under the window, about to start drawing again, when Franco and Narcissio burst into the room. Narcissio had a flyer that he had torn from a lamppost. From the dirty white sheet of paper her own face stared back—younger, hair combed hair, but it was her face. Above, a heading, was the word: *Runaway*. Underneath were her name, age, the date of her disappearance, and *Have you seen this girl?* Five thousand dollars was offered for information leading to her return. A choked sort of laugh came out of her, though she didn't know why. She was worth five thousand dollars!

Franco made a stab at pronouncing the name on the poster. "You are not Clara."

Narcissio said, "You are thirteen year olds," not accusing her.

"Years old," she whispered, and started to cry.

They were instantly tender. Narcissio held her hand. Franco gave her a handkerchief. She closed her eyes, opened them. They were still looking at her. "Get out of here!" They started laughing, and she too, more comfortably—relieved, touched that they didn't hate her for lying. They didn't blame her for being rich enough, her family important enough for her face to appear on posters up and down Clark Street. But would they turn her in for five thousand dollars? It was a lot of money.

Seated on the floor by the couch she told them a more elaborate lie. Her mother was a famous artist who got phone calls from people like President Clinton. Which provoked her father, a plastic surgeon who worked on movie actors, to bouts of jealous rage. And then—she put a horrified hand over her mouth—her father, who naturally had to take out his anger on someone, had tried to molest her. She stopped for a confused moment, remembering that a few days ago she had told Guin that he never paid any attention to her (neither he nor her alcoholic socialite mother). But Guin, out somewhere, wasn't about to unmask her, and besides, "true" and "false" meant nothing to these kids, who lied more purposefully and inventively than she'd ever imagined. She told them she'd fucked her principal and he went to jail, and the day after the trial—she giggled harshly as if pretending it didn't matter when it really did—her father grabbed her arm and broke her wrist. "Please don't tell on me," she said, rubbing her purportedly injured wrist. "If I have to go back, he'll kill me. Or she will." She wiped at the tears that sprang to her eyes God knows why, because she didn't at all feel like crying.

When the boys left, she gazed for a while at the name under the picture, Hadley Alana Winger, after her mother's father Harry who died of a heart attack the year before she was born and her father's brother Alan, who had died in a car crash in college. She looked through the burglar bars out onto the street, trying not to feel like a prisoner. There were cars, shoppers, moms with strollers, kids hanging out. She had liked watching them, but right now they made her feel depressed—women younger than her mother walking like they were old, buying things because that was all they could think of. Their lives were over. And it occurred to her now that for most people life was like a gradually narrowing cave; after a small number of years it closed in. Even Cheeta, so beautiful and thin, just slept all day and woke up in a terrible mood; she wouldn't talk to you. Hadley felt sorry for Cheeta, and for her mother and father. She walked to the kitchen and dialed home, just to hear the ringing.

She listened hard, picturing the soft bleats, one, two, coming from all the phones in their house, the lilac-colored phone that matched the wallpaper in her mother's bedroom, the little white phone up in Nora's room, the old-fashioned black one on the telephone table in the hall, the two cordless that could be anywhere, that were always getting lost and having to be beeped for and losing their charge. Oh, what was she doing? As if something her mother could say would make a thing un-happen. As if she could ever tell her mother or Nora or anyone what had happened to her. Stupid, stupid. Still, she waited one more ring. If she turned herself in, she'd get five thousand dollars? Then she heard footsteps. Nat getting up. She stuffed the poster into the bottom of the garbage can, ran up the stairs and outside.

Guin sat on the curb out front with a cup and a crayoned sign that read: *I need it more than you do.* The cup was empty. Hadley was so glad to see her that her hands shook. "Hi, girl." Her voice shook, too. It was her first time outside in God knows how long. She breathed the air rapaciously, although it was cold and exhaust-filled. She sat down beside Guin, eyed the empty cup. "Business sucks, huh."

Guin shrugged. "This is my coffee break. Soon I'll get back to work."

Hadley laughed and leaned against Guin. Liking Guin. "Hey, girl. What day is today?"

"Friday? I don't know."

Hadley nodded, absorbing the fact that she was gone a week now. It felt longer than that. She watched the people passing close in front of them, walking fast, hunched against the wind, their faces shiny, pinched. "It's funny. I haven't smoked or anything but I feel like I'm high today!" Her teeth were chattering.

"You're a strange person," Guin said. "I never know if you're for real or not."

"Why do you say that?" She felt hurt—unaccountably, since real and unreal were a dead issue to these people. Guin smiled, but Hadley was still uneasy. "I mean, why does it matter if I feel high or not? I'm as real as you are."

"You have a point, Clara." Guin motioned toward a flyer stapled to a telephone pole a few feet away. It was identical to the one Narcissio had showed her. There was another on a building across the street. "I didn't know you were famous."

The street was spinning. "God. When did those appear?"

Guin shrugged. "Are you Clara or Hadley, by the way? 'Hadley' is so—no offense—preppy?"

267

Hadley opened her mouth—to protest her innocence or against Guin's sarcasm, she didn't know which—but Guin cut her off. "If you don't want to get caught, you should go back inside. What's the matter? I won't tell on you."

"Not for five thousand dollars?"

"Would you turn me in for five thousand dollars?"

"Never. Not for anything."

"I believe you," Guin said. "Not that anyone's offered a quarter for me."

They hugged each other, Hadley feeling oddly protective of Guin, whom no one was tracking. "Help me tear those things down, will you?"

"For sure. But first things first. If you want to walk around outside we have to do something with that preppy hair of yours."

Guin stowed her cup and sign just inside the door, and they walked quickly inside, into the bathroom. Hadley sat down on the toilet seat and Guin covered her shoulders with a towel and began clipping. A couple of years ago, Hadley had let her mother convince her that short hair was the style. She had sat down happily in the beauty-parlor chair, and watched her cut hair hit her shoulders and fall to the floor. She emerged with hair barely covering her ears, in tears that recurred for a week at least, every time she looked in a mirror. Now, though, she didn't care about the brown hair piling up on the bathroom floor. She sat calmly while Guin cut every lock to a length of an inch and a half. "Do you want to take a look?"

"When it's all done." Hadley held the towel over her eyes and forehead while her hair was sprayed blue. When it dried, Guin applied gel, sculpting the clumps of her hair into eight or ten little blue teepees. Then Hadley looked. Her neck was snaky long. She must have lost weight because her eyes were huge, her cheekbones jutting like a magazine model's. She smiled and her cheeks jutted higher. Her skin looked white against the blue, her forehead oddly long, topped with those dinosaur wedges. She belonged, she thought tranquilly, on *Star Trek*.

Guin patted her shoulder. "You're not Clara anymore. Well, not that you ever were."

"Shut up."

Guin laughed her pleasant growly laugh. "But what should we call you? How about Blue?"

Hadley put on white lipstick and regarded her new face. "Blue," she said aloud.

As Blue, she walked with Guin down Clark Street. On buildings and lampposts every twenty yards or so was another damning flyer, but they agreed that removing them now was worse than leaving them up. They would take care of them later tonight. In the meantime they strolled like tourists looking in windows, at other shoppers, testing Hadley's disguise. The sidewalks were gray and cold in the cold air. People like her mother glanced at her, then politely away, as if she were missing an arm. "You look outstanding," Guin said, and Hadley kissed her cheek. Guin's face always looked pretty to her now. Guin's wild hair was magnificent, blown back from her face. Hadley glanced in a window to check out her own reflection and had to wave just to locate herself. They continued walking, Hadley observing the two of them in store windows, car windows, all reflecting surfaces, till they arrived at the building that housed Linens 'N' Things. "I could use a down comforter," Guin said with a merry, criminal lilt. Hadley giggled, eager to see Guin on the job. Inside, though, a salesman followed them around the store; they made a brief circuit and walked out.

Now the goal was to shoplift something, anything. Guin didn't like the ambience of Marshall's, and Blockbuster's was full of security mirrors, but Sportmart, undergoing construction, was so packed you could probably shoot off a gun and no one would notice. They marched down the congested aisles, looking at tennis racquets, boxing gloves, soccer balls, too large to fit under their T-shirts. They fingered sports bras, nylon running suits, too yuppified even to try on. "I don't know how to choose," Guin said. "There's so much great stuff."

"Let's browse," Hadley said. "We're in no hurry. We have all the time in the world."

Guin laughed and said, loudly, "But tomorrow I have my Vassar interview and then my mom is taking me shopping for the prom!"

Hadley saw a couple of women eyeing them curiously. She said in the same stage-voice, "Mine too. As long as our new Lexus gets delivered on time. You know those delivery people!"

They high-fived each other, delighted with the impact of their routine on the local populace, and went on browsing. Hadley found a bikini that consisted of three black triangles and a tangle of strings. Along with a couple of other two-piece suits, she took it to the fitting room and put it on. She took her mother's bracelet out of her pack and put that on, too, then knocked on Guin's stall. "No anti-theft tag," she declared, turning to show off the back of the suit. "I bet I could walk out of the store like this."

Guin laughed. "With the punk do? You're kind of noticeable."

"If I acted like this was normal, they wouldn't look twice. Mind control." She touched a peak of her stiff blue hair.

"You're a wild and crazy girl, Blue. I mean Clara. Or is it Hadley?"

"Will you stop that?"

Hadley stared at herself in Guin's mirror. Crazy, sane. Smart, dumb, pretty, ugly, good, bad—if these were word-pairs to select from to describe herself, she wouldn't know which to circle. She widened her mouth, observing her reflection. She raised her braceleted arm. Rainbows swam across the mirror.

"That's an exceptional touch," Guin said, indicating the bracelet.

"I borrowed it from Marshall Fields. The one in the Loop. During Christmas, when they were really busy." It didn't matter what she said now. Even if there were consequences, and there could be consequences, they didn't hurt a person who didn't care what happened to her. She gazed at the bracelet musingly. "Too bad it's just rhinestones."

Back in her own stall, she put her clothes on over the suit, gave a last approving glance to her smooth, narrow hips and rib cage. With a blatantly confiding smile at the fitting-room clerk, she handed over the other suits. "They're way too big." The girl smiled back automatically. Guin couldn't get the anti-theft tag off the spandex biking pants she'd tried on and began looking for unencumbered merchandise. Hadley ripped the price tag off a red baseball cap and put the cap on Guin's head but it kept falling off. "My head has gotten so big lately," Guin said, which Hadley found excruciatingly funny. She and Guin laughed so hard and long that people turned away embarrassed, but it was fine. She was a girl who laughed. A laughing girl.

Still smiling, tufted head high, she walked past the registers, pushed through the heavy glass door. Guin followed, her cap anchored by a tail of heavy hair out the opening in back. Then she heard her name. Her old name, a net too frail to hold her now. Across the street out of the blur of the crowd something blue disentangled itself. "Hadley!"

The name flies out into the gray, windy afternoon and disappears, but Claire calls louder, stepping down onto the street. The girl she saw looked ten years older than Hadley, and her hair was insane, and she was with someone in a Cardinals hat, a little heavy, not pretty, not the kind of friend Hadley normally had. But Claire knows her daughter's height and posture and the way her face looks blank for a second before it takes on any expression.

She's halfway across the trafficked street against the light when a bus cuts off her view. It doesn't stop, thank God. Heart fizzing in her chest, Claire runs after the girls, sees them rounding Clark onto Belmont.

When she turns the corner they're gone, but she has the address. She checks out the stores on the odd-numbered side of the street—a Starbucks packed full, a used-CD store trendily denominated Ruptured Disc. She peers through the windows but sees no sign of Hadley or her friend. None of the stores have address numbers. Beside Ruptured Disc, however, is an alcove with a door of black-painted steel marked with the number she found on the Internet. To one side are three mailboxes, one unmarked, two with unfamiliar names. She presses all the buttons at once. Hears, after a moment, the buzz-click of unlocking.

Inside, two staircases lead in opposite directions, up, down. The carpets are equally gummed and grimy. She tries up. Through the door on the second floor she hears a baby crying and a woman singing an old camp song, *I've got sixpence, jolly jolly sixpence* . . . She meets at the top of the next flight a grave-faced Indian man who extends his arms to welcome her into his apartment, out of which wafts smells of incense and curry. "You're so kind," she smiles at him, almost falling backward down the stairs.

The door to the basement apartment is closed; she puts her ear to the door, hears nothing. Tries to turn the knob. Knocks though it makes no sense. As if Hadley, who ran upon seeing her, would answer the door for her. She can perhaps look for a cop to

273

get her into the apartment, but knows from television how long it takes to get a warrant. If only Eileen or Janice were here to watch the back door, if there is a back door. She pictures Hadley running out the back. Starts knocking like crazy.

Hadley sits across from the locked door, crying from authentic terror. The mother in the tacky blue sweats with the big dangling purse isn't the selfish bitch who left her with a nanny for an entire year (in Guin's version) while she jetted around Europe, and that's part of the problem. The two bad mothers (bad in different ways) are running toward each other on the same track. The air is full of cinders. "If you're my friend, don't let her in!" That's all she can say.

Guin pats her arm. "I won't. But, girl, what does she want with you?"

The knocking goes on, harder. Hadley stands, her legs shaking. "Please?"

"Okay, but she left you alone all those times. Why do you think she wants you back now?"

She takes a breath. Does Guin think she ought to go home? For a moment she wonders why she is afraid to be found. She wasn't mistreated in any way she could explain, even to herself. She wasn't punished physically. At worst, she was grounded, but below Ruptured Disc with her picture all over the street what is she but grounded? She's stopped for a moment, paralyzed by logic. Still, what would she say, eye to eye with her mother? *Hi. I guess I'll come home now.* Her cheeks burn with the shame of it.

"She thinks she wants me, but she doesn't. She's crazy!" Hadley says. "Please, Guin?" She takes Guin's hand, gives it a shake. Her legs are shaking badly now.

Told so infrequently, the truth feels like a lie that she'll be punished for. But Guin laughs conspiratorially. "I know what you mean."

Hadley squeezes her friend's hand hard, without knowing it; Guin stifles a yelp. "Thank you! I mean, sorry." She tosses over her shoulder a last despairing glance, and runs down the hall.

Claire knocks till her hand throbs. The door opens the width of the chain.

"May I help you?"

The voice is lower than Hadley's but clearly female. Claire plants her feet, says as firmly as she can, "I'm looking for my daughter."

She expects resistance and is ready for it. But the girl starts to laugh. "That's a new one!"

Claire peers through the crack into the dim interior. Sees nothing. But she has rehearsed her speech. "Her name is Hadley Winger."

"Who?"

"Do you mind if I come in?"

The girl laughs again, more stridently. "Are you kidding? You might be a burglar. I'm joking. Are you a cop?"

"What?"

"Yeah, sure. Look, I'm sorry, Ma'am. There's just me and my roommates. So you can go back where you came from."

It's brighter in the hall where Claire is standing than in the apartment; through the slot Claire feels the girl's eyes on her. Feels her own visual impact, the lack thereof. Who would back down before a middle-aged woman in a royal-blue velour running suit? Her throat starts to close. There are tears in her voice. "I'm not a cop but I can get a cop. If you don't let me see my own daughter!"

The girl says amiably, "If your Hadley Weiner comes by I'll say you were looking for her."

"Winger," Claire says.

The girl tries to shut the door but Claire, who has never before, to her knowledge, violated the edicts of courtesy, places her foot in the doorway. "I saw her with you. I don't know what she told you but it's probably not true!" Planted firmly on the threshold, Claire explains the circumstances of Hadley's flight. The girl remains politely amused, as if it's Claire who is lying. "Wait! Look at this!" Claire takes Hadley's picture out of her purse, thrusts it through the opening. "Please, I just want to talk to her. I'm not going to hurt her, I'm her mother, for God's sake!" The girl takes hold of the picture and seems to be examining it but Claire is afraid to let go of her end. "Please?"

The girl says, "There's no one here who looks anything like this."

She sounds sincere but Claire pushes on, "I know she doesn't want to see me. And I can see you're her friend. But she has a father and a sister. We love her. We might have made some mistakes with her, but we miss her." Claire has been trying not to weep but the tears come now. She tries to speak clearly. "She's only in seventh grade, she doesn't know what she's doing. . . ."

"Seventh grade?" says the girl.

"Look, here's her school ID. She's thirteen. Barely."

"Shit. All right, just move your foot. How can I take the chain off?"

Claire doesn't know whether or not the girl is fooling with her. She decides to obey, holding onto the latch to keep the door from locking.

Standing in the kitchen Hadley hears her mother's alternating hesitancy and insistence, Guin's growly laugh. Her mother sounds like a mouse and Guin a bear or a wildcat. Then the tones even out. Hadley starts to worry that they're getting along too well, they've come to an understanding. She remembers her mother on the phone with their HMO, making them pay what they were supposed to pay. But Guin, she knows, can be a great actress. When the front door clicks shut she takes a small breath, ready to celebrate victory with Guin. But the voices are louder.

Guin: "Get the fuck out of here!"

Her mother, gushier than she has to be: "If you were a mother you'd understand."

"Lady, I'll call the cops. I swear . . ."

The back-door lock needs a key, which Nat has. Hadley freezes between terrors. Runs to Nat's door. The padlock is gone. She turns the knob and the door opens.

"So what have we here? More ghosts in the house?"

His whisper is gruff but he sounds happy with her presence. She shuts the door behind her and takes a breath, though her teeth are chattering. "I'm sorry. To disturb you. But my parole officer saw me and followed me here. They'll just put me back in the girls' detention home if you don't—oh, please lock the door!"

"Parole officer? For what?" He laughs. "For skipping study hall? Copying someone's homework? By the way, your hair looks like crap."

He locks the door. She runs to the window, lifts the blind. Burglar bars. "I'm sorry, Nat, it's my foster mother. She treated me like dirt and I stole some of her jewelry, this bracelet—" She raises her arm to show him. The room is dim and she can barely see. Her head seems to be full of water. No thoughts, no planning or choosing, just her voice rippling on like an animal in panicked flight, not expecting to be believed, just hoping to be allowed to carry on the lie. "It's real diamonds. You can have it, Nat. I'll give it to you." She starts to take it off. He shakes his head, puts his arms around her.

"Have you been missing me?"

Tears fill her eyes. Yes, it seemed to her now, she has missed him. She wants to be with him. "Oh, God, save me."

He touches a tuft of her hair, then wipes his hand on his pants. "Sorry." He kisses her eyelids, individually, then the side of her face. He, too, is trembling.

Claire runs to the back of the apartment, rattles the locked exit, then bounds forward again, peering into closets, the bathroom, the pantry off the kitchen. The girl, hatless but recognizable as Hadley's companion, doesn't get in her way. Claire stops by the one closed door, turns the knob. It's locked. "Who's in there?"

"Nat," says the girl. "Off limits. We're not supposed to bother him."

Claire runs into the living room again, looks in the closet, looks under the couch against the wall. Lying on the couch in the center of the room is a girl in shorts and a tank top, so skinny Claire is stopped a moment. Her eyes are closed, her face flushed, breathing labored. She seems dangerously ill; Claire reaches out to touch her forehead. Then remembers her primary goal and runs back to the closed door, before which Hadley's friend has remained standing. "She's got to be in there!" The girl shrugs helplessly. Without her cap, her hair is a rat's nest; Claire could pull it out by the roots. She labors to restrain herself. She used to believe the world had rules, and if you broke them you paid the price, a harsh system but fair. She'd followed the rules. Then she doubted the price, and the system of reward and punishment. Is this it, the price? She bangs on the door. "Hadley, open up! Hadley, answer me!" She turns to the girl. "Is that guy with her? If anything happens to her, I swear I'm going to kill someone!"

Hadley holds onto Nat, cringing with each rap of her mother's fist. If her mother finds her, if her eyes just look at her, she imagines herself turning to stone or shutting off like a light. Turning back into an embryo or the tiny, flimsy husk of a seed. "Please."

The doorknob shakes. She stares at it, waiting for the lock to break. The door rattles its hinges. Nat steps back, pulling her with him. "Jesus Fucking Christ!"

"Please be quiet," she breathes into his shoulder.

"Are you kidding me? Who is that woman?"

The pounding continues. "Hadley, if you're in there, talk to me!"

"Who the fuck," he says, "is Hadley?"

The door is being kicked now. The hinges groan. Suddenly Hadley wants to laugh. That her mother is kicking the door she's crouched behind. She labors not to pee her pants. Squeezes her muscles tight and small against Nat's hard body.

"I'll call the cops!" her mother cries. "Honest to God, you'll be arrested for kidnapping!"

"Nobody kidnapped anybody," Guin says in a voice Hadley finds soothing. "You'll be arrested yourself, lady. You forced your way in."

The banging stops for a moment. Her mother says, "Listen,

Hadley. Should I apologize? I know I haven't been as good a mom as I should have been—"

Her voice trails off. In the dark Hadley nods grimly, clinging to Nat. Hating her mother.

"Had," her mother says more softly, "why did you run off? I hope you'll tell me one day."

She sounds oddly respectful. Hadley sees her in her mind in her Crayola-blue jogging suit, kneeling on the floor, her forehead against the wooden door, wavy black hair spilling over her face. Hadley stares at the doorknob, which is still now. In the silence she can hear her own pulse. Oh, let this be over.

"Honey, I've learned something," her mother says.

Hadley closes her eyes, willing herself gone from consciousness. She thinks of last year at school, the girls in the bathroom compressing each other's midriffs to make each other faint. She hadn't been able to faint.

"Happiness isn't our birthright," her mother says. "Are you listening, Hadley? We have to work for it and even then we can't be sure."

"Whatever that means," she says under her breath.

"Hadley, is that you?"

She shakes her head no, silently.

"Hadley, I love you, honey."

The words are soft against her eyelids, but, so? Maybe her mother loves her, but as far as she knows, her life isn't improved by it. Isn't *affected*. She wonders why people make such a big deal about love, and tries to remember if she ever loved someone. Rachel comes to mind. But it's hard to picture Rachel except as a school photo, glossy and unreal. Nat massages the back of her neck. Rubs down her back. Hadley shivers. Maybe she loves Nat.

"Hadley," her mother says, "I can hear you breathing."

Nat pats her butt. "What the fuck are you wearing, girl?" His hand slips down the back of her jeans. "Is that a thong you have on?"

She pushes away from him. "Cut it out."

She can hear her mother gasp, hear the actual air sucked into her mouth. Her mother screams. "What are you *doing* in there!" Her mother is pleading, "I won't call the police, just open the door. Please, just give me my daughter back."

Nat looks at her, eyebrows in the air. "She sounds serious. You want to go with the lady?"

She shakes her head violently, no, no, no, no, no!

Then Guin raises her voice, "What's the matter, lady? Ma'am? Mrs. Weiner!" There's a strangled moan, a thud. Guin screams, "Oh my God. You guys, come out! Help me! Oh, this is so *weird*."

Hadley is still shaking her head. At the same time her hand reaches out and opens the door.

CHAPTER TWENTY-ONE

And Then

I n the cab on the way home, her mother tries to explain. She has epilepsy. She had a lover but gave him up. She and Leo might be divorcing. She didn't try to kill herself, had never even been tempted—where did that idea come from? Hadley shrugs, pretending she's on her way to prison. "Hadley," her mother says, "Not now but at some point I want to hear about what happened to you. You'll need to talk about it. For your own sake." Hadley looks out the window. Her mother takes a patient breath. "You have to promise me one thing. You'll never, I mean never, ever..." Hadley says nothing.

Once upon a time Hadley told the whole truth and nothing but, to her mother who was her self, fount of pleasure and sustenance and judgment. Then she lied to her mother and everyone. She gave up on judgment and sustenance and even pleasure. Banished self and other-than-self. Erased the lines between where she could and couldn't be. How could she promise anything?

Her eyes on the ground, hands at her sides like a bound captive, she walks into the house behind her mother. Her father hugs her so hard it hurts. His cheek is wet. "Oh boy," he keeps saying. "Thank God."

Nora lies on the couch with a book. "Nice do," says Nora.

"Nora," their mother says, "give your sister a hug."

Nora follows instructions. Hadley lets herself be hugged. Their mother says something bubbly to their father, then walks into the kitchen, calling out, "Nora honey, would you mind washing up? I want to make dinner." Nora turns a page. Their mother returns, eyes Nora hopefully.

"Ask Hadley," Nora says. "She hasn't done it for a week."

"She has to rest. Do you see how skinny she is?"

"Right, Mom. She's a real holocaust survivor."

Claire takes Nora's book and waves toward the kitchen. She laughs giddily. "I'm looking forward to you two fighting again." She shakes her head from side to side. "I am so fucked up."

"Don't say fucked," Nora says.

"Sorry. You'll have to remind me."

"I don't want to remind you. That's not my responsibility."

Claire's laugh is apologetic.

Nora motions toward Hadley. "She has your good bracelet on."

"Does she?"

Hadley doesn't try to conceal it. It hangs from her wrist, diamonds glinting.

"God. Well, I didn't miss it." Claire's eyes roam, then fall on Nora again, stretched out on the couch in passive mutiny. "I don't need this from you right now."

Leo has been sitting in an armchair with his face in his hands. "Help your mother."

"Like always." Nora stomps out of the room.

"Well," says Claire, "she doesn't try to hide her feelings now. I guess that's good."

"For whom?" Leo says.

With some of her old, automatic triumph at any discomfort of her sister's, Hadley picks up her sister's book from the table where her mother put it. The title is *Maus*. The subtitle, *A Survivor's Tale*. It's actually a comic book, but the print is too small to read. "Sit up straight," her mother says. "Your eyes don't like it so close to the page." The words touch her ears and float on by.

From the time of her emergence from Nat's room, having seen her mother alive, Hadley refused to acknowledge her. Or Nat. Their dual presence seemed impossible, as if a carton of milk could be full and empty at the same time. She tried other contradictory pairings—the book is blue, the book is not blue,

I'm here, I'm in Florida—while Guin and Nat helped her mother over to a chair in the kitchen. "It was bizarre," Guin said. "You were flopping like a fish all over the place. Are you really her mother?" Hadley kept her eyes on a squashed grape on the floor while her mother looked around as if she didn't know anything. "Hadley," she said. Yes, that was her name. But when she reached for her hand, Hadley withheld it. She wanted nothing to do with her mother's hands that wouldn't stop twitching. "Get your things," said her mother, "we're going home."

They proceeded down the hall, Hadley trailing behind with Guin. "How could you?" she hissed.

Guin mouthed, I couldn't help it, which meant exactly nothing. Guin said, "I'm sorry. I really tried, but...I think she cares about you."

But Guin seemed, for once, uncertain. Her words didn't stick. Hadley was planning her escape. Outside was large, with many hiding places.

Then in the living room her mother saw Cheeta on the couch. She felt Cheeta's forehead, turned to Nat and asked—angry, incredulous—how long this girl had been sick and when she had stopped eating. She said to Cheeta, whom she didn't know or need to care about, "Honey, you're burning up," and produced two Tylenols from her purse. She called an ambulance, made them wait till it came, said to the driver with tears in her voice, "We don't know where her parents are," and Hadley forgot about her plans to run. She didn't like her mother, in fact she hated her, but there was no more choosing. They were mother and daughter, a blood bond that could be stretched and torn but not ignored or forgotten. Her mother called a cab. Hadley got in.

Now Hadley walks to the kitchen where Nora is cleaning up from lunch and breakfast. "You rinse, okay, and I'll put them in the dishwasher?" While they work, a nasty, funny remark bubbles up in her. She tries to quash it, then lets it go. "How's Jesus?" she says, trying not to smile. "Does He still turn you on?" She holds still, awaiting Nora's anger or scorn.

Nora says quietly, "Jesus is a partial truth,"and turns back to her job, but Hadley can't stop.

"God, are you turning normal now?"

Nora doesn't reply. Hadley feels her mother's eyes on her back, the familiar heat of her disapproval. She passes a dishwater-wet hand across her own forehead. "Honey," she says to herself, "you're burning up."

Although Hadley won't speak a detail of her saga, now or ever, Claire will see her as almost (or maybe entirely) unscathed. She'll go to school, see Rachel, and even Fletcher sometimes. She'll do her schoolwork perhaps more diligently than before. She'll grow the blue out of her hair. She'll pass the intersection of Clark and Belmont (in the car, heading toward Lake Shore Drive) without turning her head.

Claire will try to meld again with the rhythms of dailiness. She'll cancel Kara. She'll see Patel, who will increase her dose of

Tegretol. Back at work, full time, she'll discover Josh Potrero admitted again. In bad shape but hanging on. She'll take sculpture at the Evanston Art Center, go with Leo to counseling, and even after the separation and divorce have him to dinner sometimes. They'll get along better in some ways, their talk more varied. But still, passing infamous Clark and Belmont—that anomaly, that cleft in the ordinary scheme of things—she'll feel a surge of fear. That during her daughter's seven-day sojourn something was planted in her or implanted, an alien seed or infernal microchip that will eventually draw her back there.

One Saturday in early fall—with Hadley in eighth grade, and Nora a junior—Claire double-parks in front of Ruptured Disc. The alcove door is ajar; she walks down the steps and knocks on the door of the basement apartment. It's answered by a man in overalls with an electric saw in his hand. Under his feet the pale, narrow boards of new hardwood stretch to the hallway. Where are the old tenants? He shrugs, smiles. He doesn't speak English. She hopes this is his place, that he's working for himself, though probably it's for someone turning the building into condos who doesn't pay him enough. She smiles back, drops her car keys. He kneels faster than she, places them in her shaking hand.

A few months later she goes on a date, an uncomfortable, wearying, post-divorce evening. Her face hurts from smiling. I will never, she thinks, get married again. By now she's almost sure that Hadley has forgiven her. Hadley has a part in her high-school production of *Hair*. Nora goes out every weekend with her track friends, who have momentarily replaced her nerd friends. A good thing, says Hadley. Claire took the girls to Greece over winter vacation and they enjoyed it, as far as Claire can tell; England is coming up next summer. It's nice in Chicago, too, in their condo on the lake, with high ceilings and light and varnished sweeps of floor.

But every once in a while, on the elevator or the running path, she'll smell the cologne Bodey wore sometimes, along with a scent of rank adult male, and she'll feel again for a moment utterly known, fully given over, as to the tornado that set Dorothy's house down safely on the Witch of the West, or the whale that spit Jonah out on dry land, a force that could have destroyed her and generously declined.

For Hadley, too, there's a residue, a low-level itch on hidden parts of her skin, that she feels even bathed and freshly dressed as she was, the night of her homecoming. Her mother dimmed the chandelier and lit candles. It was so dark that even with twenty-twenty vision Hadley could barely have seen the food on her plate, but she was aware of her body—of her blood circulating, her cells taking in what they need and giving off what's used up. She imagined her cells plumping up so fat there was no choice for them but to divide. In her chair at the table she crossed and uncrossed her ankles. Tried to relax her shoulders. Had a crazy urge to sing a song. In six months, just before the start of her last year of middle school, she'd sit behind her father's eye machine and walk from then on with prescription glass between herself and the world (and later the barely detectable glaze of contact lenses). But tonight in the flickering candlelight, the world's surface was blurred, and the only thing distinct and knowable was the buzz and hum of her body at work, a private pleasure close to pain. She kept her eyes open in the dark, and tried to see.

THE AUTHOR

Sharon Solwitz's first collection of stories, *Blood and Milk* (Sarabande, 1997), won the 1998 Carl Sandburg Prize from Friends of the Chicago Public Library, the prize for adult fiction from the Society of Midland Authors, and was a finalist for the National Jewish Book Award. Her short stories, published in such magazines as *TriQuarterly*, *Mademoiselle*, and *Ploughshares*, have won numerous awards, including the Pushcart Prize, the Katherine Anne Porter Prize, and grants and fellowships from the Illinois Arts Council. Currently, along with her husband, poet Barry Silesky, she has worked as fiction editor of *Another Chicago Magazine*. She teaches fiction at Purdue University in West Lafayette, Indiana.